THE NICEST GUY IN AMERICA

Praise for Angela Benson's work:

"BANDS OF GOLD is a love story that touches all the hidden corners of the heart . . . Readers won't be able to turn the pages fast enough."

—*Romantic Times*

"FOR ALL TIME is a tremendously realistic relationship novel . . . Five stars."

—*Affaire de Coeur*

". . . With FOR ALL TIME, Angela Benson has proven that she has a voice to be heard in the African-American romance genre."

—*Storyline Treasures*

". . . With THE WAY HOME, she emerges as a writer of great depth, sensitivity, and unparalled talent."

—Cheryl Ferguson, *Romantic Times*

THE NICEST GUY IN AMERICA

Angela Benson

Pinnacle Books
Kensington Publishing Corp.

http://www.pinnaclebooks.com

PINNACLE BOOKS are published by

Kensington Publishing Corp.
850 Third Avenue
New York, NY 10022

Pinnacle, the P logo, and Arabesque are Reg. U.S. Pat. & TM Off.

First Printing: October, 1997
10 9 8 7 6 5 4 3 2 1

Printed in the United States of America

Prologue

"But I'm a nice guy, Kim. Why do I get this kind of treatment? It's like I always say, women don't want a man who'll treat 'em right."

Kimberla Washington twisted the phone away from her mouth and turned her lips in a snarl. "Yadda, yadda, yadda," she said after pressing the mute button. She didn't know why Derrick Thompson thought she had nothing better to do than listen to his relationship problems. It seemed their friendship had turned into a Dear Abby saga, with her playing Abby. Well, she was tired of it and she was tired of him. She pressed the mute button again. "Look, Derrick," she said, interrupting his sob story, "I've got work to do. I'll talk to you later." She hung up without waiting for his response. "I've got to get some new male friends," she muttered. "I'm about tired of these *nice* brothers crying on my shoulders about how women don't want a nice guy."

"What'd you say, Kim?" Jim Whittaker asked from the doorway of her office cubicle.

Kim looked up at the short, balding man who'd hired her to work at Urban Style Magazine when she'd first moved to D.C. five years ago. "Nothing," she said.

Jim came fully into her cube and propped on the corner of her metal desk. A chubby man of about fifty-five, he didn't seem to mind that his stomach rolled over the waistband of his pants as he made himself comfortable. "Didn't sound like nothing to me," he said. "And from the smirk on your face, it wasn't nothing to you, either."

Kim sighed. Sometimes Jim was nosy—there was no other way to describe it—but she knew that if she didn't tell him what he wanted to know he'd hound her until she thought she was going crazy. He was known in publishing circles as a bulldog, a moniker he relished. Word was that he'd been a helluva reporter before striking out and starting his own magazine. "I was talking to Derrick," she explained and wasn't surprised when Jim's lips turned down. She and Derrick had started dating soon after she'd been hired at the magazine, so Derrick's face had become a regular around the office. Unfortunately, their break-up a few short months later followed by their decision to remain friends had become fodder for office gossip. "He's complaining again that women don't appreciate nice guys like him. In other words, he got dumped. Again."

Jim rubbed the faint stubble on his chin. As usual, he'd been in such a hurry to get to the office that he'd left home without shaving. "This makes what—the third time this year?"

Kim rolled her eyes toward the ceiling. "And it's only April."

He dropped his hand from his chin and snapped his fingers. "Kimmy, girl, you haven't been learning what I've been trying to teach you."

Kim leaned back in her chair and waited. She knew the twinkle in Jim's eyes meant he had what he thought was a great angle for a story. "I'm waiting. What are you gonna teach me today?"

Jim grinned and stood up. He framed his hands as if he

held the headlines of a magazine. "Can't you see it, girl?" he said, but he didn't wait for her answer. "Why Nice Guys Get Dumped." He grinned a smug grin. "The title alone will sell thousands of magazines."

Kim leaned forward as Jim talked through his idea. Okay, so the idea intrigued her a little—just a little. Her attention faded in and out as she thought through how she'd handle the story. Why did nice guys get dumped? She could think of a thousand reasons why *nice* guys like Derrick got dumped and she was getting excited just thinking about putting those reasons on paper and getting paid for doing it. Boy, did she have a lot to say on the subject.

She'd start with the fact that *nice* guys like Derrick weren't really interested in regular women. No, they wanted the Jet Magazine swimsuit types who wouldn't give them a cold stare on a hot day. Not that she had anything against the women who posed in Jet. It was just that Kim knew that Derrick and guys of his ilk were more interested in beautiful faces and perfect bodies than in building committed relationships with real women. She'd been through enough of his type to be an expert.

"Hey," Jim shouted, drawing her attention back to him. "I've got it. A contest. We can do a contest. Kimmy girl, this is pure genius. We can sponsor a contest for the nicest guy in America. Only our nicest guy has to be nominated by a woman who's dumped him."

"Wait a minute, Jim," Kim began. She chastised herself for not paying more attention to Jim's thinking out loud. "The article has some merit, but a contest? I think we'd be overplaying it with a contest."

Jim shook his head and his meaty jaws wobbled. "The Nicest Guy In America Contest. Kimmy, this idea is gonna make us a bag of money. Now you get on the copy for the contest. We can probably get it into this month's issue." He rubbed his fat hands together. "Then we'll sit back and wait for the money to roll in. This oughta raise circulation. If we're lucky, we'll make a run at Upscale's number three position."

"Jim," Kim said again, but it was no use. He ignored her and walked to his office. She knew he was already counting the new subscribers he hoped to get.

Chapter 1

"You've got yourself some losers here, girlfriend." Kim's longtime friend Leslie Montgomery tossed a black-and-white photograph on the mound of black-and-white photos covering Kim's dining room table. "Thank God it's Saturday and I have a date tonight. You two are about as boring as some of these guys here."

Kim rolled her eyes in the direction of her other friend, Tammy Williams. The three women had been friends since they were freshmen roommates at Spelman. Pledging Delta Sigma Theta sorority together their sophomore year had cemented what had now become a lifetime friendship.

"Give it a rest, Leslie," Tammy said with a sigh. "Kim didn't force you to help out. If you want to go, just go."

Leslie got up from her seat directly across the table from Tam and stretched her lithe, five-foot-four-inch, one hundred ten pound body. Her orange shirt, which had been tucked in her short orange shorts, rose up and exposed her flat pale-brown stomach. Kim knew Leslie's innocent stretch was a not-so-subtle taunt at Tam, who'd been in a losing battle with the weight monster since her divorce six years ago and she found her friend's display offensive. Who did Leslie think she was pulling a stunt like that with them?

"Yes," Kimberla agreed. "Give it a rest, Leslie. If you gotta go, then leave. Don't stay around here complaining all day."

Leslie made a production of pulling her top down. Then she reached over and grabbed her shiny gold shoulder bag that matched her shiny gold sandals, earrings and choker in typical Leslie fashion. "If that's the way you feel about it—"

"Please, Leslie," Tam said. "You know you want to go so just leave."

Leslie turned and headed for the front door of Kim's small one-bedroom apartment. "I'll be sure to call you two and let you know how my date went. I *did* tell you he was a fine brother, didn't I?"

Kim shot another glance at Tam whose now-full face showed disgust and maybe something akin to envy. But Kim knew Tam wasn't envious of Leslie. No, Tam was envious of the slender girl she herself had been back in college when all was right with the world. Feeling as though she was intruding on Tam's private thoughts, Kim turned and watched Leslie sashay through the front door and close it with a whack.

"That chick needs to learn some manners," Tam said.

Kim didn't want to be put in the position of talking about Leslie behind her back, even though she agreed with Tam's remark, so she turned the conversation back to the contest. "What do you think, Tam?" she asked. "Do we have any winners here or is Leslie right—they're all losers?"

Tam brushed her straight, shoulder-length dark brown hair back behind her ear in the self-conscious manner she'd adopted since her divorce. "I don't think they're all losers and I bet you don't, either." Tam shuffled the stack of photos in front of her. "Look at this one."

Kimberla took the offered photo and immediately recognized the dark, handsome face smiling back at her. Reggie Stevens. God, he was a fine man. She guessed he was about six-foot-two and spent a great deal of time in the gym. The brother definitely had a buff body. Why in the world had so many sisters dropped him? She shook her head. Fine. Fine. Fine.

"So, what do you think?" Tam asked.

I think he's so fine that I should take him for myself, she thought, but of course, she didn't say it. Tam, though upset with Leslie now, would be on the phone within five minutes of leaving her apartment telling Leslie that Kim had the hots for one of the *Nice* Guys. "He seems like a *real* nice guy."

Tam picked up another photo and slapped Kim on the shoulder with it. "What do you expect, silly? It's a Nice Guy contest."

"I know, Tam," Kim said, remembering the day two months ago Jim had come up with the contest idea. "At first I thought the whole idea was going to blow up in our faces. Thank god, other women had *real* nice guys in their lives because the ones I've had have been the pits."

"Like Marcus," Tam said, speaking of her ex-husband. "I still can't believe that jerk left me so he could marry that sleazy nurse. Hell, I practically put his behind through medical school *and* I gave him a daughter. I get mad every time I think about how stupid I was to think he ever cared for me or Melissa."

"Don't beat yourself up," Kim said, not for the first time. "It's not your fault Marcus was a jerk. Hell, we've all had our share of jerks. Remember that I had Derrick, the man with the roving eyes." Kim let her eyes scan the dining room without moving her head similar to the way Derrick used to do. As she'd hoped, Tam laughed. "The brother was always looking for something, or shall I say, someone."

Kim shook her head. While she knew she didn't have the kind of looks that made men stop on the street for a double-take, she also knew she could hold her own in the company of most women. At five-eight, she wore a size twelve, which meant she wasn't skinny but then neither was she fat. Her skin was dark, which she knew turned some men off, but those men she didn't want anyway. She liked her complexion, and except for a few weak moments in high school and college, she always had. And on top of all that, she was a kind and intelligent woman with a good job and good friends. As far as she was concerned, her break-ups with Derrick and the others like him who'd passed through her life was their loss.

"I hope Derrick hurries up and finds whoever he's looking for," she said, "because he's been through almost every woman in D.C. by now."

"And he still hasn't figured out why he keeps getting dumped?"

Kim shook her head again. "What can I say? Mr. Roving Eyes is slow. He still thinks he's a nice guy being mistreated by cold-hearted women."

Tam chuckled. "You should have nominated him for the contest and I should have nominated Marcus."

Kim laughed with her friend. "I thought about doing it, girl. Then we began getting nominations and I saw how serious the sisters were about the brothers they nominated. Some of these guys sound like real princes." She glanced at Reggie's picture. "If one of them had come through my life, you can bet I wouldn't have let him go."

"You know," Tam said. "I bet a lot of your women readers will feel the same way. You're going to be getting letters in droves after they see these brothers."

"I know you're right," Kim said. "I just hope Jim hires someone else to go through all the mail. He's definitely not paying me enough to do it in addition to my regular responsibilities." As a feature writer, her tasks usually included special projects like the Contest which required a great deal of time—on and off the job.

Tam plucked the picture of Reggie out of Kim's hands. "This brother here is going to get his share of mail. I can already tell you that. Looks, a good job, knows how to treat women. Can you believe somebody gave him the boot?"

Kim glanced down at the full-length picture of Reggie on the stack of photos in front of her. "And it wasn't the first time."

"How do you know?" Tam asked, eyes wide. "Did someone else nominate him?"

Kim pursed her lips. "More like some *ones.*" She picked up the short stack of letters next to the tall mound. "Look at this."

Tam took the offered letters and began to read. After finishing the first one, she went on to the second. "You mean he was nominated twice?"

"Keep reading," Kim said.

Tam shook her head and went to the next sheet. "Three times?" she said with obvious surprise. "But he seems like such a nice guy. I wonder what's wrong with him."

Kim's sentiments exactly. Sure, Reggie Stevens was fine, had a good job and seemed to possess the qualities women always said they wanted, but something had to be wrong with him. He'd been entered in the contest so many times by so many women.

"Wait a minute," Tam said. "You mean to tell me that this guy was nominated six different times by six different women? Dag, something must be seriously wrong with this one. I don't think he should make the finalist cut, Kim. The guy's probably a drug addict or something."

Kim smiled. Tam's overly imaginative mind was now in high gear. "You read those letters, didn't you? Those women love that guy." She thumbed through the letters Tam held. "Here, let me read you parts of this one. It's from Christina Duncan from Boston. Apparently, she and Reggie dated before she got married. Here goes."

"Reggie is a very special man. I could tell from our first meeting that he was open, honest, considerate and fun to be with—traits that are becoming more and more difficult to find in men. And he never proved me wrong. When he learned I hadn't gone to many amusement parks during my childhood, he took me to Six Flags Over Georgia and we spent the day like kids. I still have wonderful memories of that day. What I remember most is having tired feet from all the walking and having Reggie pull my feet on his lap and massage them. I almost fell in love with him that night.

"I think I would have fallen in love with Reggie had I not had already met the one love of my life. When it seemed my love and I weren't going to make it, Reggie offered the most wonderful of sacrifices which I'll leave to him to tell you about. He's indeed a man among men and I wish him the happiness I found."

"Reggie told me once that he thought I'd get over the love I felt for my now husband, but I knew then he was wrong. I told him that one didn't get over love, but I don't think he believed me. He will when he finds that special woman. She'll be a lucky woman whoever she turns out to be."

Kim's heart filled with wonder as she read again the words she'd read many times before and she knew she had to meet Reggie Stevens. "What do you think?"

"I wonder what great sacrifice he made and I wonder why she, and all those other women, dropped him if he was such a great guy. I don't know, Kim. I'd be careful with this one if I were you. Dumped six times," she continued with a shake of her head. "If he's been nominated this many times, just think how many times he must have been dumped. What do you think? Sixty?"

Kim picked up the full-length picture. There was something about Reggie Stevens that told her he was a man worth getting to know. Maybe it was the kind eyes and the sweet smile set in the most masculine of faces. Or, Kim thought as firecrackers went off in her belly, maybe it was his wide shoulders, tapered waist and firm thighs.

"You're not getting hung-up on this guy, are you?" Tam asked, leaning over her shoulder.

"Of course not," she answered quickly. "I'm just doing my job."

"You're not gonna make him a finalist, are you?"

"I'm not sure," Kim lied. Reggie Stevens was definitely making the finalist cut. She had to meet this man and find out for herself what about him attracted her and what about him had sent so many other women packing. "Let's make it through the stack and then decide."

Reggie knew he wasn't going to like what he found when he walked into his house as soon as he turned his blue Nissan Maxima onto Southwest Atlanta's Roman Street. Cars were lined up and down both sides of the street. Although he hoped he was wrong about where all those drivers were now, he knew deep inside that he wasn't.

He heard the music even before he reached his drive and found it blocked by four cars. Luther had to go. This was it. His neighbors were probably already getting a petition together to force him out. He slapped his hand against his steering wheel and continued down the street looking for a place to park. He really didn't need this. Not tonight. After his date with Deborah, he needed some chill time. A brother needs time to lick his wounds after a sister breaks his heart.

He found a spot around the corner from his house and grudgingly pulled his car into it. *Why am I doing this?* he asked himself. *I have a house with a two car garage and I'm parking around the block. Luther has got to go. This is the last straw.*

Reggie got out of his car, pressed down the lock and slammed the door shut. Yes, he had to give old Luther the boot, just as Deborah had given it to him.

"I just want to see other people," she'd said, her eyes sparkling. "For the first time in my life, I feel in control. I just want to have a little fun."

Reggie could still remember when he'd met Deborah, at the wedding reception of a mutual friend. She'd caught his eye because she'd looked so sad and so out of place. He'd immediately walked up to her and struck up a conversation, determined to see her smile before the afternoon was over.

Getting that smile had been a difficult task though since Deborah hadn't wanted to talk. But he hadn't let that stop him. He'd talked. He'd told her about himself, his family and a little about his work as a computer security specialist. But it was the stories about his nephews that got to her. First, she smiled. Then she laughed outright. There was something in the timbre of her laughter that made him think it had been a long time since she'd really laughed. He determined then to make sure she laughed more often.

As the afternoon progressed, she'd gradually opened up to him and told him about her last relationship. Apparently, she'd come home one day to find her live-in boyfriend gone, along with her stereo system, color TV and a few choice prints she'd bought. It wasn't until she got a call from her bank a few days later that she realized he'd almost cleaned out her account, too. She'd been so distressed about the entire situation that she'd been unable to function in her receptionist job and after numerous warnings, she'd been let go. The day Reggie met her had been the six-month anniversary of the day she'd come home to find the deadbeat gone.

Now, Reggie knew some brothers would have gotten as far away from Deborah as possible after hearing only part of her story. But not him. Her story had the exact opposite effect on him and he'd asked her out. Her reluctance had charmed him and he'd known pursuing her was the right thing to do. That was six months ago. And tonight she'd given him his walking papers.

Reggie sucked in his breath when he reached the walkway to his house. *Luther had to go,* he told himself. No more excuses. He made his way up the walk and into the house. It was a miracle the loud music that greeted him didn't shatter his eardrums. And as loud as the music was, he was surprised it didn't sound louder outside. He thanked God for his thick exterior walls.

A small hand grabbed one of Reggie's buns and he jumped. "Hi, handsome," a soft, sexy voice purred.

He turned and looked down into the smiling eyes of a Halle Berry look-alike. "Hi, yourself," he said, trying to keep the irritation out of his voice. It wasn't this woman's fault that he'd had a bad day.

"Wanna dance?" she asked. He could tell by the smile dancing at her lips that she fully expected him to say *Yes*. Women like her always did. And men usually complied. There was a confidence and a surety about this woman that was the exact opposite of what he'd seen in Deborah when he'd first met her. But, he realized with a jolt, the confidence in this woman's eyes now had been in Deborah's earlier tonight.

"Save one for me," he said with a forced smile. "I've got to find the host and take care of some business."

She gave a practiced frown that said she was disappointed. "I'll be waiting for you. Don't forget me."

"How could I?" Reggie said with the teasing grin he knew was expected and the woman walked off. The male in him didn't miss the invitation in her hips as she moved away from him.

He forced his eyes away from the Halle look-alike and scanned the living room for Luther. He spotted him behind the bar, preparing drinks and no doubt giving a line to the three women seated around him. Only three women tonight, Reggie mused. Luther must be off his game. Women usually fell all over themselves for what Luther called his Ed Gordon-ish looks and his Denzel-ish charm.

With purpose, Reggie walked over to them. "What's up, man?" he said to Luther.

The surprise in Luther's eyes was almost reward enough. Almost.

"Ahh, ladies," Luther began, "You'll have to excuse me for a minute." He winked. "I gotta see a man about some business. But I'll be back. Have a good time while I'm gone, but not too good."

Luther quickly moved from behind the bar and clapped Reggie on the shoulder. "I didn't expect you back tonight, partner. I figured you'd be spending the night with your lady."

"Well, you figured wrong. What's going on here, Luther? I can't believe you've turned my place into a nightclub when you have a real one across town."

Luther laughed, all the while leading Reggie away from the party crowd and back to his bedroom. When he stepped in front of Reggie and eased the door open, Reggie knew he was making sure no one was *using* the room. A relieved look on his face, Luther turned and let Reggie enter the room before him.

"What were you doing, Luther? Making sure none of your friends were making use of *my* bed?"

Luther grinned. "You know how parties are, man. I just didn't want you to be embarrassed."

Reggie dropped down on the foot of his king-sized bed, not even bothering to turn back the comforter as he normally did. "This isn't working out, man," he began. "You have to find your own place."

"I'm looking," Luther said. "But you know it's hard to find the right house in the right neighborhood at the right price. I'll be outta here as soon as I find something that's right for me."

Reggie didn't even want to think about how many times he'd heard that spiel. Luther had been living with him for almost a year now, when they'd originally planned for him to only stay a couple of months. "Well, you'd better start looking harder. I'm giving you a month, Luther. Four more Saturdays and you're outta here."

Luther pulled up the burgundy leather armchair in the corner of the room and sat down facing Reggie. "What happened with you and Deborah?" he asked, concern in his voice.

"I don't even want to talk about it. Just get these people out of my house so I can get some rest."

"She dumped you, didn't she?" When Reggie didn't answer, Luther said, "I knew it. She did, didn't she?"

Reggie fell back on the bed and stared at the ceiling. He noticed a couple of cracks in the crown molding and made a mental note to call his builder. "She just doesn't want an exclusive relationship anymore."

"She dumped you, man. I don't care what pretty words she put around it."

Reggie knew Luther was right, but he didn't want to hear it right now. "Why don't you go and get your party people out of my house?"

"I knew this was going to happen, man," Luther said, ignoring Reggie's request. "I told you that chick had too many problems. Never date a woman with more problems than you. Didn't I tell you that?" He didn't wait for an answer. "Sure, I told you. But did you listen to me? No, you didn't. What did you do? You loaned the sister some cash, helped her find a new job and let her cry on your shoulder. And what did it get you? Dumped. I'm telling you, man, never date a woman with more problems than you, 'cos once they get themselves together, you're history. History with a capital H."

Reggie grabbed a pillow from the bed and threw it at Luther. "Get out of here and get these people out of my house. I need some sleep."

Luther stood up. "Okay, man," he said. "I know you're feeling down right now. But remember there are plenty of women out there. Hell, there are plenty of women at this party. Next time just make sure you don't choose a woman with more problems than you."

Kim hung up after talking to Melvin Gaines, her fourth Nicest Guy finalist. Now she only had one more finalist to call. Reggie Stevens. She picked up his black-and-white photo again. What was it about this guy that tugged at her heart so? she wondered for the hundredth time. Sure, he was good looking, but she'd come across good looking men before. It was more than Reggie Stevens's looks.

Since reading his nomination letters, she felt that she and Reggie were soulmates. She knew she sounded like some lovesick teenager, but that's how she felt. His nominators had all said he was a good guy, a nice guy. Someone they could depend on. A man who was always considerate of them and their feelings. Yes, she concluded, Reggie Stevens was truly one of the good guys. Not like Derrick. No, Derrick was a number one player in nice guy clothing. The kind of guy you had to watch. But Reggie Stevens was the real thing. At least, she thought he was.

She picked up the phone and dialed his number, telling herself there was no need to be nervous. She'd already called the other four finalists, so this one should be a piece of cake.

The phone rang five times and she began to wonder if he was even home. "Hello," a deep, masculine voice said after the sixth ring.

His voice didn't surprise her. It was strong and sure, just as she'd imagined it would be. "May I speak to Reggie Stevens?" she asked anyway. She didn't want to come across as too sure of herself.

"This is he," Reggie answered. "How can I help you?"

Such good telephone manners, she thought. "My name is Kimberla Washington and I'm a writer with *Urban Style* magazine."

"Urban Style," he said, surprised and maybe even a little impressed. "I subscribe to your magazine."

"Well, ah, thank you," Kim said. "The reason I'm calling, Mr. Stevens—"

"I'm Reggie," he said, interrupting her. "My father is Mr. Stevens."

"Well, Reggie, the reason I'm calling is to inform you that you're a finalist in a contest that we're sponsoring."

"You mean somebody nominated me for Bachelor of the Year?" he said, referring to the yearly spread the magazine did on the country's most attractive and successful bachelors.

Kim cleared her throat. "Not exactly. This is a new contest. We're calling it The Nicest Guy in America."

"The Nicest Guy in America?" She heard the suspicion in his voice. "Exactly what kind of contest is this?"

"Well, I'm surprised you haven't heard of it since you subscribe to our magazine. We ran an ad for nominations in last month's issue."

"And I was nominated?"

"More than once," she said.

"You still haven't told me what kind of contest it is."

"As I said, we're calling it The Nicest Guy in America Contest. Women nominated wonderful men they had dated who turned out not to be the right man for them."

Silence.

"You mean women nominated men they dumped? Is this some kind of a joke?"

The words sounded harsh coming from him. "I assure you the contest is being handled with utmost professionalism. It is definitely not a joke."

"It's gotta be a joke, lady. Why do you think I'd want to be featured in a contest about men who've been dumped? Who nominated me, anyway?"

Kim rattled off the six names.

"Damn," he said, again surprised. "I was nominated six times. You must think I'm a number one loser."

"Not at all, Reggie," she chimed in. "You're a finalist because we think you're a true representation of a Nice Guy. Your nomination letters all portrayed you in a most positive manner and with a great deal of respect."

"So what do you want?"

Kim knew she was on the verge of losing him and therefore she had to get to the point of her call before he hung up. "I want to interview you, along with the other finalists of course, for a spread in an upcoming issue of our magazine."

"And what do I get out of being in your magazine?" he

asked, not yet warming to her idea. "Other than having everyone in the country know how many times I've been dumped?"

"Well, we expect this article to bring the kind of response our bachelor issue brings. You'll be getting mail from women all over the country who want to meet a Nice Guy. I'll want to interview you in your home and your place of business and get some candid pictures in both places." She crossed her fingers and her toes and said a silent prayer. "What do you say I come down there next Tuesday, a week from today?"

"I say no. I have no desire to be on display in your magazine. Believe me, women don't want a nice guy. They want some player who looks good, talks smooth and is about as stable as a sand castle. Thanks for the offer, but no thanks. Good-bye, Ms. Washington."

"Wait a minute," Kim said. She couldn't let him get away.

"I was on my way out the door when you called. I don't have all night."

"Won't you just think about the interview? I promise you this article will in no way be embarrassing. It will be an honest look at Nice Guys. We may even use your suggestion and explore why women drop Nice Guys for the not so nice ones. What do you say?"

"I say "no," Ms. Washington. Now, if you'll excuse me, I really do have to go."

"Wait," Kim said, but it was no use. He'd already hung up. "Dag," she said, "I definitely blew that one."

"What's the matter, kiddo?" Jim Whittaker asked.

She looked up, not surprised to see him standing in the doorway of her cubicle. It was almost seven, but many of the staff kept late hours. "How do you do that?" she asked.

Jim perched his bulk on the edge of her desk. "Do what?"

"Show up unexpectedly and jump into the end of my phone conversations." She eyed him closely. "You don't have listening devices in the phones, do you?"

Jim laughed. "Now that's funny, Kimmy. Come on, what's got you so upset?"

"I just called Reggie Stevens, my fifth Nice Guy finalist, and he won't agree to an interview."

"No problem," Jim said with a shrug. "Pick another guy or stick with four." He got up. "I thought you had a real problem. Take care of it, Kimmy. And you'd better start making reservations for your trips to visit these guys. That spread is due in six weeks."

After Jim scooted off to nose in somebody else's business, Kim sat thinking about what he'd said. He was right. She could just pick another finalist or she could go with the four she already had. This wasn't a big deal. So what if Reggie Stevens didn't want to participate? Maybe she'd been wrong about him. Maybe he wasn't a Nice Guy after all. Maybe he was just another guy using another angle to get over on women. Unfortunately for him, his angle wasn't working too well.

Chapter 2

"I think you should do it, man," Luther said. He propped his feet up on the wrought iron and cherry cocktail table in Reggie's den. In the background, an old Al Green tune played from the entertainment center. "A lot of women read *Urban Style*. You'd probably get a lot of play from an article."

Reggie leaned forward and placed his beer bottle on the table. He, Luther and their friend Nate Brown had just returned from their regular Wednesday visit to the Boys' Club. "Is that all you can think about? Meeting women?"

"What else is there?" Luther stretched his arm across the back of the teal leather sofa and tapped Reggie's shoulder. "I figure it this way. I've only got one life and I've got to make the best of it. Like they say, so many women, so little time."

"At least you've stopped marrying every woman you meet," Nate said from the matching club chair next to the sofa. At five-ten, Nate was the shortest of the three friends. His boyish grin made seem the youngest, though he was actually about three months older than Luther who was only a couple of weeks older than Reggie.

Reggie laughed. "Nate has a point, Luther."

"I'm not gonna let Nate press me. He's the only brother I know whose wife filed for divorce on the grounds of boredom."

"At least I was married longer than a week," Nate said.

"Yeah, but your wife was bored to death before the honeymoon was over."

"So what do you have to say to that, Nate?" Reggie asked, getting into the jone-ing. He, Nate and Luther never failed to have a good time when they were together. Sometimes Reggie felt they reverted back to little tykes on the playground. At others, they seemed more like college boys on the make. When they were together, they rarely acted like the thirty-eight year old professionals that they were.

"Man, I don't know why you're laughing," Nate said. "At least, we've been married. You can't get even get a woman to go out with you for more than six months."

"You've got that right," Luther added. "And when you get a chance for some national publicity with the women, you turn it down. You must be losing your mind."

"Or maybe he's just embarrassed," Nate said. "Maybe he doesn't want everybody back home in Oklahoma City to know the high school star quarterback and Most Popular Guy in the Senior Class is the most dumped guy in America."

"Hey, hold up," Reggie said, tapping his toe against the wrought iron base of the cocktail table. While he was used to the teasing his buddies, things were getting out of hand. He looked at Luther. "How would you feel if they told you that you were a finalist in the Most Divorced Man in America Contest?"

"Hey, man," Luther said. "They didn't divorce me. *I* divorced them."

"Yeah," Nate added. "After they threw you out of the house."

Reggie turned to Nate. "How about you, Nate? How'd

you like to be in the Most Boring Ex-Husband in America Contest?''

"Hey, I'm not boring. I'm just shy."

"Right," Luther said with a snort. "You're shy until you open your mouth. Then you're boring." Luther made a snoring sound. "But let's not get off the subject. We're not talking about us, we're talking about Reggie. I still think you ought to do the interview," he said to his friend. "What harm could it do?"

Land another blow to his already bruised ego, maybe? "Too late," Reggie said. "I've already told them no. It's a moot point now, so let's talk about something else. Like your search for someplace else to live."

"I don't know about you, man," Luther said. "I told you I was looking."

"You've been looking for a year. It's time, Luther." Luther's last divorce, his third, had left him anxious to get away from Oklahoma and his ever-increasing number of ex-wives. The Club, a night club for the over-thirty crowd that he'd started before his first marriage, was a huge financial success, but most of the money was going to the ex-wives.

After visiting Reggie in Atlanta only one time, Luther had decided to turn his first club over to the ex-wives and start afresh. He'd gotten Nate, a commercial real estate broker, to help him make a deal on suitable property in Atlanta, and before Reggie knew what was happening, Luther was moving in with him. The exposure Nate had gotten to Atlanta's commercial real estate market convinced him that Atlanta would be a good place for him to expand his business. So, six months later, he, too, was in Atlanta. Fortunately for Reggie, Nate had chosen to get his own place.

"I don't know why you want me to leave," Luther was saying. "It's not like you have a woman or anything."

"It's his house," Nate explained as if talking to a child. "You have money. You could find a place if you weren't so cheap."

"I'm not cheap."

"Yes, you are," Reggie said. "Look at your car. You need a new one. If you ever get stopped in that rat trap, you're going to get a ticket."

"Hey, there's nothing wrong with my car. It's practically an antique."

"Not an antique," Nate said. "More like a junk heap. You're too cheap to buy a new car and too cheap to foot the bill for your own place to live. Maybe your wives divorced you 'cos you're so cheap."

Reggie smiled. He liked putting Luther on the hot seat. "And I know you have plenty of money. You spend as much time with the *Wall Street Journal* as you do in *Playboy.*"

"All right, enough," Luther said. "Just so you know, I've ordered a new car and I'll be out of here at the end of the month just like I told you. But you're gonna miss me. I was about to set you up with a Halle Berry look-alike, but I'm not so sure you deserve a fine woman like her."

Reggie remembered the woman who'd grabbed his butt at Luther's last party. "I don't need a matchmaker. I can find my own women."

"Sure you can," Luther said with sarcasm. "You're the most successful man I know when it comes to the women. Second only to Mr. Boring over there."

"Give the man the digits, Luther," said Nate. "You know you won't be getting any play from her."

Luther opened his mouth to make another crack on Nate, but obviously decided against it. He reached in his pocket and handed Reggie a slip of paper with a name and phone number on it. "Now don't mess this up," he warned Reggie. "This sister has it going on. She's not like the needy women you usually date."

Reggie took the paper and glanced at the info. So, Brandy was her name. "She grabbed my behind the night of your party."

"And that's a bad thing?" Luther asked incredulously. "You can bet if she'd grabbed my butt, I'd be at her house right now."

Reggie shook his head and placed the slip of paper in his pocket. He wasn't sure he was going to call. Brandy was attractive, but she just didn't appeal to him. He liked his women a little less aggressive.

"You're not even going to call her, are you, Reggie?" Luther asked.

"Maybe." Reggie shrugged. "I don't know."

"You're crazy, man," Luther said. "You can't do much better than this sister. She's got beauty, body and brains. You definitely won't have to help her with her rent."

Nate laughed. "He has a point there, Reggie. You might want to make that call."

The last thing Reggie wanted to do was rush into another relationship. He needed some time to figure out what had gone wrong in the last one. In the last few ones, to be exact. His track record hadn't been too good lately. "Maybe I'm thinking about taking a break from women and the dating scene. Everybody seems to be playing games. Women say they want a nice guy and then they go back to the guy who dogged them. I don't understand them."

"Who said you had to understand them?" Luther asked. "Anyway, I don't think it's all women. It's just the women you choose. That's why you need to hook up with Halle. I'm telling you, man, she's got it going on in a major way."

"I'll think about it," Reggie said, but he wouldn't commit to anything more. He was about burned-out. While he tried to be understanding of women and really didn't want to be with a woman who didn't want to be with him, he was finding it more and more difficult to understand the choices women made. For now, he'd stop thinking about it.

Kimberla couldn't stop thinking about Reggie Stevens. It was Tuesday, two weeks to the day since she'd spoken to Reggie on the phone, and she'd just gotten back to D.C. after traveling to Denver and Dallas to interview two of the finalists. Unfortunately, she hadn't been impressed with either of them. Sure, they were nice guys, in a way, but she also thought they were a bit clingy. She imagined that they smothered a girl. She didn't get that impression from Reggie Stevens. Even though he'd turned down her request for an interview and refused to participate in the contest, she still had the lingering feeling he was a true Nice Guy. A guy she'd like to get to know.

Of course, she'd been a bit disappointed when he'd turned her down out of hand, but after she thought about it she had seen his point. A private person might view the contest as a bit over the top. Left to her boss, it might turn out that way, but she was in charge and she was determined that this article would explore male-female relationships and draw some conclusions about why people choose the mates they do. She'd even spoken to a couple of family counselors and psychiatrists. Her article was definitely shaping up to be something she could be proud of. And something she felt Reggie would be proud of too. If only she could convince him to participate.

She shook her head and glanced at her antique grandfather clock, the only furniture she'd taken from her family home when she'd moved out after her mother's death five years ago. Any minute now, Leslie and Tam would be ringing her doorbell wanting to get the scoop on her latest interview. She wondered if she had enough time to call Reggie Stevens again before they arrived.

She tossed aside the paisley sofa pillow she had pulled onto her lap and got up from the loveseat to find his phone number. She thumbed through her Day Timer and quickly found it. Sucking in her breath, she picked up the phone on the wall in her kitchen and began dialing.

Her doorbell sounded after the second ring.

"Damn," she said under her breath. She let the phone ring one more time before deciding to hang up. "Coming," she called to her insistent visitors.

"What took you so long?" Tam asked as soon as Kim opened the door.

"Yeah, you don't have a man in here, do you?" Leslie

added, entering the apartment after Tam. "We don't want to interrupt anything."

"Please," Kim said. "You're not interrupting anything. It just took me a minute to answer the door." She watched her two friends make themselves comfortable on her green corduroy loveseat, then joined them by taking a seat in the matching rocker-recliner across from them.

"So tell us about the guys you interviewed," Leslie said, folding her legs under her.

Kim looked at her eager friends and almost laughed. One would have thought she'd just interviewed celebrities instead of some guys who'd been dumped by their girl-friends. "Unfortunately, there's not much to tell."

"I knew it," Leslie said with satisfaction. "They were duds. Never trust a good guy."

"How would you know, Leslie?" Tam asked. "You've never dated a good guy."

"They were good to me," Leslie said with a sly smile. "One woman's bad is definitely another woman's good."

"You ought to know," Tam smarted. "Lord knows, you've dated enough bad ones."

"Marcus wasn't exactly a saint, Tam," Leslie shot back. "Or have you forgotten?"

Kim had the feeling that things were about to get out of hand with her two friends. Tam resented the speed and ease with which Leslie went through men and Leslie thought Tam was jealous of her because she was so thin. Kim tried not to get in the middle of their brawls, knowing somebody had to be the voice of reason if the three of them were going to remain friends. "Let's not get started tonight," she said. "I'm just not up for it."

"She started it," Leslie said in a voice that indicated she was used to getting her way. "Who made her the morality police?"

"The truth hurts, doesn't it?" Tam said with a smug look on her face.

Kim thought sometimes Tam was a bit too self-righteous

for her own good. "Tam," she warned. "I think we should talk about something else."

"Yeah," Leslie said. "Why don't we talk about Tam's love life?" She covered her mouth. "Oops," she said, "I forgot. She doesn't have a love life."

Kim winced. That was it. The verbal fight was on and nothing she could do would stop it. They'd have to slug it out with words. She listened to the battle for a few minutes. Then, tiring of it, she got up and went into the kitchen to prepare a snack. She knew the combatants would be hungry and thirsty when they finished.

Sure enough, ten minutes later, they joined her in the kitchen. "You guys finished?" Kim asked.

"Finished with what?" Tam said. "We were just having a discussion."

"You didn't have to leave the room," Leslie said. "Why do you do that anyway?"

Kim rolled her eyes. Tam and Leslie's quick make ups always bewildered her. "I don't enjoy hearing my two best friends berate each other," she said, handing a tray of cheese and crackers to Leslie. "Take that back into the great room, will you?"

Leslie took the tray and turned back to the great room. "What do you want me to take?" Tam asked.

Kim pushed the pitcher of tea into her friend's thrust out hands. "You take the pitcher. I'll bring the glasses."

Kim shook her head as she listened to her friends giggling about something. They'd started out as the most unlikely roommates about fourteen years ago. The three of them couldn't have been more different in temperament. Gregarious was too tame a word to describe Leslie, while Tam was quiet and somewhat shy, and she herself was somewhere in the middle, she supposed. What they shared though was a stubborn streak and a strong sense of what they wanted from life.

Leslie's family had wanted her to get a degree and a Morehouse man and not necessarily in that order. Her Spelman graduate mother had married her Morehouse graduate father and her Spelman graduate sister had found and married a Morehouse man as well. But Leslie hadn't been interested in getting married and settling down. She'd chosen instead to major in Chemistry and to do graduate work in the subject at Howard—all without a Morehouse husband. Now, she was an award-winning sales rep for American Pharmaceuticals.

Tam had bucked her blue-collar parents and studied to be a teacher instead of a doctor like her four older sisters. She'd fallen in love with Marcus during freshman year. They'd gotten married right after graduation and she'd followed him to Georgetown University where he'd studied, of all things, medicine.

Kim's parents hadn't understood her career choice either. More than anything Kim had wanted to be a writer. For as long as she could remember, she was writing stories. In high school she was editor of the school newspaper, so it shouldn't have been a surprise to her parents when she wanted to study journalism and creative writing in college. It shouldn't have, but it had. Kim thought it was because her parents had been of another generation. They'd had her when they were in their late forties. In some ways, they'd thought more like grandparents than parents. They'd wanted her to study a safe subject like teaching or nursing which would give her a guarantee of employment when she graduated. But Kim hadn't been able to accommodate them. She'd gone against their wishes and followed her heart.

"Hey, Kim," Tam said once they were all seated in the great room again. "Did you hear about Leslie's promotion?"

"No," Kim said. She turned to Leslie. "Why didn't you tell me?"

"I'm telling you now. You were out of town on one of your interviews when I heard about it."

Kim leaned over and hugged her friend. "Congratulations! Did you get a big raise?"

Leslie grinned and her bright eyes shone. "A big raise *and* a relocation package."

"A relocation package?" Kim and Tam repeated together.

"You're moving?" Kim added.

Leslie chuckled. "Calm down. I'm just moving to Atlanta. No big deal."

"It *is* a big deal," Tam said. "I can't believe you're leaving us."

"Me either," Kim said. "You're really moving." The news unsettled Kim. Leslie and Tam, though trying at times, were the closest thing to family she had and she didn't want them to be separated.

Leslie sat forward on the couch. "I can't turn this down. I'll be in charge of a district sales office. You know how much I want something like this."

"But Atlanta?" Kim said again.

Leslie leaned over and tapped her on the knee. "Don't look so sad. Maybe I'll meet my first Nice Guy in Atlanta. Isn't that where that Reggie guy lives?"

"Sure is," Tam said. "Wouldn't it be something if you ran into him?"

"Yes, it would," Kim said slowly, thoughts of Leslie's move temporarily replaced by thoughts of Reggie. Why did the idea of Leslie and Reggie getting together bother her? "But Atlanta is a big city. Meeting Reggie would be a huge coincidence."

"Hey, I could always look him up," Leslie said. "You have his number, don't you?"

Yes, she did. "You know I can't give you the guy's number."

"Why not?" Tam asked. "It's not as if she's going to stalk him or anything."

"I know that," Kim said. "but what are you going to tell him when he asks how you got his number?"

"Good point," Leslie said. "If he'd agreed to your interview, we'd have a totally different story. Guess I'll have to forget that idea. But hey, you never know. I could still run into him.''

Kim kept thinking about Reggie while her friends moved on to the next topic of conversation. She didn't understand why she felt so possessive about him. It wasn't as though he belonged to her or anything. She didn't even know the man, for goodness' sake.

Reggie slammed his front door after he let himself in. He couldn't believe it. He really couldn't believe it. *I want to see other people,* Deborah'd said. Yeah, right! She'd wanted to see other people, all right. A specific other people.

He strode into his kitchen and pulled open the refrigerator. He still couldn't believe it. He grabbed a can of light beer and popped the top. Then he took a swig of the cold brew, enjoying the burning sensation in his throat. If he hadn't seen it with his own eyes, he would never have believed it. But he *had* seen it, so he had to believe it.

Deborah was out with Eddie! Eddie, the guy who'd moved out without a word, stolen her furniture and raided her bank account. He couldn't believe the woman! She'd dumped him—a guy who'd been good to her—for a low-life like Eddie. Well, he was glad to be rid of her. If she wanted a guy who'd walk all over her, then she deserved Eddie. Taking another swig of beer, he walked into his den and dropped down onto the couch. *Maybe she's lost her mind,* he thought as he flicked the remote and turned on the television. Surely, no sane woman would choose to go back to a man who'd so mistreated her.

"Damn," Reggie muttered. "I can't believe it. I just can't believe it."

But it was true. He'd seen the two of them all snuggled up at The Club. And he knew Deborah had seen him. At least, she'd had the decency to lower her eyes. He hadn't even bothered to speak to her. He was sure she could read the disbelief in his eyes.

Couldn't she see that Eddie is no good? he asked himself. *How could she have convinced herself to go out with him again?*

He shook his head then flipped the remote, looking for something to take his mind off what he now considered, Mindless Women. Then, Reggie flicked off the television, knowing nothing was going to keep his mind off what he'd seen tonight.

He shouldn't care, but he did. Deborah was a nice woman. She really was. A little misdirected. Maybe even a little naive, though she was thirty-five. But he thought she'd grown up a little in their time together. She'd established some goals and was well on her way to achieving them. He'd been proud of the way she'd come back after such an awful time with that Eddie character. But now she'd decided to go back with the rat and Reggie was worried.

He knew he shouldn't be. Deborah was a grown woman, free to make her own choices, whether those choices were good or bad. And this one, he was convinced, was definitely a bad one. He just hoped she didn't get hurt too much. She deserved better. She really did.

He wondered, not for the first time, what made women choose men who were bad for them. What was the appeal of the selfish, self-serving man? Sure, he knew most women would consider Eddie handsome, but there were many men, he was sure, they considered more attractive. Hell, he was pretty sure most women would think *he* was more attractive than Eddie. So, it wasn't the man's looks.

Then what is it? he asked himself. Surely, no woman enjoyed being mistreated, emotionally or physically. He grunted. Maybe it was something even more basic. Could it be that the bad boys were better lovers? *Nah,* he thought with a shake of his head. How could a man whose sole focus was his own needs be a good lover?

But, then, he really didn't know what went on behind closed doors. Maybe the guys were tender and considerate lovers. Maybe that dichotomy in their personality was what trapped the women. Maybe women expected that tenderness in the bedroom to carry over outside it. Maybe, maybe,

maybe. There was no sense in his trying to figure out women and their choices. There was no answer.

Though he wished Deborah the best with Eddie or who-ever she chose, he had the bad feeling Eddie was going to hurt her again. And he suspected she had that feeling too. Obviously, the woman couldn't help herself. She must really think she was in love with the guy. Reggie was convinced though, that it wasn't true love. No, even true love had its bounds. And he was sure Eddie had crossed them.

It's not your problem, he told himself. *It's not your problem.*

Though his words were true, they didn't change his concern. He'd seen Deborah at the lowest point in her life and he didn't want her to go back to that place. She deserved so much more. She hadn't believed that when he'd met her, but he'd been sure she'd finally come to realize it. Maybe he'd been wrong.

The ringing telephone brought him out of his thoughts. He considered letting it ring, but decided against it. He reached for the phone on the sofa table behind him.

"Hello," he said.

"Hello. Reggie Stevens?"

The voice was familiar, but he couldn't place it. "Yes, this is Reggie."

"Reggie," the soft, feminine voice said. "You probably don't remember me, but I called you about a month ago."

He remembered the voice now. The woman from *Urban Style.* Kim something.

"I'm Kimberla Washington from *Urban Style* magazine. I called you about our Nice Guy Contest."

She paused and he knew she wanted him to acknowledge her earlier call. He chose not to oblige.

"Do you remember me?" she asked when she realized he wasn't going to jump in.

"I remember telling you that I didn't want to be inter-viewed and that I didn't want to be featured in your con-test," he said. He knew he was being difficult, but he'd had a long day and this woman was not helping.

"I know that's what you said," she began. "But I was hoping I could change your mind. This article—"

"I'm not changing my mind, Ms. Washington. I don't want to be included in your article and I don't want to be interviewed."

"But the article is shaping up to be something I'm sure you'd approve."

"Look, Ms. Washington, I don't mean to be rude, but I'm really not interested in how your article is shaping up. As I told you before, I don't want to participate."

"But—"

"No buts, Ms. Washington, just no. Now, I have to go. Have a good evening."

Reggie hung up the phone rather abruptly, he knew. But the woman should learn to accept "no". Why should he participate in a Nice Guy Contest, only to get mail from women who said they wanted a nice guy, but, given the chance would choose a bad one every time?

Why did women say they wanted one type of guy and choose the exact opposite? That was the question he wanted answered. Ms. Kimberla Washington ought to do an article on that. But, he was sure that kind of article wouldn't appeal to her. She wanted to perpetrate the myth that women were looking for good guys. Well, he knew it was only a myth.

And myths needed to be exposed. Reggie got up from the couch and walked over to the burgundy leather chair and cherry desk that defined his home office. Maybe it was time for the myth to be exposed. And maybe he was the guy to do it.

He eased down into his high-back chair and flicked on his computer. First, he needed a title. If he intended to do this, he was going to do it right.

That's it, he thought, when the perfect title passed through his mind. He knew he was onto something when he typed the words, "Double Minded Women and Their Two-Timing Men."

Chapter 3

Kim was still thinking about Reggie Stevens a week later, after meeting with Jim to discuss the status of the article. He agreed that it was shaping up well so Kim should have been satisfied, but she wasn't. She knew Reggie Stevens would add a uniqueness, a spark which the article lacked without him. Too bad she couldn't convince him to participate.

She sat down at her desk and checked her calendar. She still had two more interview trips to make. Just as she was about to pick up her phone to make travel plans, it rang.

"*Urban Style,* Kim Washington speaking."

"Kim, have you seen The Papyrus?" Tam's excited voice rushed out. "Girl, you've got to see the paper."

"What's up? Tell me what you read in the paper. I haven't picked up my copy today."

"You're not going to believe this," Tam said. "You're not going to believe it."

"Come on, Tam, you're making me nervous. Tell me."

"It's that guy. You know, Reggie Stevens. He's written an article."

Kim leaned forward, her interest piqued. "About what?"

"You're not gonna believe this title. This Reggie Stevens is a bad brother. I wouldn't mind meeting him myself."

Kim understood that feeling totally. She certainly wanted badly to meet him. "Come on, Tam. Tell me about the article."

"Girl, the title is something. Double-Minded Women and their Two-Timing Men. Can you believe that?"

It was definitely an attention grabber, Kim had to agree. But a title didn't tell her enough. "So what does he say?"

"I can't explain it to you. You have to read it for yourself. I have to go now so I can finish it. Too bad you couldn't interview this guy. He definitely has some strong opinions on male-female relationships."

"Can't you—" Kim began.

Kim heard Jim bellow her name. "Kimmy!"

"Forget it, Tam. I'll get my own paper. Thanks for telling me about the article."

"Any time, girl," Tam said. "What are friends for anyway?"

Kim hung up, picked up her pad and headed back to Jim's office. A bellow usually indicated that a pad was needed.

"Did you see this paper?" Jim demanded just as she entered his office. He handed her the Lifestyle page. "Read that."

In big, bold letters were the words, "Double Minded Women and their Two Timing Men—Reggie Stevens speaks out for the nice guys in America." Kim skimmed the article. "There is much media attention these days on the black woman and her unsuccessful search for a mate," Kim read to herself. "A good man, these women complain, is hard to find. All the black men are either married, gay or in jail, hordes of single black women complain. They constantly moan, If only I could find a nice guy. I'm not looking for a rocket scientist of a Tyson double, they say, just a nice, simple guy who's not playing games and who understands the definition of commitment."

"To these black women, I say, Stop lying to yourselves

and to the nice black men that you say you're looking for.
Black women today may say with their lips that they want
a nice guy, but their actions speak a different truth. Consider the woman who leaves a hard-working, straight-forward
brother for a guy who puts her down and always wants to
borrow money from her. Or the woman who chooses a
man with four other women over a guy who believes in
monogamy. What about the other women who say they
want a nice guy, but who choose the exact opposite? From
a nice guy who's been through his share of women who
talked the talk, but didn't walk the walk, I say these women
are double-minded and have no idea what they really want.
And I also say that these women deserve the two-timing
men they choose." Kim didn't need to read any more
right now to get Mr. Stevens' drift. No, the man had been
perfectly clear. In a single article, he'd slammed the entire
black female population. She wondered if she'd judged
him a true nice guy prematurely. She looked up at Jim.
"What about it?"

"What about it?" he shouted. "Isn't this Stevens guy
one of the finalists in the Nicest Guy in America Contest?"

Kim shook her head. "We wanted him, but he refused
the interview. You remember, don't you?"

Jim waved his hands disregarding her words. "Get him
for the article, Kim. We need him."

"No, we don't. I thought you said the article was shaping
up nicely."

"That was before I saw this paper and talked to the
editor. It seems the story originated in the *Atlanta Voice*
and was picked up by the *Number One* urban radio station
in Atlanta. The DeeJays are talking up the article and
getting their listeners to discuss its merits. This means other
papers in other urban markets are going to be picking up
the story and other radio stations are going to be talking
about it. The word on the street is that Tom Joyner will
be joining the discussion in the next few days."

Kim glanced at the article again. If Tom Joyner was going
to start discussing Reggie's article on his syndicated show,

then the article would probably end up in all the urban papers. Tom had Oprah-like clout in that sense. And given the title and contents of the article, Kim wouldn't be surprised if Reggie ended up on some local, maybe even national, talk shows. She began to see Jim's point.

"We have to get him, Kimmy," Jim continued. "This is too good to pass up. Just think what this guy could do for our circulation. We could put him on the cover with Nice Guy Fights Back. You've got to get him, Kimmy, and you have to get to him before the other magazines do. I'll bet *Ebony, Essence, Upscale* and *Emerge* have already contacted him. *Upscale* might be our strongest competition since they're based in Atlanta and have the hometown advantage."

Kim understood Jim's position, but she didn't see how she could convince Reggie Stevens to participate. She told Jim as much.

"Well, you'd better come up with something because we have to have him. Consider getting Reggie Stevens on the cover of *Urban Style* your sole job right now. And Kimmy, don't let me down."

Kim knew further explanation was futile. Jim didn't want excuses. He wanted results. But how could she do it? She'd already called the man twice and he'd made it clear that he wasn't interested. "Okay, Jim, I'll do my best to get him," she finally said.

"Don't do your best, Kimmy. Get him."

Kim nodded and walked out of his office and back to her desk. The first thing she needed to do was get a copy of the paper and read the article in full. Then she needed to call her friend at WBAH, the local station that ran Joyner's show, and find out if he was really going to talk about Reggie's article. Jim's info could be wrong; in which case getting to Reggie was not as urgent. But if, as Jim expected, Joyner was taking the topic to the air waves, she had to get Reggie for *Urban Style* and she had to get him soon.

* * *

Reggie Stevens was having a hell of week. Ever since his article had run in last week's Voice and Tom Joyner had discussed it on his radio show, his phone had been ringing off the hook. It had gotten so bad at work that his partner had told him to try working from home. He was trying, but not with a lot of success. The steady phone calls and visits from reporters seeking interviews and women wanting to take him out distracted him so much that he couldn't concentrate well enough to find the security leak in his new client's program.

"Still hiding out in here, man?" Luther said when he joined Reggie in the den. His friend hadn't moved out as scheduled and Reggie had to admit that having him around was paying off for a change. His friend did a lot to keep the uninvited guests away from him.

"I'm not hiding out. I'm just trying to get some work done. I have a business to run, remember?"

"You wouldn't need to work so hard on your business if you'd take some of the offers coming your way. Have you thought about doing the column for the paper? The guy seemed pretty sure that you could join one of the major syndicates right away."

Reggie looked at his friend. "I'm no writer, Luther. I can't even believe they want me to do a column."

"Believe it, my friend. You're hot stuff right now. But you'd better pounce on it while you're still the flavor of the month. You know what they say about fleeting fame and all that."

Reggie knew what they said, but he didn't care. If someone had told him that a single article written at the height of his frustration would have garnered this much publicity, he wouldn't have believed them. He still couldn't believe what was happening and he was living it. In addition to the offer to do the column, he'd been approached by publishers with offers to do a book, a TV promotions manager about hitting the talk show circuit, and even an offer for his own local radio talk show. All because of one article.

Not that he didn't believe what he'd said in the article. He did. And he believed what he said needed to be said. But now that he'd said it and people had read it, he'd done what he'd set out to do. People were thinking about and talking about what he'd written. If just one woman made the decision not to enter a bad relationship because of his words or if one brother decided to change his ways, he would have made a major contribution to society.

He couldn't tell much from his most recent mail though. The letters seemed to be split between women who were looking for a man "just like him", to women who felt he was challenging their right to date the men of their choice, to men who felt he'd forsaken the brotherhood, and on to those men who agreed with every word he'd written. He assumed it would be a while before the life-changing letters started flowing in.

"Did you go through today's mail?" Luther asked.

"I didn't get around to it yet. Is there a lot?"

Luther nodded. "You're going to have to hire a press secretary. I can't keep up with it all."

"I can't afford a press secretary," Reggie said. "I don't even *want* one."

Luther clapped him on the shoulder. "You'd better face reality, my man. You're a celebrity now and you've got to deal with it. Maybe you should call Denzel and figure out how he handles fame."

Reggie shrugged off his friend's hand. "That's not funny, Luther. I'm not a celebrity."

"Keep telling yourself that, but in the meantime, take a peek out your window and tell me why those people are outside."

Reggie got up and looked out the den window. About fifteen people were milling around the front of his house. "What are they doing here?" he asked.

"Well, the reporters are looking for a story and the

women are looking for a date. I'll make a deal with you, you talk to the reporters and I'll handle the women."

Reggie shook his head. "This is funny to you, isn't it?"

"No way. I take my women very seriously."

Reggie peeked out of the window again. "How long have they been out there?"

Luther shrugged. "I'm not sure. It looks like the number is growing. You're going to have to do something or they may never leave."

"Do what?"

"You might try giving an interview."

"No way. No interviews. That'll only feed the frenzy. Can't you do something? You're the night club owner. Handling these people should be right up your alley."

"Okay," Luther said. "I'll go out there and see what's up. I'm not making any promises though."

"Thanks, man. I don't know what I would have done without you the last couple of days."

Luther grinned. "Does that mean I'm welcome to stay here as long as I like?"

Reggie laughed. "It depends on how well you take care of those people out there."

"Let me get on it then," Luther said and left the room.

Reggie dropped back down in his chair still wondering about the interest the article had sparked. Unexpectedly, thoughts of Kim Washington popped into his mind. He wondered what she thought about his newfound fame. He wouldn't be surprised if she called again to coax him to participate in her article. He was savvy enough to understand that his article and his subsequent celebrity would give her renewed interest in him as a subject. He wondered what tack she would take this time to get him to change his mind.

"Kim, it's perfect," Leslie said. The three friends were sharing a quiet Saturday afternoon at Kim's apartment. "You can come to Atlanta with me. While I'm looking for a place to live, you can track down Reggie Stevens. You'll have a better chance of changing his mind if you see him face-to-face. Plus, we'll get to have some fun in Hot Lanta. I could even take some time off and we could make a working vacation of it."

"I don't know," Kim said. The idea of tracking down Reggie Stevens didn't exactly appeal to her. It made her seem a little too much like the crazy women he'd portrayed in his article. She didn't appreciate the similarity.

"Hey, maybe I could come too," Tam added. "School's out so Melissa will be spending some time with Marcus and I'm not teaching this summer. It would be perfect. Come on, Kim, think about it."

"I think I'm gonna try calling him one more time," she said. "Then maybe I'll make the trip to Atlanta when I have an interview scheduled."

"Works for me," Tam said. "Either way you're coming to Atlanta. We're going to have a ball."

"And I'd better do some shopping," Leslie said. "I don't have anything fit for Atlanta. You guys want to come with me?"

Kim shook her head. "No, I'd better try to get Mr. Stevens on the phone again."

"How about you, Tam?"

Tam hopped up from the couch. "Sounds good to me."

Kim got up and escorted her friends to the door.

"Give us a call and let us know what happens," Tam said. "We're going to need to make reservations."

"Okay, I'll do that. You two have fun shopping. And don't spend too much money."

"You'd better let me handle the reservations, Kim," Leslie said, looking back over her shoulder. "American Pharmaceuticals owns a hotel there and my relocation packages allows me to stay there free for three months while I'm looking for a place to live. I'm sure I can get you two an excellent rate. I'll check on the rates for three-bedroom suites and see what I can hook up. This could turn out to be a very cheap vacation."

"Sounds good to me," Tam said and Kim agreed. She had no doubt Jim would be excited about getting a break on her travel costs. That detail covered, Kim watched her friends as they made their way to their car. Then she closed her door and headed back for the telephone. She'd give Reggie Stevens one more chance before she showed up on his doorstep.

Here goes nothing, she said to herself as she picked up the phone and dialed Reggie's number.

"Hello," she said when someone picked up on the fourth ring.

"Hello." The masculine voice didn't belong to Reggie.

"May I speak to Reggie Stevens please?"

"May I ask who's calling?"

Kim didn't really want to tell who she was, but she didn't see any other alternative. "I'm Kim Washington from *Urban Style Magazine.*"

"Oh, you're the one with the Nice Guy Contest."

"That's me. Do you think I could speak with Mr. Stevens?"

"You'll probably have better luck speaking to me. You're not too high on Mr. Stevens's list right now."

"Well, you seem to know a lot about me. Who are you?"

"I'm Luther Cross, Reggie's best friend."

Ahhh, Kim thought. *A best friend.* This could work to her advantage. "What do you think about your friend doing the interview?"

"Hey, I already told him he was crazy for not doing it. I'd volunteer myself but I've never been dumped. Women know a good thing when they meet one."

Kim erased modesty as a possible trait for Luther. "That's not what your friend said in his article. According to him, women always dump the real thing for an imitation."

"He was in a bad mood when he wrote that article. He'd just found out that his last girlfriend had gone back to her previous old man. The guy was bad news. And that's an understatement."

Some things began to become clearer for Kim. "You mean Reggie recently broke up with someone?"

"No, what I mean is somebody recently broke up with him. I think she dumped him a few nights before you called about the contest."

Talk about bad timing, Kim thought. No wonder Reggie hadn't wanted to participate in the contest. "I guess my timing could have been better, huh?"

"Just a little," Luther said with a chuckle. "Reggie's a nice guy, no joke intended. Under other circumstances I'm sure he would have cooperated. But now . . . I'm just not sure."

"Has he been contacted by a lot of people?" she asked. "Since his article, I mean." It seemed Luther was in a talking mood so she thought she should take advantage of it.

"The phone hasn't stopped ringing and people are practically camping out in the yard. It's a madhouse around here."

Just what she didn't want to hear. "Is he talking to anybody?"

"Only the people I let through to him. And then I have to fight to get him to talk."

"What do I have to do for you to get me in to see him?" she asked.

"Let me think for a minute," Luther said. Shortly, she heard him snap his fingers. "I've got it. Think about me when you do your Most Eligible Bachelors feature. I think I'm a good candidate."

Think about him? She could do that. "All right, you have a deal. Now let me speak to Reggie."

"Just remember the name is Luther Cross. Hold on a minute."

Kim held her breath while she waited for Luther to get Reggie to the phone. She knew this was her last chance.

"Hello, this is Reggie."

He didn't have to tell her. She recognized his voice.

"Hello, Reggie, this is Kim Washington from *Urban Style.* I saw your article."

"You did?" he said.

"Of course. You've become an instant celebrity."

"I don't know about all that," he said and she felt he meant it. Reggie Stevens didn't strike her as the false modesty type of guy.

"You have to know why I'm calling, Reggie. We still want to feature you in our contest. Won't you think about it?"

"I already have. It's just not something I want to do."

"But think about all the exposure you'll get."

"I think I have enough exposure right now. Believe it or not, I'm a private person."

"But don't you have some things to say? Your article indicates you're a man with a lot on your mind. Why did you write that article if you wanted to remain a private person?"

She heard his frustrated sigh. "I'm asking myself that question a lot lately. I wrote it because I thought there needed to be a voice of reason in this world of insanity."

"So you think women are insane because of the choices they make in men?"

"Some of them. Don't you think so?"

"I'm not sure I totally agree with you," she hedged, looking for an entrance to further her cause, "but I can see some of your points. Wouldn't you like to expand on them in the magazine? I assure you we'd give you wonderful coverage. My editor has even suggested putting you on the cover."

"Whoa. First you want an interview for a contest, and now you're talking a cover story. That's not me. I told you I'm trying to keep a low profile."

"Look, Reggie," Kim said, her patience growing short. "I think you'd better give up this search for a low profile. After that article, you're going to be in the spotlight for a while."

"Not if I keep refusing interviews."

"You don't know much about the press, do you? The

more you won't talk to us, the more we want to talk to you. I wouldn't be surprised if someone hasn't already contacted your family and your friends trying to get information. That's the way we do it. If we can't get to the source, we get to those around the source."

"So, who have you talked to Ms. Washington?"

"I only want to talk to you. What do you say? I can be in Atlanta in two days."

Kim waited with her fingers crossed while he thought about her proposition.

"I just don't think so, Ms. Washington. I'm sorry, but I don't want to be in your magazine."

Reggie's phone rang at midnight and he had to answer it since Luther was no where to be found. He gave a groggy hello, hoping the caller would think he was asleep and kindly hang up.

"You can't be sleeping, bro," his brother William said. "You're a big star now."

Reggie smiled at his brother's wit. "Some star. How's everybody?" He had spoken to his mother about two weeks ago but that was before the article.

"Healthy, but talking. You've made the papers out here in Oak City. You should see Mom and Dad. They're proud their son is a star, but a bit concerned about his disastrous love life. I'm surprised they haven't called you."

Reggie sighed. He was surprised too. Though he was the oldest of the Stevens boys, his family tended to treat him like the baby since he wasn't married. The attitude wore on him at times. "They probably couldn't get through," he said. "I'll call them tomorrow."

"You always were brave," William said with a chuckle. "I don't know if I'd be up to the drill. You know how Mom is about seeing you married and settled down like your younger brothers."

"Speaking of settled down, how's that beautiful wife of yours and those wild animals you call sons?"

William chuckled. "Still beautiful and still wild. Kathy sends her love. She says she has a friend she wants you to meet."

"Oh, no," Reggie said. "I'm don't need setting up. I can manage my own love life."

"Not according to that article you wrote. What's really going on, man?"

Reggie settled back in the bed and told his brother the events leading up to his writing the article. "And on top of getting dumped," Reggie continued. "I had an offer to be in a Nicest Guy in America Contest."

Reggie then explained the contest and the industrious Ms. Washington who wouldn't take no for answer.

"This Ms. Washington sounds interesting. You ought to do the interview, bro, just so you can meet her."

Reggie faked a yawn. "When your little brother starts advising you on your love life, it's time to end the conversation." He and his brother exchanged a few more quips, said good-night, then hung up. Reggie went to sleep thinking about Ms. Kim Washington.

Chapter 4

"If I had known that all we were going to do was stand around in front of the man's house, I'd have gone house hunting with Leslie."

Kim looked over at Tam and felt sorry for her friend. It was ninety degrees or more and Tam looked as though she could use a dip in a cool pool. "Well, I didn't plan to spend the day out here either. You'd think the guy had found a cure for AIDS instead of just having written an article."

"Look who's talking. You're trying to get to him yourself. I thought you called before we came over here."

"I did, but no one answered." Kim had wanted to speak with Luther again. She was hoping he'd get her in to see Reggie. "I thought that if we were here when he came home we'd have a better chance of seeing him." Plus, she didn't want the other reporters here to have an advantage over her.

Tam wiped the sweat from her brow. "You call that a plan?"

"Forget it, Tam. Why don't you go back to the car and turn on the air-conditioner?"

Tam turned up her nose. "I have a better idea. Why don't I leave the cell phone with you and go back to the air-conditioned hotel?"

"And leave me out here?"

Tam looked around at the other people milling around Reggie Stevens's house. "It's not like you'll be by yourself."

Kim considered her friend's words and decided she had a point. There were at least a half-dozen reporters present along with a handful of women looking to meet the man of the hour. "Okay, give me the phone. I'll call you when I'm ready to leave." Tam handed her the phone and turned to go to the car which was parked around the corner. "And please hang around the hotel, Tam," Kim called after her. "I don't want to have to stay here all night."

Tam threw up her hand and waved back to Kim, not even taking the time to look back. Kim just shook her head. She hoped this trip to Atlanta wasn't going to turn out to be a bust.

She walked over to Glenda, one of the reporters she'd met earlier, and leaned against the hood of her rented brown sedan. Glenda was freelancer looking to break into the big magazines like *Essence* and *Ebony*. Kim was about the speak when Glenda said, "Here he comes."

Kim turned and saw a red Spitfire turn into the driveway. "Please don't let them drive into the garage," she prayed. "Please."

The gods must have been on her side because the Spitfire, whose dealer plates indicated it was a recent buy, stopped in the driveway and the engine was shut off. *I'd never have expected Reggie to be a Spitfire kind of man,* she thought. She expected him to be a bit more conservative in his choice of vehicle.

She braced herself to see him get out of the car. A tall, thin, light brown-skinned brother wearing aviator sunglasses got out on the driver's side. Attractive guy, she thought, but definitely not Reggie.

Then Reggie emerged from the passenger side—tall,

dark, his broad shoulders exposed by a short sleeve navy T-shirt and hairy legs left bare by his knee-length shorts. The brother was fine. No other way to say it. Reggie Stevens had it going on and then some.

Some of the reporters began calling his name, but he just threw up his hand in an absent wave and made his way into the house. The driver, she wondered if he was Luther, approached the crowd.

"When's he going to give us a break, Luther?" the male reporter standing next to her asked. Kim knew the guy to be from a local Atlanta paper.

So she'd been right, and the guy was Luther. She wanted to talk to him, but she didn't want to approach him in front of the others. She didn't need to alienate any of her peers by asking for special favors. Luther's gaze met hers through his sunglasses and she turned away, not wanting him to ask who she was. She eased away from the crowd and watched him from afar as he joked with the reporters and flirted with the ladies anxious to meet the man who'd penned the article they'd read.

Kim made a quick trip around the corner, pulled out her cell phone and dialed Reggie's number. She hoped he'd pick up.

"Hello Reggie," she said without preamble. "Guess who this is?"

He laughed and the sound trickled down her spine. "I don't have to guess. Hi, Ms. Washington. It's been a while," he said sarcastically. It was Monday and she'd spoken to him Saturday, just two days ago.

"You should know by now that I don't give up, Reggie. You're going to give me an interview and you're going to appear in the magazine."

He laughed again and the sound had the same effect on her. "You're pretty sure of yourself, aren't you, Ms. Washington?"

"With reason, Mr. Stevens," she said, enjoying the lightness of her conversation with him. "You see, I know you really want to do this interview with me. You just don't know it yet."

He chuckled. "And I suppose you're going to convince me the way you convinced Luther?"

"Luther's a smart man and he has your best interests at heart."

A snort followed his next chuckle. "If you really believe that then you must be one of those women who make poor choices in men. I admit I'm disappointed in you. And I had such high hopes, too."

She knew he was kidding, but the idea of him thinking about her gave her a certain feminine satisfaction. "Are you saying Luther's not one of the Nice Guys?"

"Why don't you ask Luther the next time you talk to him?"

"What makes you think I'm going to talk to him again?" she asked, enjoying the back-and-forth with him.

"You said you didn't give up easily and right now Luther is your only road to me. I figure you're going to try again to get him to set you up with an interview."

He'd read her right. If he turned her down again, she was definitely going back to Luther waving the Most Eligible Bachelors story bait under his nose. "Are you telling me no again, Mr. Stevens?"

"You've got it, Ms. Washington. Maybe you're a smart woman after all."

"Thanks," she said dryly. "Why don't you tell that to my boss. Want me to give you his number? Or maybe I could bring him over and you could tell him in person?"

His deep laughter sounded again. "It's been nice talking to you, Ms. Washington, but I have a life that I have to get back to. Take care of yourself."

"Reggie," she began, but it was too late. He'd already hung up.

"Well," she said to herself, flipping her phone closed. "It's not over yet, Mr. Stevens. I'm going to get my interview."

* * *

Reggie stared at the phone and thought about Kim Washington. He'd been doing a lot of that lately and he couldn't understand why. He hadn't even met the woman, but there was something about her that intrigued him. Maybe it was her undaunting determination. Sexually aggressive women usually didn't hold much appeal for him, but he found Kim's professional aggressiveness most attractive. Under different circumstances, he might have welcomed her interest. But not in this case.

"There are some fine sisters out there, man," Luther said, interrupting his thoughts. He'd finally decided to come into the house. "If I were you, I'd start giving interviews."

Reggie moved away from the phone and wiped Kim Washington from his mind. Almost. "That's because you'd do anything to get a phone number."

Luther grinned. "Not anything," he said, "But I'd certainly give a few interviews. What do you have to lose, man? You don't have to talk to all of them. Just pick a couple and be done with it. I'm beginning to get tired of the crowd myself."

"That's why you're always out there flirting with them and shooting the breeze?" Reggie took a seat on the leather couch in his den.

Luther leaned against the door jamb. "Hey, I'm just trying to be hospitable."

Reggie looked up at Luther and snorted. "Pretty soon you'll be taking them lemonade."

Luther shook his head. "A cold brew is more my style, but you may have a point. Maybe I'll end up in the paper instead of you."

"Go for it, man, if that's what you want. Just keep me and my name out of it."

Luther flopped down on the couch next to Reggie. "Why don't you come out to The Club tonight?"

Reggie considered it, but he really wasn't in the mood and told Luther so.

"You're turning into a real hermit, Reggie. All you've done since you wrote that article is make the Wednesday night visits to the Boys' Club. You've got to get out of this house. Your staying at home like this is not natural."

"And going out every night is?"

"It beats sitting here staring at the walls."

"Don't you get tired of it, Luther? We're thirty-eight years old. That's too old to be running to clubs all the time."

Luther shook his head. "Age is in your mind, brother. And besides, it's not like we're running to clubs and hanging out. The Club is a mature place with mature, going somewhere people out for a good time and some relaxation."

Reggie knew Luther was right. Most of the regulars at The Club were professional types like them. But sometimes Reggie got tired of it. "Even so, I'm not up for it tonight."

"Deborah still got you down?"

He shrugged. "Not really. Deborah's an adult. I can't be responsible for her decisions."

"But you're going to help her out once this guy dumps her again, aren't you?"

"I like her and I'll be there for her as a friend. But that's it. You know me, no backtracking." Reggie knew his limits and one was that he never went back to a relationship once it was over. He could remain friends with his ex-lady but he couldn't and wouldn't try to recapture what had been lost.

"Yeah, I do know you and that's one of your best rules because God knows you don't have a clue about picking women."

Reggie closed his eyes and leaned his head back against the sofa. "Not that again."

"Okay, I won't get into it. But why don't you let me fix you up with the Halle girl? She's still available and still interested."

Reggie shook his head as a thought of Kim Washington appeared in his mind. "She's not my type."

"Right. She has a job and good sense. I should have known she wouldn't be your type." Luther stood up and looked down at Reggie. "Look, you can sit here and stare at the walls all night, but I'm going out."

"Fine," Reggie said. "Have a good time. Are you going to call Nate?"

Luther snorted. "I want to have a good time. Bringing Nate along is like bringing your own wet blanket. You should invite him over to spend the evening with you. That way you two could be boring together."

"I just might do that."

Luther shook his head. "I was joking. Man, you really do need to get a life."

The phone rang and Luther turned and picked it up. Reggie's immediate thought was that Kim was calling again, but he didn't ask. If Luther thought he was interested in Ms. Washington, he'd have her in the house before Reggie could count to ten.

Reggie wondered what a Kim Washington looked like. Was she thin, heavy? Tall, short? Light, dark? Did she smile a lot or was she reserved? He'd guess she was open and friendly. Probably had lots of friends, male and female. Of course, she was determined. Probably had a list of goals that she clicked off with regularity. A level-headed woman for a change.

He looked back at Luther who was now whispering into the phone. *Must be one of his women,* Reggie thought. Luther probably wouldn't be going to The Club alone after all.

Kim closed her flip phone. She couldn't believe her good luck. Luther had come through for her and she was going to get her interview with Reggie Stevens. All she had to do was be at the back door of Reggie's house in ten minutes and Luther would let her in. Unfortunately, she had to do this without her colleagues noticing her. Now, how was she going to accomplish that feat?

She peeked around the corner and saw that her colleagues were still in place in front of Reggie's house. That made simply walking around to the back of the house out of the question. No, she'd have to come in through the yard of the house behind Reggie's. That in mind, she continued around the corner to the next street and made her way down to the house that was directly behind Reggie's. The brick ranch was almost identical in style to his.

Her first thought was about whether the occupants of this house had a dog. She tossed the question aside and counted her blessings that they didn't have a fence. She walked across the lawn and around to the back of the house, only to find that a four-foot redwood fence separated the two yards. Now what was she going to do?

She looked down at her short blue skirt and cursed the unsuitability of her attire for climbing fences. Thank God, she had on sensible shoes. After looking around and making sure that no one was watching, she hiked up her skirt and heaved herself across the short fence.

Male laughter greeted her once she was on Reggie's side of the divide. "Nice legs," Luther said. "Maybe you ought to be interviewing me instead of Reggie."

Kim righted her skirt, uncomfortable with Luther's staring. "You could have told me about the fence," she said.

He continued to stare at her. "Would it have made any difference?"

She pursed her lips and strode toward him. "You know it wouldn't have, but you still could have told me."

He chuckled. "Hey, if I had told you, you might have figured out that you could have opened the gate over there and walked through. Then I would have missed that grand showing of leg."

Kim looked behind her, and sure enough there was a gate in the fence. She had to look closely to find it, since it blended in so well with the fence, but it was there. "No wonder you didn't make it to The Nice Guy contest," she said. "You're definitely *not* a nice guy."

Luther flashed a grin that Kim imagined had blown the mind of many sane women. "Now how can you say that? I'm setting my best friend up for an interview that I know he doesn't want to do and I'm doing it just for you. That alone should tell you I'm a good guy."

He had a point, but Kim wasn't ready to concede it just yet. "I haven't gotten the interview yet. For all I know, Reggie is going to throw me out of his house."

He shook his head. "You don't know Reggie, if you think that. He'd never throw a woman out of his house."

Luther's words gave Kim a bit of reassurance. At least, she'd have a chance to make her case face-to-face.

"No, Reggie wouldn't throw you out," Luther continued. "He'd just escort you to the front door."

Her lips turned up in a grim smile. "Cute, Luther. Now do I have to stand out here all afternoon or are you going to let me into the house?"

Luther pushed the storm door open and stood back so she could enter. She crossed the concrete patio and entered before him.

"Nice perfume," he said as she passed him.

She turned back and cocked a brow at him. "Are you sure you and Reggie are friends?"

He laughed. "I think that's an insult."

"Smart man," she said, surveying what she expected was an immaculate house, judging from the state of the ultra-modern and ultra-clean kitchen. Every imaginable kitchen appliance was there and every counter looked as if it had been recently scrubbed clean. "Now where's Reggie?"

Luther inclined his head toward the door leading out of the kitchen to the rest of the house. "He's in the den. Are you sure you're ready to meet Mr. Nice Guy?"

She sucked in her breath. "The real question is, is he ready to meet me."

Luther stared at her for a long second. Too long a

second. "Hmm. I think he may be more ready than even he realizes."

Before Kim could ask Luther what he meant, he'd taken her hand and was guiding her through Reggie's house and, she hoped, to Reggie.

"Hey, Reggie," he called out when they were in the living room. "You have company."

"Nice announcement," she murmured sarcastically.

"Thanks," he said.

While they waited for Reggie, Kim took in the soft tones of his living room and was pleased that Reggie wasn't a brother who leaned towards dark colors and hard woods. The linen sofa and loveseat covered with pillows in shades of red, green, blue and beige gave the room an intimate, yet open, feel.

"I didn't hear the—" Reggie stopped mid-sentence when he saw her. He captured her gaze and wouldn't let it go. "A reporter?" he asked.

"Not just any reporter," Luther said, ushering Kim toward Reggie. "*The* reporter. This is Kim Washington from *Urban Style*. Kim, I guess you know who this is."

Kim tore her gaze away from Reggie's piercing one and extended her hand. He stared at it for a second too long and she wondered if he was going to leave her hanging. Evidently, the gentleman in him took over and he clasped her hand in both of his.

"Well, well, well," he said, his large hands warm and comforting. "You *are* industrious, aren't you?"

Kim had the feeling he was laughing at her, but for some reason, it didn't bother her. His laughter didn't make fun of her. Rather, it applauded her efforts.

"I told you," she said, gently easing her hand from the warmth of his. There was something sensual in the way his hands wrapped around hers. "We were destined to get together. Just as you're destined to appear on the cover of *Urban Style*."

"I'm not too sure about that." His smile told her he was flirting with her. "Let's take this one step at a time."

She joined in his game. "And what's the first step?"

Luther cleared his throat. "I'll take that as my cue to leave. This seems to be getting serious."

Kim watched as Reggie shot his friend a glance that said he wanted to talk privately with him. He turned to Kim, his smile in place, and said, "Why don't you make yourself comfortable?" He pointed to the linen sofa she'd admired earlier. "I need a minute with Luther then I'll be right with you."

Kim looked from him to Luther and back again. "No problem," she said. "Take your time. I'm not going anywhere."

He smiled at her again. "For some reason, Ms. Washington, I didn't expect you would be." He turned then and followed Luther out of the room.

Chapter 5

Reggie joined Kim in the living room a few minutes later. She wondered about the words he'd had with Luther, but decided not to inquire about them. She was here to get an interview and she didn't want to get distracted. Maintaining her professional distance would be hard anyway given her physical response to the man.

"Thank you for the interview, Mr. Stevens," she said as a peace offering.

He gave her a smug smile. "I didn't have much choice, did I? You and Luther pretty much railroaded me into this."

"You can always kick me out," she said, hoping he wouldn't take her up on her offer.

"I could," he agreed with a nod.

"But you won't?" she said, more a question than a comment. *Please,* she prayed, *don't let him escort me to the door.*

His smile turned real and her insides turned to mush. It's just a smile, she reminded her racing heart. "You're right. I won't. Do you want something to drink before we get started?"

She shook her head. "I'm fine. But get yourself something if it'll make you more comfortable."

"I'm fine too." He took a seat on the couch next to her and turned his body slightly so that he faced her.

Kim felt his warmth and wondered at it. What was it about Reggie Stevens that tugged at her senses? "All right, then. Are you ready to get started?"

"As ready as I'm ever going to be. Shoot."

She reached into her purse for her pad and pencil, thankful for a reason to turn her gaze away from him. "Okay, let's start with the easy questions. Where are you from?"

"Oklahoma City," he answered. "Born and bred."

Kim didn't know anyone from Oklahoma City, not that it mattered. "Family still there?"

"Mother and father. Two brothers, two sisters-in-law, two nephews and a niece."

She heard the pride in his voice as he spoke of his family and automatically her eyes scanned the room for family photographs. She wasn't disappointed. The glass-topped end table behind him and next to the sofa was cluttered with photos. An only child who'd always wanted siblings, she envied the closeness she suspected he shared with his rather large family. Unfortunately, her parents had been much too old to consider other children after they'd had her. She inclined her head toward the pictures on the end table. "Those are family photos?"

His broad smile charmed her as he reached for a gold and wood frame holding a photo of an older man and woman whom she guessed were his parents. "My parents. Now these people knew and still know about relationships. They've been married forty-one years."

Kim's parents had been married twenty years longer and she told him so.

His eyes widened. "And I thought my parents had been married a long time. Do you come from a big family?"

She shook her head. "It was just me and my parents. They were in their late forties when I was born."

"Well, at least they did it right for the first time," he said and she felt the kindness in his words.

"Thank you," she murmured, then remembered she was doing the interview, not him. "Looks like you have a fairly large clan."

He gave a wry grin. "My parents weren't as smart as yours. Even though they had a perfect first child, they kept at it. As you can guess, perfection only strikes a family once."

She chuckled. "I guess that means you're the oldest."

"Smart women." He replaced the picture of his parents and picked up a group shot. "Here's the Stevens clan." He pointed to his Mom and Dad. "Those two you know." He pointed to a shorter, bulkier version of himself. This guy looked like a weight-lifter. "This one here is my youngest brother, William. And this is his wife. And these are his two children."

"How do you like being an uncle?" she asked, hoping someday she'd get to be an aunt *and* a mother.

"I love it," he said with a grin. "But I didn't realize how much until this little lady came along." He pointed to a baby, no more than a few months old, in the arms of another man who shared his features.

"Another brother?"

"You got it. That's Greg. He's the middle son and that cute lady there is his wife. I'll never know what she sees in him. I keep telling her she picked the wrong brother."

Kim felt the love and respect that Reggie had for his brothers and their families, despite his words. "And I bet they love every minute of it."

"Maybe not every minute. But they tolerate me."

"Now you've got me curious," she said. "What are you doing in Atlanta when all your family is in Oklahoma City?"

He chuckled. "Now you sound like my mother. I'm here because of my business. Atlanta is a progressive town and I'm a progressive kind of guy."

"What kind business are you in?"

"I do some computer consulting," he said with a shrug.

Kim sensed there was more to it than what Reggie said and made a note to follow-up on it later. "How long have you been here?"

"Not long," he said. "About eighteen months."

"That explains it," she said, more to herself than to him.

"Explains what?"

She looked up and met his eyes. Big mistake. They seemed to penetrate her mind. "The nominations. You received nominations from Atlanta, Boston and Oklahoma City. Have you ever lived in Boston?"

He shook his head. "No, but I have a friend who lives there."

Kim sensed the subject made him sad. Maybe he hadn't gotten over his friend from Boston. She flipped the page on her pad. What was her name again? "Christina Duncan?"

"That's her," he said in a faraway voice. "The one who got away."

"You sound as though you really cared about her."

He nodded absently. "Christina was the best. Too bad she was in love with another guy. I never really had a chance. Not really."

His honesty disarmed her. Was he still in love with this Christina or had he gotten over her? Kim couldn't tell. "She had wonderful things to say about you."

He smiled. "I'm sure Christina did. That's the kind of woman she is. Definitely one of a kind."

Kim felt a sprinkle of jealousy. Christina Duncan still had a place in Reggie's heart. She was sure of it. "In her nomination letter, Christina mentioned that you'd offered to make a grave sacrifice for her, but she didn't say what it was."

"I'm not surprised," he said. The look on his face said that he was enjoying his memories of his lost-love. "But it wasn't really a sacrifice. I just asked her to marry me."

His words hit Kim hard. She hadn't been unrealistic enough to assume he hadn't been in love before, but to know that he'd already found the woman he wanted to spend the rest of his life with cut deeply. "Did you ask any of the others to marry you?" she asked, trying to keep her professional demeanor.

He shook his head and his eyes seemed to focus again on her. "None of the others got that serious."

She glanced down at her notes again. "That's strange."

"What?"

She looked up at him, not realizing she'd spoken aloud. "Christina, the one you asked to marry you, is the only one of the six who doesn't seem to regret letting you get away. The others gave the impression that they very much wish they had handled your relationship differently."

"It's strange to me, too," he said. "Why is it women don't realize how good you are when they have you?"

Kim knew his question was a sincere one, but she didn't have a good answer for him. She chose instead to play it light. "You know what they say. Hindsight is always twenty-twenty."

"That's no answer. Come on. I answered your questions. Now tell me what you think."

Kim didn't want to turn this session into an interview of her so she deftly turned the question back on him. "I read your article, Reggie. I think you already have your answers. Do you really believe everything you wrote?"

"Of course, I believe it," he said. "And it's the truth."

"Your truth, maybe," she challenged.

"You're right about that," he agreed. "I'm the nice guy women say they want. I have a good job, own a house, understand and appreciate monogamy and feel that women should be treated with kindness and respect. I also understand the difference between sex and making love and am well-acquainted with foreplay."

"On the physical front, I've been told that I have a handsome face, and not just by my mother, and a fit body. I'm not bragging here. I'm just stating fact. I'm sure most of the ladies out there would tell you they're looking for a guy just like me. Well, these women are lying. And I have the walking papers to prove it.''

"For example?'' she queried, somewhat disappointed in his monologue. He sounded like Derrick and some of the other brothers she knew.

"The woman who recently broke up with me. If you stopped this woman on the street, she'd probably tell you she wanted a nice guy. A man she could love and build a life with. A man she could count on to be there for her when she needed him. A man who would love her and cherish her and who she could love and cherish in return. Mind you, this is the same woman who just went back to a man who deserted her after stealing her stereo system and raiding her bank account. I don't know about you, but I think there's something wrong with this woman's logic. And I don't think she's alone. Given a choice, most of the women who say they want a nice guy will choose the opposite every time.''

"Some might think that your observation is a case of sour grapes. That you're complaining because you're the one who always gets dumped.''

Reggie stared at her for a couple of seconds before responding. "Well, some might think that, but they'd be wrong. The article was not about my ego.''

"What was it about, then?''

"I thought it was obvious. It's one man's exasperation and total bewilderment with the female population.'' He leaned closer to her. "My mother raised me to be a gentleman. To treat women with respect. To cherish them. But women don't seem to want that.''

He was so close that Kim could smell the light, masculine scent of his cologne. "So you take your experience with a few women and extrapolate it to mean that all women are the same?''

"Of course not all women are the same. My sister-in-laws are different, my mother is different, Christina is different. A lot of women are. But the majority of you are exactly as I described in the article."

"Have you ever considered that it's you and not the women?" she asked, feeling as though he'd included her in his blanket indictment of the female population.

"Sure, I thought about it. For a second or two." He lifted his shoulders slightly. "But, and I'm not being immodest here, I know the kind of man I am. My only fault is being nice to women."

"Yeah, right." Kim heard Derrick's melody from Reggie's lips and she didn't like the sound.

"You don't believe me?"

"Look, Mr. Stevens," she said slowly, wanting to keep her irritation in check. Why did he have to sound so much like Derrick? "You're not the first guy to complain about women not appreciating a nice guys. It's been my experience that these guys contribute to their situations."

"Can you be a little bit more specific?" he challenged, forcing her to go from the general to the specific just as she'd done with him earlier.

She could be *very* specific. "First," she said, "The guys who call themselves nice guys usually say they're looking for nice women."

"Yeah, that's exactly what we're looking for. A woman who'll treat us with the same kindness and respect with which we treat them."

"I know that's what you *say,*" Kim said, "but it's been my experience that it's not what you mean."

Reggie leaned back against the sofa, his dark skin a brilliant contrast to the tan coloring of the upholstery. "So what do we mean?"

Kim rested her pad and pen on her lap and primly folded her hands across them. He'd asked for it, so she was going to give him both barrels. "What do you mean when you say *nice*, Reggie? Tell me about a nice woman."

"I told you. She treats men with kindness and respect."

"Are you sure there's nothing else?" She knew there

was, so she waited for him to dig his own grave. Then she planned to calmly push him into it.

"I don't know what you're looking for."

Okay, she'd give him a nudge. "It's been my experience that brothers who say they're looking for a nice woman usually consider a nice woman a Vanessa Williams clone with long hair and very light skin."

His chuckle surprised her. "You're joking, right?"

"Not at all," she said. "And if you're honest with yourself you'll admit I'm right."

He shook his head as if he couldn't believe what she was saying. "You really think this is what men want? What I want?"

She nodded. "Are you suggesting that I'm wrong?" A part of her wanted him to offer some explanation to prove she was wrong. About him, at least.

"I'm not suggesting anything at this point," he said, giving her a curious look. "I'm just listening."

"It's been my experience," she explained, "that men who toot their own horns and always complain about a lack of acceptable women are usually pretty shallow."

His flinch told him he knew she included him in that group. "Oh, no you don't," he said. "You can't lump all men together that way."

"Why not? You lumped all women together in your article. What's the difference?"

His silence told her that she had him there. She wasn't surprised though since most men had the decency to shut up when they realized how ridiculous they sounded. Maybe one day she'd meet a man who was different. Unfortunately, Reggie Stevens wasn't that man. She looked down at her pad. "Maybe we should get back to the interview now. Tell me some more about your job."

She'd dismissed him as shallow. She'd done everything but come right out and say it. He could even feel the change in the air around them. When the interview had started, he'd felt a warmth from her, a connection. Now he felt a chill. And all because of some ridiculous notion she held that men were stupid creatures looking for trophy women.

Not that Ms. Kimberla Washington wouldn't make a perfect trophy woman. She was beautiful. From her short-cropped hair to her long, lean fingers to long, full legs that plainly told her of soft and feminine virtues. On top of that, Kim Washington had a quick mind and an aggressive spirit that he found enticing. He knew, though he'd only just met her, that she was a woman who knew what she wanted and who refused to take anything less. He bet she didn't give a brother a second chance. One misstep and he was out the door. He guessed her experiences had caused her to develop the thick outer shell that he now wanted desperately to penetrate.

"Look, you're trying to make me out to be the bad guy here and I'm not."

"Of course, you're not," she said with a fake, sugary sweet smile. "You're just a nice guy, looking for a nice woman. Maybe we should get back to the interview now." She picked up her pen and pad and asked the next question, hoping she'd finish the interview before she threw up. "Tell me some more about your job as a computer specialist."

Reggie opened his mouth to tell her that she'd read him all wrong, but the tightness of her lips and the rigidity in her stare told him there was no use trying to change her mind now. So he let her lead him through a series of questions about his work as a computer security specialist. Her questions were succinct and his answers matched.

"Well, that's it," she said after about an hour. "If you don't mind, I'd like to bring my photographer over to get some shots of you here and in your office."

"Sure," he said, looking for some way to make amends. "Just let me know when."

Kim stood up. "Fine. Thank you, Mr. Stevens," she said, extending her hand. "It's been an interesting interview."

Reggie took her hand. It felt so soft and smooth in his that he didn't want to let it go. For some reason, it was very important to him that Kim not think badly of him. "Look, Kim," he said. "I think we've suffered from some miscommunication this afternoon and I'd really like to show you that I'm not as shallow as you seem to think. How about having dinner with me tonight so we can get to know each other."

Kim removed her hand from his. "I'm sorry," she said, "But I already have plans. Thanks again, Mr. Stevens."

Reggie knew she was lying about her plans for the evening, but he saw no alternative but to escort her to the door. After he opened it, he turned to her, "I'm feeling pretty bad about how things went today. Won't you let me make it up to you."

Again, she shook her head. "You've done enough. I appreciate the interview. Thanks again."

She stepped outside and didn't look back. She never would have guessed she'd be so disappointed in Reggie Stevens. She'd thought he was different. But he wasn't. He was just another man looking for a goodlooking woman to squire about on his arm. Why couldn't he have had more depth?

Why was the sky blue? That's just the way it was. With that brilliant conclusion, she decided to push Reggie Stevens out of her mind.

Feeling eyes on her, she looked up and saw all the other reporters looking at her. It was only then that she realized she'd exited the house via the front door. Bad move.

"How'd you get in?"

"What'd he say?"

"I'm glad somebody got in to see him."

Kim tried to ignore the questions of her colleagues and she was almost successful.

"Hey," Glenda said, tugging her away from the others. "Good work. You know we all hate your guts."

"It figures."

"It's just jealousy." Glenda waved her hand dismissing

the notion. "What's your angle on this guy, anyway? Are you following up on his article like the rest of us or are you working on something else?"

Kim's antenna went up. "Something else like what?"

Glenda shrugged. "Wouldn't it be something if one of the finalists in your magazine's Nice Guy contest was the man who wrote "Doubled Minded Women and their Two Timing Men?"

Kim smiled. So Glenda had read about the contest. Well, she wasn't going to get any information from Kim.

"You can't blame a girl for trying," Glenda said when realized Kim wasn't going to respond.

Kim smiled again. This time a real smile. She really couldn't blame Glenda. Were she in her shoes, she'd be doing the same thing.

"So what did you think of Reggie Stevens? Was he at all what you expected?"

Disappointed summed up her feelings, but she couldn't very well say that about the man who was going to grace the cover of her magazine. "Interesting," was all she'd say.

"Is that interesting good, interesting bad or interesting weird?"

Kim laughed. "You're good, too, you know. But I'm not going to answer that one." She looked at her watch. "Excuse me, I have to call my girlfriend to come pick me up."

She pulled her cell phone out of her purse and dialed the hotel number. She was grateful when Tam answered after only two rings.

"I'm ready," Kim said.

"I was about to get worried. I called your cell phone, but of course, you had it shut off. Did you get to talk with him?"

"Sure did," Kim said. "How long will it take you to get here?"

"Tell me," Tam said enthusiastically. "How'd it go? What's he like in person?"

Kim didn't want to get into it then, and said so.

"All right, then," Tam said. "Be that way."

"How long before you get here?" Kim asked again.

"I'm walking out of the door as soon as I hang up."

"Good. I'll see you in a little while."

Chapter 6

"She's not here," Tam said after looking around The Garden Restaurant. "She said if she wasn't here, we should get a table. She's probably running late. You know how it is with real estate agents."

Yes, Kim knew how it was with real estate agents. After her parents' deaths, she'd considered selling her family home and had called in an agent to help with the sale. In the end, though, she hadn't been able to part with that part of her heritage, much to the realtor's dismay.

"Let's get a table," she finally said, even though she wasn't really hungry. Dinner out had been Tam and Leslie's idea and she hadn't had the energy to argue with them. She'd learned a long time ago that sometimes it was easier and less frustrating to just go along with her friends.

"Sounds good to me," Tam said. "Now if we could just get a waitress."

Kim turned and scanned the room for the missing waitress. She found her and caught her eye. The restaurant wasn't that busy, so the one waitress meant they were short-staffed.

"Tell me about Reggie Stevens," Tam prompted. "And I want details."

Kim was saved from responding by the waitress who chose that moment to seat them. She gave them leather bound menus, said she'd be back with water and quickly went off toward the back of the restaurant.

"I don't think we're going to get much service this evening," Kim said.

Tam picked up her menu. "I'm in no hurry. We'll just hang out." She closed the menu. "I already know what I want. Now tell me about Reggie. What was he like?"

Kim didn't know where to start. She felt foolish every time she thought about the high hopes she'd had about Reggie Stevens. But he'd turned out to be no different than the other brothers she knew. "He's just a guy, Tam. A guy looking for a pretty piece to sport on his arm."

"Damn," Tam said. "Aren't they all?"

Kim sighed. From her experience with the men she'd dated, Derrick included, they were. "I thought Reggie was different. From his nomination letters, I just thought he was different. That article he wrote should have warned me though."

"I thought he was right on with most of what he said in the article. A lot of woman don't really know what they want."

"On the surface he made a few good points," Kim conceded, "but his whole message was that women are too stupid to make wise choices. Could be he's the one who's too stupid. Could be he's just another jerk."

Tam shook her head. "Girl, sometimes you're tougher on men than I am. You've only talked to the man once. Give him another chance before throwing him in the dung heap with the others. Now, the important question: Did he look like his pictures?"

Kim had to smile. Tam had gone from talking like a wise old woman to a giddy teenager. "I never said he wasn't fine. He's definitely fine. But fine isn't everything. A man has to have some substance. He has to want more in a relationship than a pretty face."

"Did he hit on you?" Tam asked.

Kim placed her menu on the table in front of her. "Now why would you ask that?"

Tam shrugged her shoulders. "Just wondering. You make him sound like a player so I figured he hit on you."

"Please, girl. I'm definitely not his type. Probably a little too dark and a little too heavy for his taste."

"Girl, you are not heavy," Tam said, getting her attention. "And you have a beautiful complexion. Why do you put yourself down? Have you looked in the mirror lately?"

Of course, Kim had looked in the mirror. She looked in the mirror every day. "I know how I look, Tam. I'm not talking about how I perceive myself but how others perceive me."

"You don't seem to have too much trouble attracting your share of men."

Kim heard a bit of accusation in Tam's words that she didn't understand. Sure, she attracted men, but she'd never met a man who appreciated her kind of beauty, who stirred her passion, who was stable mentally and financially, *and* who believed in monogamy and commitment. She wanted it all and she felt she deserved it. She wasn't going to settle for less. "Neither do you, Tam, so what's the problem?"

"No problem," Tam said. Kim didn't believe her.

"Come on," she encouraged. "Tell me."

"It's Leslie," Tam confided in hushed tones. "I'm getting tired of her telling me about every new diet that comes along. You'd think I was as big as a house."

As one who was no stranger to diets, Kim felt for her friend. "Girl, you know, Leslie. You'd better ignore her. Anyway, next to her, we're both as big as a house. You'd better not let her get you down."

"I'm not down," Tam said. "I'm just tired of Leslie."

"What have I done now?" Leslie said, breath short from

exhaustion. She pulled out the vacant chair between her two friends. "So tell me, what have I done?"

Tam gave Kim a look that said she'd rather change the subject. "We've been waiting for you," Kim said. "What took you so long?"

Leslie went on to give a long spiel about her house hunting trip and the ignorant real estate agent who'd hosted her. "You can bet *she* won't sell me a house," Leslie said. "I told that woman I wanted to live in South DeKalb and she kept telling me I wanted to live in Gwinnett. What's with these people?"

"You know what's with them, Leslie," Tam said. "They probably figured since you had a little money you didn't want to live on the black side of town." Tam lifted her nose. "She wanted you to go North and live with the "better" folks."

"Better, my behind," Leslie said. "That agent just lost herself a big fat commission and got a piece of my mind to go along with it. I can't stand that kind of crap."

"This is Atlanta," Kim said.

"And what's that supposed to mean?" Leslie asked.

"In case you haven't looked recently, this is the *Old* South."

"Old South," Leslie snorted. "Don't get me started. I just may have to come here and get some of these people straightened out."

The waitress returned with their water and an additional menu for Leslie. "Do you need more time?" she asked.

Both Kim and Tam looked at Leslie. "You go ahead and order," Leslie said. "By the time you're finished, I'll have made up my mind."

Kim and Tam ordered and sure enough, Leslie had decided what she wanted by the time they finished.

"Now, tell me about Reggie Stevens," Leslie said, leaning toward Kim. "And don't leave anything out."

Kim rolled her eyes. "What's up with you two and Reggie Stevens? He's just a man."

Leslie leaned back in her chair. "That's what I told you

at first, but you didn't agree. So don't hold back now. Tell
me what he was like."

Kim sighed again. She really didn't want to spend her
entire dinner thinking about Reggie Stevens, but she knew
she had to give her friends something to satisfy their curios-
ity. "He's a guy, Leslie. A guy who's got an attitude because
so many women have dumped him. I think he wrote that
article to get back at women."

"What makes you say that?"

"I interviewed him, remember? Reggie Stevens may
think he's a good guy, but in my opinion he's just a brother
trying to get over."

"Too bad," Leslie said. "I was actually hoping you two
might hit it off."

"What?" Kim asked, unwilling to admit that she'd har-
bored similar thoughts. Ridiculous thoughts, given that
she hadn't even met the man.

"You heard her, Kim," Tam joined in. "We saw you
mooning over his picture."

"I was not mooning over his picture. I was doing my
job."

Tam and Leslie shared a knowing smile. "Sure, Kim.
Anything you say."

Kim stared wide-eyed at her friends and they began to
laugh. She knew it would do her no good to try to stop
them. She just sat back and waited for the waitress.

Later that night as Reggie was getting ready for bed, he
was still thinking about Ms. Kimberla Washington. He just
knew she'd gotten the wrong impression of him. It was
obvious to him that she had a chip on her shoulder. He
wondered what crazy brother had put it there. Well, he said
to himself, it wasn't his problem. *She* wasn't his problem.

He was about to climb into bed when he heard the
front door open. Luther, he assumed. A short knock at
his bedroom door confirmed his assumption. "Come on
in," he said.

Luther swaggered into the room. "What's up, man?" he said, dropping down in a chair and propping his feet up on the edge of the bed. "I'm dog tired, you know."

"They say partying will do that to you."

"I wasn't partying," Luther said. "I was socializing. There's a big difference. Not that you'd know the difference. What'd you do? Call Nate?"

Reggie shook his head. "Nah, I wasn't up for company tonight."

"I know I'm crazy for asking, but did you call Halle?"

Brandy. Reggie realized he hadn't even thought about the woman. "Maybe another night," he hedged.

"Uh-huh. By the time you call her, she'll be married with three children."

"Why are you talking about me? You can't even remember the woman's real name."

Luther slid his legs off the bed. "But I *can* remember that body. And that face." He closed his eyes and grinned. Then his eyes shot open. "Hey, what happened with Ms. Washington? She wasn't too bad. A little on the heavy side, but nice legs and a nice smile. What was she like?"

Reggie had been pondering that question himself. When the interview had begun, he'd quickly formed a positive opinion of Kim as a level headed woman. "First of all," Reggie began, "She's not on the heavy side. She looks like a woman, and not like a little girl."

"Don't get mad. I said she had nice legs."

"I'm not mad."

"Sounds like you're mad to me. Did you ask her out?"

"Of course I didn't ask her out," Reggie answered, though he wasn't being truthful. He had suggested she have dinner with him, but she'd turned him down. Flat. "She came for an interview, not for a date."

Luther got up and stretched. "Who says one can't lead to the other? Man, you've got to take advantage of your opportunities. Now, this Kim has a good job, a good head on her shoulders. You could do worse." He gave a wry laugh. "Come to think of it, you *have* done worse."

Reggie wondered, not for the first time, how he and Luther had managed to stay friends for so long. The brother definitely got on his nerves at times.

"So, are you going to see her again?" Luther asked.

Reggie shrugged. "She's bringing a photographer by to take some photos. She should be calling to arrange a time. I'm sure you'll talk to her."

"Maybe I will," Luther said. "Seems to me you need somebody to run interference for you."

"Look, man, I don't need your help. I can find my own woman."

"Sure you can," Luther said, clearly not convinced. "Just look at your track record."

"We *could* look at yours."

"Well, as Nate says, at least we've been able to get a woman to the altar. You don't seem to be able to do that and I bet you'd handle married life a lot better than either of us did."

Reggie felt as if he'd been insulted. "What makes you think that?"

Luther shrugged, walking to the door. "Much as I hate to say this, you're a good guy, Reggie. You're the type who'd enjoy the wife, the house, the two and a half kids."

"And you're not?"

Luther shook his head. "But sometimes I wish I were. Maybe I just haven't met the right woman yet."

"And maybe you've met her and let her get away."

Luther's eyes widened. "Don't even think it. I'm like you in that respect. I don't look back. Once it's over, it's over." He yawned. "Night, man. I've got to get some shuteye."

After Luther left the room and closed the door, Reggie lay back on the bed and thought about what he'd said. Luther was right. Reggie very much wanted the wife, the house, the kids. His parents had it. His brothers had it. And he wanted it too. Though he'd dated his share of women, he'd only come close to having the love and the life he wanted once. With Christina. She was the first and only woman he'd asked to marry him. And she'd turned him down.

He should have seen it coming since she'd made no secret about being in love with Jackson Duncan, her co-worker and a friend of the Stevens family. But he'd fallen quickly for Christina. When he'd seen her on the bus that day in Mobile, something about her had tugged at his spirit. Maybe it had been the uncertainty in her beautiful brown eyes. Or maybe it had been something more profound. Maybe her spirit had reached out and touched his.

Thinking about her no longer hurt. She and Jackson had been married two years now and she was pregnant with their second child. He hadn't spoken with her since the day she'd told him she was marrying Jackson, but her friend Liza and Liza's husband, Robert, had become casual friends in the time he'd been in Atlanta, and they kept him up-to-date on the Duncans.

Thoughts of Christina quickly turned to thoughts of Kim. The women couldn't be more different. Christina was definitely more reserved than Kim, and a bit more conservative, he'd guess. But there was a similar spirit in the two women. Both seemed to reach out to him in some indescribable way.

Reggie rolled over and turned off the bedside light. All this thinking about women was making him tired. His last thought before he went to sleep was that he'd like to see Kim Washington again if only to correct the unfavorable impression she'd somehow gotten of him.

Two days later, Kim woke to the sound of her ringing telephone. Wiping sleep from her eyes, she picked up the phone and mumbled her greeting.

"Kimmy girl, is that you?"

It was Jim. Why in heck was he calling her so early in the morning? What time was it, anyway? She squinted to make out the numbers on the bedside clock. Six o'clock.

"Kimmy, wake up. I know it's you. What are you doing

down there in Atlanta? You're supposed to be writing the news not making it."

Kim shook her head to clear away the sleepiness she still felt. She, Tam and Leslie had gone to a play at the Fourteenth Street Theatre last night and had a late supper. Then, at Leslie's insistence, they'd accepted an invitation for some dancing at a private club. It had been a good evening, but they'd gotten in much too late.

"What are you talking about, Jim?"

"I'm talking about this article. What are you doing in the paper, Kimmy? You're supposed to be writing articles not being interviewed. What's gotten into you?"

"Article?" She sat up in bed. "Slow down a minute, Jim. I have to get my thoughts together."

"The papers, Kimmy," he clarified. "The radio stations will love this one."

"What paper?" she asked impatiently. "Tell me exactly what you're talking about."

Kim heard Jim sigh and knew he was growing impatient with her. "What I'm talking about is an Atlanta Voice article titled, Good Guy Not So Good After All."

"What?"

"You heard me. And your name is all over this piece, too. Too bad it's not a byline. The magazine could have used this article, Kimmy. It would have gone well with the contest article. So tell me, why are you down there giving interviews to the competition?"

"Look, I'm still not sure what you're talking about, but you can rest assured that I haven't given an interview to anyone."

"Maybe it's one of your friends then," Jim said. "You know how that Leslie talks."

Sometimes Kim regretted the family atmosphere that prevailed at *Urban Style*. It would be nice to have a private life outside work. "Leslie wouldn't talk about my work," she assured him. "And neither would Tam."

"Well, somebody's been talking. Listen to this: Reggie Stevens is no different than any other get-over, brother,

Urban Style features editor Kim Washington said." "Did you say something like that?"

Even if Kim didn't say it, she agreed with it. "How am I supposed to remember every thing I say?"

Jim read the byline. "Are you familiar with the name?

Kim definitely was. Glenda was the reporter who'd tried to get information out of her after her interview with Reggie. But how had the woman gotten the quotes?

"Don't let this happen again, Kimmy. You're down there to get a story, not give one."

"All right, Jim," she said. *Don't get your shorts all twisted,* she added to herself.

"Good. Now that we've gotten that clear, there's a good side to this article."

"What's that?" she asked, though she really didn't want to know. She had a feeling Jim had an idea for another scheme.

"This could actually help us, Kimmy," he began and she knew she was right. "The paper and radio stations are already getting calls about the article and expect to get even more. It seems your article has stoked the fires. You know what this means, don't you?"

"That it's even more important that Reggie Stevens appear on the cover of *Urban Style?*"

"That's exactly what it means, but it also means that we may be able to turn the Nice Guy contest into a series. Maybe I'll fly down to Atlanta and talk to Reggie Stevens myself. The two of you could do something like a "He Says, She Says" column. The readers would eat it up."

Kim didn't know about all of that. She hadn't seen Glenda's article and couldn't comment until she did. "Wait awhile before making the trip, Jim. As I've already told you, Reggie is skittish about the press. He's already gotten offers for columns and talk shows. He's just not interested. At least, not now."

"Well, Kimmy," Jim said tersely. "You *get* him interested. This magazine could use a boost. You know as well as I do that things have been difficult around here. I'd hate to have to start laying off people.''

Kim had heard that veiled threat more than once. And while she didn't like it, it no longer bothered her as it once had. Threats were the cornerstone of Jim's management style. If she had the extra money, she'd pay for him to attend a class so he could develop some *real* skills. ''Look, Jim, I'm going to get dressed and see if I can find a copy of that article. I'll get back to you later in the day.''

''You do that, Kimmy girl. You just do that.''

Kim hung up the phone wondering why fate seemed determined to mix her life with Reggie's.

Chapter 7

"Have you seen the paper?"

Reggie just stared at a wide awake and fully dressed Nate standing in his front doorway. He'd heard the incessant *bams* on the door and had dragged himself out of bed to find the fire. And here Nate was talking about some article. "Man, you must be crazy." Reggie turned to walk back to his bedroom and to his bed. "See yourself out."

He heard the front door close. "You've got to see this, Reggie," Nate said, following him down the short hallway leading to the bedrooms.

"What's all the racket about?" Luther called, sticking his head out his bedroom doorway.

"You've got to see the paper, Luther."

"Man," Luther said, walking past Reggie and toward Nate.

"I'll see you guys after I wake up." Reggie wasn't at all interested in whatever the paper had to say.

Luther laughed. "Good picture, Reggie."

"Yeah, yeah," he said. His picture in the paper was no longer a big deal. Since his article, his face had become as common in the newspaper as the masthead.

"Yeah," Luther said. "But what about this one of Kimberla Washington? You two look good together."

Reggie stopped short and turned around, his sleepiness gone. "What are you talking about?"

Nate took the paper from Luther and turned it around so Reggie could see it. "This time somebody else made the headlines," Nate said with a chuckle.

Reggie snatched the paper out of his friend's hand. He couldn't believe what he was reading. "Good Guy Not So Good After All," the title read. Under the title was a photo of Ms. Washington and one of him. "What the . . ." He skimmed the article quickly, taking note of Ms. Washington's many comments. Most of them negative. And about him. "Just who does she think she is?"

Nate snatched the paper back. "If you're the voice of reason for men, I'd say she's the voice of reason for women." He chuckled again. "How do you like the part where she says you only wrote your article because you'd been dropped more times than the ball atop Times Square?"

Reggie didn't like it one bit. "What's on this woman's mind? What did I ever do to her?"

Nate clapped him on the back. "Guess that interview you had didn't go too well."

Reggie shrugged off his friend's hand. "But . . . this. How could she say these things? They're not true."

"Looks to me like she's dumped you before she even went out with you," Luther teased. "That must be a record, even for you."

"This isn't funny, guys. This is *my* name and *my* picture in the paper."

"It's her picture, too," Nate said with what Reggie considered a bit too much interest. "If you got hundreds of letters from women, I'll bet this sister gets thousands from brothers. I may just drop her a line myself."

"Be sure you get somebody else to write it," Luther quipped.

That began a back-and-forth insulting match between Luther and Nate that didn't interest Reggie in the least. He was still thinking about Ms. Kimberla Washington. He slipped the newspaper out of Nate's hand, left his friends arguing in hallway and went into his bedroom, closing the door behind him.

"Men kill me," the article quoted Kim as saying, "They talk about wanting a nice woman, but what they usually mean is they want some fashion model look-alike who's going to worship them as if they're a god or something."

He kept reading and the article got progressively worse, at least from his perspective. "In this day and age," the article quoted Kim as saying, "it's hard for a woman to tell a good guy from a bad one. The mode of today seems to be the wolf in sheep's clothing. The bad guy has the good guy role down to a science. Women have to go out with lie detectors. We never know what kind of line we're going to get." Reggie skimmed some more, but he didn't have to skim long to realize Ms. Washington hadn't said a single positive word about him.

Reggie stared at her picture. Even though she'd cast aspersions on him, he still found her appealing and saw something special in her eyes. What was it about this woman that drew him? he wondered with a sigh. What was it about him that repelled her?

Man, this was a first for him. He'd never had a woman turn on him so quickly. He was being rejected out of hand based on a single meeting and he didn't consider that fair treatment. As a man he couldn't allow Ms. Washington to go unchallenged.

No, he thought, she'd entered into the fray and he was honor bound to defend himself. He got up from the bed and headed for the bathroom. His schedule suddenly had a very important meeting on it. Ms. Kimberla Washington had attacked his honor and his manhood. He couldn't let her or her words go unchecked.

* * *

Reggie's phone rang just as he was about to step into the shower. He swore, then reached for the green body towel on the rack next to the shower and headed for the phone. A part of him hoped it was Ms. Washington calling to apologize. Unfortunately for her, an apology wasn't going to suffice.

"Hello," he said when he picked up the ringing phone.

"You're definitely having problems with the women, brother." Reggie recognized his middle brother's voice immediately. "What are you doing down there in Atlanta? First you're writing articles complaining about women and next they're writing ones complaining about you."

"Don't start with me this morning, Greg," he said. "I'm definitely not up for it." Actually Reggie had been expecting Greg's call since he'd gotten the one from William. His brothers routinely called to razz him about one thing or another. "How do you know about the article already? What time is it out there anyway?"

Greg chuckled. "We're an hour behind you as usual. And don't worry about how I found out. Just know you're a celebrity here in OKC and we know everything you do."

Reggie interpreted that to mean that one of Greg's friends had called and told him about the article. He didn't even want to piece together the pipe line of gossips that had transmitted the news from Atlanta to Oklahoma city in such a short time.

His brother laughed again. "What did you do to this woman anyway? William told me he thought you were interested in her."

Reggie sighed. At times like this, he felt like the youngest brother instead of the oldest. Why was it that his younger siblings thought their marital status made them his keeper? "Have you ever known William to know what he was talking about?"

"Don't try to change the subject. What did you do to

this Washington woman? The way you're alienating women you're never going to get married."

Here it goes, Reggie thought. His marital status. "Don't worry, brother. There are a few women who still talk to me."

"Must not be many though. Just think of all the candidates you've lost because of this article."

"If you just called to razz me," Reggie said, standing up. "I think I'll hang up."

"You can run, Reggie, but with this article you definitely can't hide. Just wait until Mom sees it."

Reggie didn't want to think about his mother seeing that article. If his brothers had forgotten his elder status, his mother had forgotten that he'd graduated high school. He knew she worried about him much more than she worried about his brothers and he knew his single status was the cause. Did she think a wife would actually make his life safer? "I'll handle Mom," he said. And he would. He'd had enough experience. "Now get a life and leave mine alone."

"Anything you say, brother. Now be careful. That Kim Washington seems to be out for you."

"Good bye, Greg," Reggie said. He hung up the phone without responding to his brother's wise crack and stomped back to the shower. Greg had it wrong, he thought as he stepped into the shower. Kim wasn't out for him. No, she'd already gotten him. Now he was out for her.

"Girl, you know you told the truth," Leslie said, reading the paper over breakfast in one of the hotel's dining rooms. "And you just started the story."

"That's right," Tam added. "What about thirty-five and forty-year old brothers talking about they don't want a woman who already has children? Of course, they can have five or six of the little crumb snatchers running around and think nothing of it."

"But I didn't say half that stuff," Kim complained. "And

I definitely didn't say it to Glenda. I knew the woman was eager, but I never thought she'd make stuff up."

Tam placed her juice glass back on the table. "Maybe she didn't make it up."

Kim stared at her friend. "Come on, Tam. You know I'd never say something like this to a reporter. I'm not stupid."

"I didn't say you were stupid. I just said that you might have said some of those things. You were pretty upset after your interview with Reggie."

"Yes, I was upset, but I think I'd remember if I'd given an interview. Maybe you guys are the ones who've been talking to reporters."

"Please," Leslie said. "If I had talked to a reporter, you can bet *my* picture and *my* name would be in the paper, not yours. You ought to know how I operate by now."

Kim did, so she turned her attention to Tam. "What about you? Who've you been talking to?"

"I haven't been talking to anybody. Not about this, anyway. Come on, Kim, you know better. I'm telling you. Some of this does sound like some of the things you were saying at The Garden Restaurant. Don't you remember?"

Kim shook her head. She remembered being disappointed, and maybe a little upset with Reggie and not really wanting to talk about her interview with him. But she'd acquiesced and done so because of her friends' interest.

"Tam may have a point, Kim," Leslie said. "Do you think Glenda could have eavesdropped on our conversation? Do you remember seeing her in the restaurant?"

Kim hated the possibility that Leslie's supposition could be right. "No, I didn't see her. But that doesn't mean she wasn't there."

"But do you think she'd really do something like that? Tam asked. "How did she seem when you spoke with her outside Reggie's place?"

Eager. Hungry. Common traits for good reporters so Kim couldn't hold them against Glenda. When it came right down to it, she couldn't blame her for eavesdropping on her conversation, if, in fact, she'd done so. As a reporter, Kim had done much the same herself. But what she hadn't done was write an article without contacting the source. That's where Glenda had broken the rules. Professional courtesy should have made her give Kim a chance to clarify her words.

But, Kim knew, it was the rawness of the quotes that made Glenda's article believable, real. Had the reporter spoken with her, she would have explained away a lot of what made the article appealing to readers.

"Don't worry about it, girl," Tam said. "You didn't say anything that wasn't true. If the brothers out there are honest with themselves, they'll agree you were dead right in everything you said."

"She's right, Kim," Leslie said. "You told the truth and I, for one, am glad you did. The only thing I hate is that my picture didn't get in the paper. What do you want to bet that you start getting letters from men all over the country?"

"Can't you think about anything other than attracting men?" Tam complained to Leslie. "I swear you have a one-track mind."

"Don't worry about my mind," Leslie returned. "My mind *and* my body are in perfect control."

"Too bad your mouth isn't," Tam volleyed. "You always have to go too far. You're like a kid. You always have to go too far."

Kim blocked out her friends' exchange. She wondered what Reggie thought about the article. Though she wanted to take satisfaction in telling him off in the media, she couldn't get rid of the feeling that maybe she'd done him a wrong. What if she was wrong about him? What if he was the good guy that she'd originally thought him to be?

Come off it, Kim, she told herself. *You've met the guy. He sounds too much like Derrick to be the real thing.*

"What about you, Kim?"

"What about what?" Kim said, looking at her friends who were both now staring at her.

"Where were you, girl?" Leslie said. "Tam's going with me to check out a couple of houses. I've decided to search out the South DeKalb area myself. Hell, this isn't the first house I've bought. I can find a place on my own and save that seven percent commission. Why don't you come with us?"

Kim thought about Jim and knew he'd have a fit if he knew she was out house hunting with her friends instead of hunting down Reggie Stevens. Well, she decided, she needed a break from Jim *and* from Reggie Stevens. She placed her white cloth napkin on the table. "It sounds like fun." And she hoped it would be. She definitely needed to stop thinking about Reggie Stevens.

Kim saw Reggie as soon as she and her friends entered the hotel lobby after their house hunting venture. "Oh, no," she said, covering her mouth with her hand.

"What is it, Kim?" Leslie asked.

"He's here."

"Who's here?" Tam asked.

"Reggie Stevens," she said, inclining her head to a section of overstuffed chairs to their far left. His head was bowed as he looked at what she thought was a magazine.

Leslie craned her neck in that direction. "I don't see him," she said. "Where is he?"

Kim tugged on her friend's hand. "Stop staring in his direction, Leslie. The man's going to know I'm talking about him."

"Oh, I see him," said Tam. "Uh, oh, I think he sees us too."

Kim dropped Leslie's hand. What was she doing anyway? So what if Reggie Stevens was in her hotel? It was a free country and the man could go where he wanted. "Let's go on up to the suite. He's probably here to meet somebody."

"Uh oh," Tam said. "Maybe that person is you. He's heading in this direction."

"He'd probably mind his business if you'd stop staring at him."

"I don't think so, Kim," Tam said.

"Hello, Kim." Reggie nodded his head to Kim, then to her friends. "Ladies." The deep timbre of his voice tickled her senses.

"Hello, Reggie," Tam and Leslie said at the same time.

"It's good to meet you in person," Leslie continued, offering her hand. "Your photograph doesn't do you justice."

Kim wished she could blink and make herself disappear. She couldn't believe Leslie was flirting with the man.

Reggie took Leslie's hand and massaged it with his, or so it seemed to Kim, before releasing it. "You ladies have me at a disadvantage," he said. "You both know my name but I don't have the pleasure of knowing yours."

Leslie introduced herself, then Tam. Then all three of them turned and looked at Kim.

"Hello, Reggie," she said. What else could she do?

His gaze met hers and held it. "Do you have a minute?" he asked. "I've been trying to get in touch with you all day."

"It's my fault," Leslie said with a short feminine—make that flirtatious—laugh. "Kim and Tam went out house-hunting with me."

Reggie slowly released Kim's gaze and looked at Leslie. "You're moving to Atlanta? All three of you?"

Leslie giggled. She actually giggled. Kim wanted to go through the floor. "No, just me. My job is transferring me to Atlanta."

Leave it to Reggie to ask questions about Leslie's job. After what seemed like an hour but was probably only a few minutes, Leslie finished her long winded answer.

"Well, I hope you like our city." He reached in the back pocket of his well-fitting tan trousers, pulled out his wallet

and handed her a card. "If you need any help getting
settled, give me a call. I'll be glad to help."

Kim rolled her eyes at the smile that spread across Leslie's face. She wanted to remind her flirting friend of her
earlier comments about Reggie, but she knew it would do
no good. Leslie had her radar set for Reggie and there
was no backing off now.

"Kim."

Her name on Reggie's lips surprised her. She'd thought
he'd been captured in Leslie's snare and forgotten that
she and Tam were even there.

"Yes," she said, not quite meeting his gaze. She didn't
want to get trapped in those eyes again.

"I wanted to talk to you," he began.

"Well, Reggie," she interrupted. "How about tomorrow? We've had a busy day and were about to have an early
dinner and head for bed."

"Of course, you could join us," Leslie added.

Kim opened her mouth to nix that idea, but Tam beat
her to it. "You're forgetting, Leslie. We have to meet your
new real estate agent later tonight."

"That's right," Kim said, silently thanking Tam for helping her out. It was apparent Reggie had charmed Leslie.
She turned to Reggie and said, "So tonight's really not a
good time."

"Yes, it is," Tam jumped in. "I'll go with Leslie to meet
with the realtor. You and Reggie can talk over dinner here
in the hotel. I really wanted to try this other restaurant
I've heard about, but I knew you were tired and I didn't
want you to eat alone. But now you don't have to."

"Well . . ." Kim tried to think of an excuse, but Tam's
betrayal had caught her off guard. What was Tam doing
anyway?

"That's a perfect idea," Leslie added, joining in Tam's
betrayal. "I wanted to try out that restaurant too." She
turned to Reggie. "You can talk to Kim over dinner, can't
you?"

Reggie turned to Kim with a sly smile on his face. "I'm

a little hungry. Sure, Kim and I can talk over dinner. I should have thought of the idea."

"Well," Tam said, "I guess it's settled." She grinned broadly at Reggie. "It was nice meeting you. I hope we run into each other again."

"My pleasure," Reggie, the perfect gentleman, said. "And," he said to Leslie, "I hope you find just the house you're looking for."

Kim watched and listened as both her friends said their good-byes with teasing smiles on their lips. The two of them knew exactly what they were doing. And, she feared, so did Reggie. This was much too embarrassing.

After her two friends turned the corner to the bank of elevators, Reggie said, "So do you really want to eat or do you just want to talk?"

What she really wanted was to get away from him. "I'm hungry," she said. "Let's eat."

"Which restaurant do you prefer? There are about three of them in here."

"It doesn't matter. Atlanta is your town, not mine. Why don't you pick one?"

He cut her a sideways glance, then turned and faced her fully. "The restaurant of my choice is not in this hotel."

"Follow me then," she said, resisting the urge to ask him what was his favorite restaurant. The irrational image of the two of them sharing a quiet dinner in a dark corner filled her mind. "We'll go to The Inn if it's not crowded."

He fell into step with her. "Fine with me."

Kim felt Reggie was walking too close to her and she wanted to scoot away from him, but she wouldn't give him the satisfaction of knowing he made her nervous. He'd come to her so she had the upper hand in their relationship, if it could be called that, and she wasn't going to yield it without a fight.

Chapter 8

Reggie told himself to keep his mind on the reason for his visit to Ms. Kimberla Washington, but the soft scent of her perfume invaded his senses and forced him to appreciate her feminine attributes. Not that he was interested in her. No, that wasn't it. But he was a man and, like most men, he responded positively to attractive. And Ms. Kimberla Washington was definitely attractive. Dressed in jeans and a silk blouse as she was today or in the soft-cut suit she'd worn the day of the interview, she made a pretty picture. The pale pink of the blouse she had on now accentuated the darkness of her skin and made her look like an ebony princess. The reddish tinge to her lips made him think about kissing her.

"Okay," she said, bringing his thoughts back to safer topics. "It doesn't appear to be crowded in there."

They stood in front of The Inn, a bar/restaurant with a country inn motif. He followed Kim inside and they were quickly seated. In short order, their waitress had delivered their drinks and was off with their meal requests.

"So what did you want to talk to me about?" she asked.

He sipped from his glass of white wine. "As if you didn't know."

She lowered her eyes in a gesture of innocence, but quickly lifted them as if she realized what she'd done. "The article."

He nodded. "Yes, the article. I thought you'd come here to get an interview, not to give one."

"I didn't give an interview," she explained, recalling Jim had made a similar comment. "I never talked to that reporter."

He studied her, surprised she would lie. He'd thought Ms. Kimberla Washington above that type of behavior and told her so.

"I'm not lying," she said, eyes blazing. "I didn't talk to that reporter."

He studied her face, flashing eyes and all. He must be losing his mind because he truly believed she hadn't spoken to the reporter. "Then how do you explain the article in the paper? Do you expect me to believe the reporter made it all up and attributed all those quotes to you?"

"Not exactly," she said. "I didn't say that I didn't say those things. I only said that I didn't talk to a reporter."

At this moment, Reggie understood how Ricky Ricardo felt when he got tangled up in one of Lucy's adventures. "I'm not following you," he said, using the kindest phrase that he could think of. "You said those things, but you didn't say them to the reporter?"

She nodded. "It's like this: after my interview with you, the reporters outside your house all wanted to know what I'd found out."

"And what did you tell them?"

She sighed impatiently. "I didn't tell them anything. I didn't want to see my story in their papers or their magazines so I kept my mouth shut."

"But . . ." He just knew a *but* was coming.

"But there was one reporter, a woman, Glenda, who was more persistent than the others."

"And you said some things to her? Off the record, I imagine?"

Her eyes blazed at him. "Will you stop finishing my sentences? If you'll listen, I'll tell the story."

He lifted both hands in supplication. "Hey, I'm sorry, but my reputation was smeared in that article. Excuse me for wanting to get to the bottom of the matter."

She looked contrite as if she understood his position and felt bad about it. "I didn't tell her anything. But my friends and I figured out that she must have followed us to the restaurant where we ate dinner and listened in on our conversation. Then she wrote the article without giving me a chance to clarify what she heard or what she thought she heard."

Reggie's hopes rose. "So you were misquoted? You didn't say the things attributed to you in the paper?"

"I didn't say that I didn't say them. I just said the reporter didn't give me a chance to clarify them. To put them in some context."

"So you did say them?"

Her lips turned down. "I guess so."

"What do you mean—you guess so? Either you said them or you didn't?"

"I said a lot of things that afternoon. I don't remember exactly what."

"Then maybe she did misquote you. That's good. We'll just call the paper and ask for a retraction. I should have known you wouldn't say those kinds of things about me. You're too fair a woman to make blanket statements like the ones in that article about a man you don't even know. We can go down to the paper together tomorrow."

Reggie looked so pleased with his conclusion and his plan of action that Kim hated to disappoint him. But she had no choice. "It's not that simple, Reggie."

"Yes, it is," he said. "We go down there. We tell them those words don't reflect your opinions and ask for a retraction."

"I can't do that."

"Why can't you?"

"Because even though I don't remember saying those exact words, the article pretty much captures my sentiments that day."

Reggie's mouth dropped open. It didn't take a genius to figure out he was disappointed in her. "I know you were a bit peeved when you left our interview, Ms. Washington, but what did I do to make you think so little of me?"

"It's not one thing you did, Reggie," she said, feeling a need to be honest with him. "It's more an attitude. But it's not just *your* attitude—it's the attitude of too many men those days."

"This sounds like a stereotype, Kim."

"Most stereotypes have their roots in truth. Can you honestly say that you don't know any men who consider the "Nice Guy" persona the best way to get over on a lady?"

"Well," Reggie sputtered. "I'm not "any men". I'm me. And that article was about me."

"Well," she said, becoming irritated with him. "From what I can see, you're a lot like "any men." You use that Nice Guy persona, but you're just like the others. You say you're looking for a nice woman, but I bet you're looking for some long-legged, light-skinned centerfold who'll cater to your every fantasy."

Reggie didn't say anything. He just stared at her. And stared at her for a long time. When he finally spoke, his voice was low. "I don't know about the guys you've been with or the guys you've been around, but the man you just described is not me."

Kim was about to tell him he was wrong, but the waitress chose that moment to return with their meals. They exchanged pleasantries with the young woman, then waited for her to leave.

"I didn't want to believe it was you either," she said, picking up where she left off. "But I think it is, Reggie."

"It is not me."

She shook her head, then stabbed her fork into her

salmon. "Sometimes it's hard for us to look at ourselves objectively so I can understand that you don't see yourself. And I can even understand why you are the way you are."

"Why don't you tell me how I am?" He sat back in his chair and folded his arms across his chest. "You seem to be such an authority."

She lowered her fork and met his gaze. "I know the man those women described in those nomination letters was a nice guy. But I think something happened to you. Maybe you got tired of being dumped." She shrugged. "Maybe you got tired of being a nice guy."

"Go on," he said.

"Aren't you hungry?" she asked, noticing that he hadn't touched his food.

He shook his head. "I'd rather finish this conversation."

"But you ought to eat before your food gets cold."

He dropped his folded arms and leaned toward her. "I'm a thirty-eight year old man and I've been feeding myself for quite a few years now, so I think I can handle dinner." He leaned back. "Go on with your analysis."

"Well, you've had some bad experiences with women." She shrugged. "Maybe you've put on a new persona. Maybe you've given up on being a nice guy in substance and chosen to be a nice guy in name only."

"And what makes you come to that conclusion?"

His words were calm but the tic in his jaw said he was anything but calm. "That article you wrote for one. On the surface it seems to be a candid analysis of male-female relationships but underneath I hear a man saying that women can't be trusted to make decisions for themselves. A man who thinks that just because a few women have decided he's not right for them that those women are somehow weak-minded or double-minded or whatever it was you called them."

He leaned forward, his tic working harder. "If you came to this conclusion based on my article, then why in the world did you interview me for the Nice Guy contest and article?"

Because I couldn't stop thinking about you. "Because the contest is my job. Your nomination letters and your article present totally different men. I guess I was curious to see who the real Reggie Stevens was."

"And you think you know now?"

She nodded, though she really wasn't sure. Even now, there was something about Reggie that made her want him to be the nice guy the women spoke of in their letters.

"After a ninety minute interview, you think you know?"

She nodded again. "It doesn't take long, Reggie."

"It must not, Ms. Washington. As I remember it, we were getting along well initially. Them bam! I'm still trying to figure out what ticked you off."

"I was not ticked off," she explained. As she remembered the interview, they'd started out flirting, which she'd enjoyed. Then he'd told her about his family and, feeling pretty comfortable with him, she'd even told him a little about hers. But then he'd made his comments about looking for "a nice woman" and her hackles had gone up. How many times had she heard a brother give her that line? "I don't think this conversation is getting us anywhere," she said. "Why don't we just finish dinner and call it a night?"

"Not on your life," he said. "That article could end up in newspapers and discussed on radio stations across the country. You've given people the idea that I'm some kind of jerk. I can't just call it a night. I have to get my reputation back."

Kim gave a silent prayer of thanks. There might be a way for her and Reggie Stevens to get what they wanted. She couldn't have asked for a better opening. "I have an idea," she said.

He eyed her suspiciously. "What? You want to put my face on a dartboard and let the women of America take out their frustrations on it?"

She chuckled. "Not exactly. I was thinking of something a bit more positive."

Reggie tasted his food for the first time. "I'm listening," he said.

"My boss still wants you on the cover of *Urban Style*. In addition, he thinks the two of us should write a column together expressing our differing views on male female relationships."

He lowered his fork slowly. "You've got to be kidding. First, you blast me in the paper and now you want to blast me on a regular basis in your magazine. Thanks, but no thanks. I'll pass on that opportunity."

Kim sensed the power base changing. She was losing ground because she still needed him for the article and he really didn't need her. "But you are still going to let me do the photo shoot for the magazine, aren't you?"

He shook his head. "Given what you think of me, why do you want me in the article, much less on the cover of your magazine?"

Kim finished the last of her salmon and pushed her plate away. "The Nice Guy Contest is about what the readers think, not what I think."

"But how do I know you're not going to blast me in the article? I know what you think of me."

"And I told you that reporter didn't give me a chance to put my comments in context. I can assure you that my article will be more than fair to you."

"And I'm supposed to take you at your word?"

"Of course."

He laughed then, out right laughed. "You must think I'm stupid. No way."

Now she knew the tables had turned. Jim was going to kill her if she lost Reggie. "Don't make any hasty decisions. Think about it. We've already had the interview. Let's go ahead with the photo shoot. Think about the column. You don't have to decide now."

He leaned forward again. "And what do I get?"

She licked her lips. She had the strange feeling he was talking about more than the article and the photos. "You get exposure."

"I've already got exposure." He grimaced. "More exposure than I want, in fact."

"Okay," she said, trying to think of an appeasement. "What if you write a rebuttal to the article with my comments in it and we print it in the magazine? Wouldn't that make the photo shoot worth your effort?"

Reggie cut off another bite of his steak. He could enjoy his dinner now that he had Ms. Washington on the ropes. Yes sirree, bob. She needed him. If he guessed correctly, she was probably getting pressure from her boss.

Yes, this was indeed a fine piece of beef on the plate before him. He took another bite, chewed it slowly, savoring the juices while watching Ms. Washington squirm in hers. "To answer your question, no, I don't think writing a rebuttal would make the shoot worth my while. I could probably call up any of a dozen radio stations or newspapers and make my case, but I want the words to come from you." He pointed his fork at her. "I want *you* to say that you were mistaken. I want *you* to tell the world that the real Reggie Stevens is a nice guy."

"You want me to lie?"

Reggie wanted to laugh. He knew if it were left up to her, she'd tell him to stuff it. But it wasn't up to her. "No, I don't want you to lie," he said. "I want you to tell the truth about the real Reggie Stevens."

"I doubt that," she mumbled under her breath.

"What did you say?" he asked, though he'd heard her clearly. For some reason, he took pleasure in watching her squirm. "I didn't quite hear you."

She cleared her throat, clearly impatient and frustrated by his request. "You know what I think, Reggie. Don't put me in this position."

"What position?" he asked. "All I'm asking you to do is help repair a reputation you've helped ruin."

She rolled her eyes. "I think you're going a bit far. I haven't ruined your reputation. What I've done is keep you in the limelight for a few minutes longer."

She was getting a bit too upset so he decided he'd best

bring his proposal to closure before she got up and left the restaurant. "You consider yourself a fair person, don't you, Ms. Washington?"

He watched as she sat up straighter in her chair as if offended by his question. "Of course, I do. I know I'm a fair person."

"In most cases, I assume you are, but I don't think you've been very fair in your assessment of me."

"I just go with the evidence presented," she stated with finality.

"That's just it," he said. "What evidence do you have? A few letters from women you don't know and a brief interview. Do you really think that's enough to go on? Do you really think that's enough to build a newspaper story?"

He had her there. She didn't think the newspaper article had been done responsibly, but she knew there was no sense asking for a retraction when she basically agreed with the statements made. "Let's just say if I had been the reporter doing that story, I would have handled it much differently."

"So you agree that the newspaper article was written prematurely?"

Hadn't she just said that? "I do."

"At least we agree on something. Now what are we going to do about it?"

The gleam in his eyes told her that he had a suggestion. It also told her that she probably wouldn't like it. "You tell me," she said.

"It's simple. How do most people get to know each other?"

"Look, Reggie, enough with the guessing games. Out with it." Kim knew he was toying with her and she didn't like it one bit. If Jim hadn't been so adamant about having the guy in the magazine, she'd—

"All you have to do is spend some time with me."

It was worse than she'd imagined. "Spend some time with you?"

He grinned. God help her, even though he was talking crazy, his grin made her stomach do flip-flops.

"You may be young, Ms. Washington, but I'm sure you've heard of the concept."

"You're talking about dating? You and me?" She pointed from herself to him.

He nodded.

"You can't be serious. I'm here to work, not date." This was a crazy idea. She couldn't believe he'd even brought it up. "You've got to come up with something else."

He shook his head. "I don't think so. The only way you're going to know for sure how I feel about women, how I treat women, is to be the woman in my life. For a short while anyway."

"Reggie, this isn't making sense. I don't have time for dating."

"I'm not asking for a lifetime commitment, Ms. Washington. Just a couple of weeks."

She shouldn't even consider this crazy idea. She knew she shouldn't. Then why was she? "My article is due in a few weeks. I don't have time for this."

Reggie ignored her excuse and took the last bite of his prime rib. This was the best meal he'd had in a long time. He couldn't wait to order dessert.

Chapter 9

"I don't know, Kim," Leslie said from her perch on the couch. She and Tam had been in the suite when Kim had returned from her disastrous dinner with Reggie and, as usual, they wanted details of the ill-fated event. She'd been able to put them off until she'd showered and changed into her pajamas, but now all her excuses were gone and she had to talk.

"Me neither," Tam added. "What's so bad about going out with him?"

Leslie popped a frozen strawberry in her mouth. "You don't have to marry the guy. Just go out with him. Who knows, he may have a couple of friends for me and Tam."

"Speak for yourself, Leslie," Tam said. "Every conversation is not about you finding a man."

"This one ought to be," Leslie said. "I'm the one who's going to be living in Atlanta. I think it would be great to meet some eligible men. The way I see it, if this Reggie turns out to be a good guy, or—" she added with a smile "half as good as he looks, he could introduce me to some decent men. That way I don't have to waste time filtering through the dross."

"Something must be wrong with me tonight, Kim, but I think Leslie has a point. Besides, Reggie sure seemed like a nice guy to me."

Kim rolled her eyes. "You only met him for five or ten minutes, Tam. Even a serial killer could fake it for that short a time."

"Yeah," Tam said, reaching for a strawberry from Leslie's bowl. "But I don't think he's a serial killer. Kim, he can't be all bad. Maybe you two just got off on the wrong foot. I say give the guy another chance. What do you have to lose?"

Kim had a feeling she had a lot to lose. There was something about Reggie Stevens. That something she'd felt when she'd first seen his picture. That something she'd felt when she'd first shaken hands with him and looked into his dark eyes. That something she'd felt over dinner tonight when he'd made his outrageous proposal. Reggie Stevens could get under her skin if she allowed him. Which wouldn't be a bad thing if she was sure of him, but she refused to waste her time or her emotions on a player.

Leslie slapped her on her knee. "Come on, Kim. Just go out with the guy. If you want a chaperone, Tam and I will chaperone for you. Just tell Reggie to find us a couple of dates."

"Good idea, Leslie," Tam said. "What do you say, Kim? We'll be right there with you and we might all have some fun? Come on, say you'll go out with the guy. Just one time. Please?"

Kim knew she'd end up giving in to the cajoling of her friends, but not without some token resistance. The triple-dating idea did have merit though. How much could Reggie get under her skin with two of her friends and two of his around? And if Luther turned out to be one of the friends who was around, she was sure he'd keep all the attention focused on himself. Maybe, she reasoned, this wouldn't be so bad after all.

"I don't have time to get to know Reggie in the way he wants. I have a job to do."

"Aw, come on, Kim," Tam said. "You know Jim will love the idea of you and Reggie dating. He'll start seeing increased circulation numbers in his head."

"You're right," Kim said slowly. "That's why Jim can't know about Reggie's proposal." Jim would try to turn this getting to know you dating into a news story and she definitely didn't want that. She was the reporter, not the subject. Her role had gotten mixed up in the Good Guy article, but she'd make sure it didn't get mixed up again. No way was she going to have Jim turn a few dates with Reggie into a feature story. She shook her head. "I can't do it, guys. You're right about Jim. He'd want to use the situation to the magazine's advantage and I won't be a party to it."

"Spoilsport," Leslie accused. "We just want to have a little fun. We won't tell Jim if you don't."

Kim shook her head again. "No way. Sometimes I think Jim has eyes and ears everywhere." She thought about the way he always seemed to appear at her desk when she got an interesting phone call. She hoped he didn't have the phones bugged as she'd teasingly accused. "I can't risk it. I know he'll find out and then *my* picture will be on the cover of Urban Style."

"That doesn't sound like a bad thing, girl," Leslie said. Her eyes widened. "Look, I have an idea. Why don't I stand in for you with Reggie?"

"Stand in for me?" Kim asked, an uneasy feeling bubbling in her belly. She still remembered Leslie's not-so-subtle flirting with Reggie in the lobby.

"Sure," Leslie said. "Reggie wants a woman to get to know him, right?"

"R—ight," Kim said, not liking the direction of the conversation. She should have known Leslie would somehow work this situation to her advantage.

"Well, what if *I'm* the woman? I'll go out with him and then you can interview me about the kind of guy he is. What do you think?"

"It's a dumb idea, Leslie," Tam said. "I think Reggie's

interest in Kim goes beyond the magazine. What they don't need is you jumping in the middle."

"But if Kim doesn't want him—"

"She never said she didn't want him," Tam interrupted. "Can't you see she's just nervous about it?" Tam turned to Kim. "Come on, Kim. Aren't you just a little bit interested in him?"

Kim didn't answer because she didn't want to give voice to her conflicting emotions. She could be interested in Reggie, if she allowed herself. But something told her that, regardless of the good feelings she sometimes had about him, in the end, he'd disappoint her.

Groggy with sleep the next morning, Kim reached for the phone. "When do you sleep, Jim?" she asked before she heard his voice.

"Kimmy, girl," he said. "How'd you know it was me?"

"It's five o'clock in the morning. Everybody but you is asleep. Now what do you want?"

"You sure are a grouch in the morning, Kimmy. You'd better work on that before you get married. I'm telling you no man wants to wake up to a grouchy wife."

"I'm not going to respond to that chauvinist comment, Jim. Tell me what you want so I can go back to sleep."

Jim chuckled. "Oh, no, Kimmy, there'll be no going back to sleep for you. You've a busy day ahead of you."

A feeling of dread surrounded Kim. What had Jim done now? "And how do you know what my schedule is?" she asked cautiously.

"Hey, I'm the boss. I know everything."

"Jim—"

"Guess who called me last night, Kimmy girl. You'll never guess. Not in a million years."

Kim rolled her eyes toward the ceiling. Sometimes Jim was nothing but a big kid. She could handle that side of him on most days, but not at five o'clock in the morning.

"Since you know I'm not going to guess, why don't you just tell me?"

"But that wouldn't be any fun, Kimmy. Come on, one guess."

Understanding that Jim wasn't going to tell her his news until she guessed, Kim asked, "Is this about a new story?"

"That's not a guess. That's a question. I want a guess."

"Okay," Kim said, sinking back down in the bed in preparation for a long conversation. If she was lucky, she'd be able to get in a nap or two while Jim babbled on. "Babyface finally returned your call and we're going to get to interview him."

Jim sighed. "Don't I wish? You know I'm beginning to think he has something against *Urban Style*."

Kim didn't think so. She guessed Babyface was tired of talking about his break up with L.A. She'd tried to tell Jim that the break up was the wrong angle to take with the musical genius, but he hadn't heeded her advice. "Okay, so it wasn't Babyface. I've guessed. Now tell me what's on your mind at five o'clock in the morning."

"I'm gonna tell you even though you didn't try to guess. Reggie Stevens called me."

Kim sat up straight in the bed, her sense of foreboding at its highest point. "Reggie Stevens? Why did Reggie Stevens call you?" Since their ill-fated dinner last Thursday, she'd had no luck in convincing Mr. Stevens to allow the planned photo shoot. She was running out of time.

"Calm down, Kimmy. The man called because he wanted to talk to me. It seems you've been doing a good job down there."

Kim wondered what Reggie had said to Jim. Not being able to accomplish a simple photo shoot in a week's time was not her idea of doing a good job. "Of course, I am. What do you expect?"

"Hey, I was just passing on a compliment. No need to get huffy."

"So that's it? Reggie Stevens just called to tell you I was doing a good job?" Kim knew there had to be more to

Reggie's call. A simple compliment wouldn't have resulted in a five o'clock call from Jim.

"We talked for a while about the article, the contest, you know. By the way, the photographer will be there this afternoon. You have to be at Reggie's house at three."

"You scheduled the photo shoot? I thought that was my job." So what if she'd been having a hard time getting it done.

"It's nothing to get upset about, Kimmy. I know it's your story and I'm keeping my nose out of it, for the most part. It's just that it came up when Reggie and I were talking, so we just scheduled it."

"Uh huh. Come on, Jim, what else just *came up* when you were talking to Reggie?"

"Well, we did toss around a few ideas. And I must say Mr. Stevens has a good head on his shoulders."

Kim sank slowly back down in the bed. *No, please God, no,* she prayed silently.

"Aren't you going to tell me, Kimmy?"

"Tell you what?"

"Reggie said you wanted to keep this under wraps, but I wouldn't think you'd keep it from me. How were you going to explain your extended stay in Atlanta?"

"I don't know what you're talking about, Jim," she said, hoping that what she thought he knew wasn't what he knew.

"There's no need to keep it a secret. Reggie told me all about it and I think it's a great idea. I couldn't have thought of a better one myself. As a matter of fact, I'm ashamed I didn't come up with it."

Kim knew there was only a slim chance Jim wasn't talking about what she was thinking about. "Why don't you just tell me what Reggie told you?"

"If you're going to be that way, I guess I'll have to." Jim sighed. "Reggie told me his idea that the two of you get to know each other better."

She'd known it. She'd known it. But she still couldn't believe it. Reggie had actually gone behind her back and over her head to talk to her boss. He had some nerve. "That's a stupid idea, Jim, and I told Reggie so."

"What are you talking about, Kimmy? This is a great idea, a great way for *Urban Style* to capitalize on the contest, Reggie's article about male female relationships and your article about Reggie."

"I haven't written an article about Reggie," she clarified.

"You know what I mean, Kimmy girl. That article that quoted you from A to Z. The idea of you and Reggie dating is a good one. It'll give you more to work with in your column."

"You've got to be kidding. I don't want to date Reggie." She paused because the words sounded false on her lips. "And I think we should just forget the column idea. I just want to finish the interview and companion article on Reggie and get back home. I still have two other finalists to interview. Or have you forgotten them?"

"Hold on, now, Kimmy," Jim said. "I haven't forgotten the other finalists, but let's be reasonable about this. Reggie thinks you didn't give him a fair shake in that newspaper article and he wants a chance to show you the real him. I don't see anything wrong with his request. If anything, I'd say the magazine owes the man. You've—I mean we've— probably ruined his reputation."

Kim could see that Reggie had done a good job on Jim. Not that it would have taken much. She guessed that the mere idea of their joint column spiced with tidbits from their dating relationship had Jim salivating. "We have not ruined that man's reputation and we don't owe him anything."

"I can't believe you're saying that, Kimmy. You're the one who's always doing everything above board. Do you honestly think that newspaper article was done fairly?"

She didn't and that's where he had her. She was going to be forced to go along with Reggie's idea unless she could come up with another one, a better one. "Hey, Jim, I think I have an even better idea. You remember my friend, Leslie, don't you?"

"Sure. Cute little thing."

"Yeah. Well, what if I do a story on her having a relation-ship with Reggie. That way I could write it from the angle of the unbiased third party."

Jim didn't speak immediately and she assumed he was considering her suggestion. She crossed her fingers and her toes for good luck.

"No, Kimmy," Jim finally said. "Not that your idea doesn't have merit. It does. It's just that with the article and radio discussions, I think our strongest angle is you and Reggie."

Kim didn't want to acknowledge the irrational relief she felt when Jim rejected her idea. She really didn't want to see Leslie and Reggie together. He wasn't her type, anyway.

"And to top it all off," Jim continued. "Reggie has agreed to give us an exclusive."

"An exclusive on what?"

"Don't be dense, Kimmy," Jim admonished. "He's giv-ing us an exclusive on him. He's only talking to us; no other magazines or radio shows will get him until after our article runs."

Kim couldn't deny she was impressed, but she wondered why Reggie was treating them so well. Her opinion of him couldn't mean that much to him, could it?

"The way I'm thinking right now is that we'll push back the deadline for the Nice Guy contest. The radio station in Atlanta and one here in D.C. want to hold their own contests. The way I figure it, we can have forty or fifty finalists, each representing a radio station or an area of the country. Something like that. What do you think?"

Kim could find no fault with the idea. Actually, she thought it was a good one and told Jim so.

"In the next few issues," he explained, "we'll have a list of participating stations with information on how to nominate candidates. That should keep interest in the magazine high. I think we've got a winner on our hands, Kim."

"It looks that way," she said, accepting the inevitable.

"But if we're going to turn the contest over to the stations and push the date back, what will I be doing?"

Jim cleared his throat. "You'll be in charge of the selection committee for the winner of the contest and you'll continue to work with Reggie. I think we'll run your first column in the issue that presents the contest finalists.'

"What do you mean by work with Reggie?"

"You know, Kimmy. You guys will do the dating thing and come up with ideas for your column. Your first column should discuss the status of your dating relationship. We want our readers to really get involved in your relationship."

"But it's not a relationship, Jim," Kim reminded him. "We're just getting to know each other for the magazine."

"I know that, Kimmy, but the readers don't have to know it. At least, not in the first column. Trust me, this will work out beautifully."

Kim didn't trust him and more importantly, she didn't trust Reggie Stevens. If the man had gone behind her back with his outrageous idea, what could she expect from him in this dating they were supposed to do? There was no use trying to explain her concerns to Jim though. Her boss thought he was sitting on a gold mine. It would be up to her to protect herself from Reggie Stevens.

Kim and Marty, the photographer, arrived at Reggie's house at exactly two-fifty that afternoon. She'd get the photos taken, then have a nice long chat with Mr. Stevens. There were some things she needed to get off her chest.

She was pleased when Luther opened the door. Seeing Reggie a minute before it was necessary was not something she needed.

"Well, if it isn't Ms. Washington from *Urban Style*," Luther said. "Long time no see."

Kim smiled, but before she could speak Reggie walked up behind Luther. "Hello, Ms. Washington," he said with a teasing smile. "I was hoping it was you."

"Our appointment was for three, wasn't it?" She tried to keep her voice free of emotion, but she wasn't sure she was doing a good job. "I'm on time for all my appointments. It's part of being a professional."

He laughed. He actually laughed. His laughter charmed her and aggravated her at the same time.

"That's right, Kim. You're a professional. That's what I like about you. You'll do whatever it takes to get the job done."

The teasing glint in his eyes told her that he was intentionally baiting her. He knew she'd talked to Jim and he knew the outcome of the conversation. He'd probably known even before he made the call to her boss.

"Well, should we get started?" she asked.

He nodded and she and Marty entered his house. They quickly decided to start the shoot in Reggie's den since that's where he spent most of his time. Then she got out of the way and let Marty do his job.

It was only natural that she study Reggie as he posed for the shots. He was a man who seemed comfortable in his own body. He didn't try on smiles before choosing one for the camera. No, Reggie Stevens, just smiled. And what a smile it was! It reached from his chin to his eyes. And Reggie Stevens's smiling eyes should have been illegal.

She continued to watch as Marty took shots of him on the phone at his desk, on the couch with his remote in hand. This room fits him, she thought. The dark woods exuded strength and warmth even as he did. The collection of East and West African masks on his wall and the collection of black figurines on his sofa table told her he appreciated his heritage.

When the shoot moved to Reggie's patio and he changed into the knee-length shorts Marty had suggested, she had a chance to study him more. Just as she'd always thought, the brother was fine. Too fine, if you asked her. It just wasn't fair that he had those dreamy brown eyes and that buff body. It just wasn't.

Again, she wondered why those women had dumped

him. After being held in those strong arms, feeling those big, muscular thighs against hers, and resting her head against that broad chest, she knew it must have been difficult. Those women must have sensed something seriously lacking in Reggie to let him go, because the brother was too fine to let go on a whim.

But fine didn't say anything about character, she knew. And that's where she suspected Reggie was lacking. Though none of the women had mentioned his character flaws in their nomination letters, there could be no other answer. Hadn't she herself gotten a glimpse of his shallowness and selfishness?

"That's it," Marty said. He went over and shook Reggie's hand. "You're one of the best subjects I've shot. Most people are so uncomfortable that I have to take three times as many shots to get half as many good ones as I've shot today. You're a natural. Have you ever thought about modeling?"

Reggie chuckled, as if he thought the idea was ridiculous. "Who? Me?"

"Yes, you."

Reggie shook his head. "I think I'm a bit too old. Maybe when I was younger."

"Don't reject the idea out of hand, man," Marty said. "Advertisers are trying to reach men in your age group because you're the ones with the cash." Marty checked his watch, then turned to Kim. "If you don't have anything else for me, I'm going to try to check out the lab at the local paper and see if I can get these prints developed so we can see what we've got."

"No, that's it for today, Marty. Thanks. You did a great job."

"I'll show you out," Luther said. Kim turned to him, realizing that she'd forgotten he was still there.

"Want something to drink?" Reggie asked, walking toward her.

She stepped back so he could open his back door. "A cold soda would be nice."

He flashed her his smile. "I think I can provide one of those. Follow me."

She followed him to the kitchen and took a seat on the stool at the counter.

He grabbed a couple cans of soda from the refrigerator and handed her one. "So," he asked. "Where do you want to go on our first date?"

Chapter 10

"What makes you think I'm going out with you?" she asked, taking the can of soda he offered. His fingers brushed hers and their eyes met. She lowered hers first and he wondered if Ms. Washington was as immune to him as she said she was. "Going behind my back to my boss is not the way to win me over."

He popped the tab on his can. "Desperate times call for desperate measures. I couldn't think of any other way to persuade you to give me another chance. You left me no choice."

"So now it's my fault," she said. "Typical male response: always shift the blame."

Reggie chuckled. She sure was cute when her eyes flashed as they did now. "You'd better watch it or that chip on your shoulder is going to fall off and break your foot."

"I don't know what I'm going to do with either you or Jim." She sighed a frustrated sigh. "Why is what I think of you so important anyway?"

Reggie couldn't explain that to himself. "I'm just concerned about my reputation." The half-truth fell easily from his lips. "Wouldn't you be concerned about yours?"

She shook her head. "Do you really think people are playing that close attention?"

He sipped his soda. "My family in Oklahoma City are. I've already gotten two calls from them. I wouldn't be surprised if I got a call from my mother asking me what I did to make that cute little lady so upset."

"Cute little lady, huh? Are you sure those are your words and not your mother's?"

He grinned. No, he'd use other words to describe her. Sexy. Alluring. Inviting. "I'm sure. Now tell me about this boss of yours. He seems like a real character."

"Hmph. You should know. I'm beginning to think you two were separated at birth."

Reggie chuckled. "Somehow I get the feeling that isn't a compliment to me or your boss. Show the man some respect, even if you have none for me."

"I do respect Jim," she said. "To a point. But I don't agree with him on this issue."

Reggie propped his elbows on the counter, rested his face on his hands and looked at her. "I gather this isn't the first time he's pulled rank on you."

"Hardly. Jim's management training came straight from a drill Sergeant's handbook."

Though her words were harsh, the near smile on her face told him that she really liked Jim. "That sounds like him," he said. "What's it like working for him?"

Kim sipped from her can of soda. "He's gruff but overall he's fair. As far as bosses go, he's all right."

"You sound as though you'd prefer not to have a boss. Tell me what Ms. Kimberla Washington does prefer."

She eyed him skeptically as if wondering about the sincerity of his request.

"Humor me," he said. "We're supposed to be getting to know each other. Unless you're one of those women who'll only talk to a man after he's spent a bundle of money on her."

She placed her soda can on the counter and leveled a stare at him. "If we're going to get to know one another, as you put it, you're going to have to stop with the insults."

"What insults?" he said. "Some women do want a man to spend money on them. It's as if their interest in a man is in direct proportion to the size of his wallet."

"And you consider that a problem?"

He shrugged. "Seems to me money shouldn't have anything to do with how a woman feels about a man."

"I'm not surprised you have such strong feelings on this subject."

At her look of disdain, he asked, "What do you mean by that?"

"Well, I just think it's a typical *hypocritical* male statement."

He leaned back from the counter and reached into the overhead cabinet for a bag of chips. "And that sounds like a typical *stereotypical* female statement." He opened the bag and offered some to her. After she refused, he reached for a chip. "What exactly does it mean?"

She sighed and his eyes went to the rise and fall of her full bosom. *Nice,* he thought to himself.

"It means, Mr. Stevens, that I get tired of men complaining about women judging them on the size of their wallets when they do the same thing."

"So, you're talking about gigolos. I don't think many men fall into that category."

She reached for a chip. "I'm *not* talking about gigolos, though I suppose they could be placed in the same category. I'm talking about the brothers whose interest in a woman is in direct proportion to her dress size." She looked directly into his eyes. "Or in direct proportion to the size of her bust."

Reggie felt royally rebuked for looking at her chest earlier. "Some busts can't be ignored," he said and his words surprised even him. He was not the type of guy to get this outrageous with a woman. But something perverse in him made him want to provoke Ms. Washington.

"And some men beg to be ignored," she returned without a pause. She slid off the stool. "Thanks for the soda. I have to be going."

Oh, damn, Reggie thought to himself. *Now you've gone too far.* "Kim," he called, rushing after her. He caught up with her in the living room. "Look," he said when she turned and faced him. "I'm sorry. I don't know why I made that stupid remark. Believe me, I've never before said anything like that to a woman I barely know."

He could tell she didn't believe him and he couldn't blame her. If he could kick himself, he would. Instead, he extended his hand to her. "What if we start over? Pretend this is our first meeting? I swear I'll make a better impression this time."

She looked at his outstretched hand, then at his face. "Why should I?" she asked. "Give me one good reason why I should start over with you."

The first thought in his mind was the obvious one: She ought to give him a second chance because her boss would rake her over the coals if she screwed up this idea. Fortunately, he had enough sense to refrain from voicing that sentiment. "Because I need to show you that you've gotten the wrong impression of me. And I need you to help clean-up the damage that article did to my reputation."

She looked down at his outstretched hand again. "You can go ahead and drop your hand because I'm not going to shake it. I'm not making any deals with you."

"But—"

She raised her hand to stop him. "Let me finish. We're going to do this get to know each other thing because you've got my boss thinking that my working with you is going to mean big bucks for him. But I'm telling you, Reggie, I'm not going to lie. I'm going to tell the readers exactly what I think of you."

Reggie dropped his hand, relieved that she'd agreed to go through with the deal. He'd prove to her that he was one of the nice guys.

"Don't look so relieved," she said. "You have a long row to hoe in order to win me over."

He wanted to give her a stern look, but his relief turned his face in a wide grin. "So where do we go on our first date?"

A visit to the Boys' Club had not been on Kim's mind when Reggie had mentioned their first date, but she'd been relieved when Luther had reminded him of his regular Wednesday night commitment. She also took satisfaction in the knowledge that Reggie had almost forgotten his weekly commitment in his effort to get her to go out with him. Though she knew their being together was strictly a business arrangement, his interest definitely stroked her feminine ego.

Now that she was here at the Boys' Club, she couldn't imagine a better evening. She liked sitting in this large gym watching Reggie, Luther and their friend Nate try to get the dozen or so teens ready for their first basketball game of the summer season. Watching Reggie run around on the court in his shorts didn't prove a hardship either. No, not at all.

His gaze met hers across the court and he smiled at her. As he lifted his hand to wave, one of the boys stole the ball from him. Needless to say, she was soon forgotten as he scrambled to redeem himself.

"Having fun?"

She looked up to see Nate standing before her. "A lot. How about you?"

Nate dropped down on the bleacher in front of her and turned his body so he faced her. He was a handsome, light-complexioned guy with a face that looked thirty or so instead of the almost forty that she knew him to be. Like Reggie, he was in good shape. His easy stride said he was a laid-back guy. She wondered what Tam would think of him. She was very much aware that Reggie had two unattached male friends and she had two unattached female friends. She was already planning her next "date" with Reggie—a triple date.

"It's tiring," he said. "But I enjoy it. These are some okay kids. They just need a little direction."

"How long have the three of you been coming down here?"

"Not long," he said. "Reggie started coming when he first moved here from Oklahoma City. He recruited Luther and me as soon as we arrived in town."

So, this had been Reggie's idea. Definitely a plus for him. "So the three of you are friends from Oklahoma City?"

He nodded. "We grew up together and have been friends since elementary school."

Kim wondered what it was like to have known someone that long. She'd been pretty much a loner growing up. A situation she knew was a result of her over-protective parents. She hadn't had any long standing friendships until she'd gone off to Spelman and met Leslie and Tam.

"So what do you think about Reggie and everything that's going on?" she asked Nate.

He studied her curiously before answering. "I don't know," he said. "At first, I thought his participation in your contest was a good idea. It seemed harmless enough. That article you wrote—"

"I didn't write," she corrected.

"Okay, that article that quoted you so much. Anyway, at first I thought it was funny, but now I'm not sure. Reggie's a good guy and he doesn't deserve some of the things you said about him."

"Those things weren't said about him specifically," she said, feeling a need to defend herself. "They were statements about men in general."

"And that makes it better?"

"Did his article make anything better?" she challenged.

"That's different," Nate said. "Reggie was writing from experience in his article. That other article was written from pure speculation and had nothing to do with him."

Kim admired Nate's loyalty to Reggie, though she wondered if it was misplaced. She was about to follow up on his comment about Reggie's article being written from experience when Reggie joined them. "Your turn, man," he said to Nate. "I need to take a breather."

Nate cut Kim a quick glance. "Translated that means I've been talking to you too long." He got up and hopped off the bleachers. Looking back at her, he said, "Think about what I said." Then he ran and joined the action on the court.

"What did he say?" Reggie asked, dropping down next to her.

"Oh, nothing," she said. "We were just talking."

"About me, I assume."

"What makes you think we were talking about you? Maybe we were talking about Nate. He's a nice guy."

Reggie lifted a questioning brow. "Nice guy?"

"You know what I mean. He seems like one of the good ones."

"And I don't?"

"That's not what I said."

"But it's what you meant."

She didn't want to start arguing again, so she swallowed the smart retort that came to her lips. "Has it occurred to you that you have two unattached male friends and I have two unattached female friends?"

He grinned. "Don't tell me you want to play matchmaker?"

She shook her head as much in answer to his question as to stop her heart from responding so wildly to his arresting grin. "No way. I was just thinking that my friends don't know too many people in town and your friends seem nice. I think it might be a good idea to get them together."

His eyes showed his skepticism.

"For the article, of course. You can learn a lot about a man from the company he keeps."

"So you're suggesting we pair your friends up with mine so they can glean information about me."

She nodded. "And maybe they could have some fun in the process. As a matter of fact, the six of us could. Think about it."

"I *am* thinking about it," he said with a smirk. "I didn't have a group meeting in mind when I said I wanted us to get to know each other."

She knew he didn't think so, but the triple-dating was the perfect plan. "Maybe you're right. It might be best if I talked with them myself. Do you think they'd mind spending some time with me?"

"Oh, no you don't," he said. "You're getting to know me, not them. Remember it's my reputation that's being trashed, not theirs."

"That's what I'm trying to tell you. By getting your friends in on the article, I'll be able to present a more rounded picture of you. Do you think they'll go for it?"

Reggie looked out at his friends on the court. "I've seen your friends. Nate and Luther will go for it, all right."

Reggie sounded so disappointed that Kim wanted to laugh. She refrained though and kept her face straight. She might enjoy dating Reggie Stevens, after all.

"So when's our next date?" Reggie asked after he'd escorted her to her car. She'd learned some things about him tonight that were more compatible with the Reggie she'd imagined him to be than with the Reggie he'd seemed since she'd known him here in Atlanta. "And this time I want to pick you up."

"That's not necessary," she said. *Or safe,* she thought. Her best bet was to keep as much distance between her and Reggie Stevens as possible. Now that he was becoming a good guy in her eyes, she knew she'd have to fight falling for him. "Besides, my girlfriends will be coming along. We'll meet you there."

He shook his head. "That's not the way we do it in Atlanta."

"How do you do it?"

"Well," he said, leaning close to her, "in Atlanta the man picks the woman up for the date then drives her home when the evening is over. We even meet and greet parents."

He was so close that she stepped back. Unfortunately, the car behind her didn't give her much maneuvering room. "I hope that doesn't mean you're dating teenagers."

He laughed outright at that statement and his deep chuckle caused a shiver down her spine. "You'd be surprised," he said. "There're some pretty o—, I mean mature, woman still living with their parents."

She chuckled. "Good save."

"You keep me on my toes, Ms. Washington. Independent women like you demand political correctness."

"You sound as though you have something against independent women. Do you?"

"Not me. Maybe it's the other way around. Maybe independent women have something against me."

She couldn't imagine what any level headed woman would have against Reggie Stevens. She was beginning to think she liked him better when she didn't like him. This Reggie was dangerous to her mind. "And why do you think independent women have something against you?"

He looked deep into her eyes. "Can you stop being a reporter for about five minutes?"

"Why?" she asked, but the look in his eyes made her add, "Don't answer that. I think it's time for me to say good night."

"Running scared, Ms. Washington?"

"Hardly, Mr. Stevens. Unlike you, I need my beauty rest."

He grinned then and she knew she'd spoken the wrong words. "So you don't think I need any beauty sleep? That's the first positive thing you've said about me since you met me."

She stepped away from him and opened her car door. Then she slid in and looked up at him. "Don't be so sure. It could be that no amount of sleep will make you look better." She started the car and he started laughing. She had a smile on her face as she backed out of his drive.

Reggie stood in the driveway long after his laughter subsided. Now that Ms. Washington was no longer in his presence, he was able to look objectively at his recent actions.

What in the hell are you doing, man? he asked himself. *Why are you pursuing this woman?*

He wanted to offer the excuse that he wasn't pursuing her, that he was just trying to prove to her that he was one of the good guys. But he knew his motives were more complicated. Ms. Kimberla Washington intrigued him. There was a distance in her eyes, a look of aloneness that reached out to him. She'd masked it pretty well in the beginning, but he'd seen it as he stood close to her tonight. When he'd looked down into her eyes, he'd seen her struggle with that aloneness. But instead of struggling to let it go, it seemed she was struggling to hold onto it. And he couldn't let that happen. He wanted to see her smile a smile that involved her whole body. He wanted to hear deep, full laughter bubble forth from her throat.

Reggie turned and went back into his house. Ms. Washington was going to be a challenge, he knew—she wouldn't succumb easily to his charm—but he was assured she was worth the effort. She deserved to have that distance and aloneness erased from her eyes and he was just the man to erase it.

Chapter 11

Kim saw Reggie, Luther and Nate as soon as she, Leslie and Tam stepped off the elevator for their triple date Saturday night. They looked like three male models standing there in the crowded hotel lobby. All three men wore jackets and matching slacks—Reggie's blue with a red shirt and string tie; Luther's black with a black high collar shirt, and no tie; and Nate's tan blazer with a white shirt and standard tie. They could have been posing for a hunk calendar.

"They're here," Kim said to her friends. "See them over there." She pointed to the guys.

"Yes, girl, I do see. You did good this time," Leslie said. "Are you sure I can't have Reggie? He looks good enough to eat."

Kim took pride in Leslie's appreciation of Reggie's good looks, though she knew she had no right. "If it were left up to me, you could."

"But he's not interested in you, Leslie," Tam added.

"Doesn't matter," Leslie said. "I want the one on the left anyway. He looks like my kind of guy."

Kim wasn't surprised Leslie chose Luther. She had no

doubt he'd pick her as well. "That's Luther," she said. "He lives with Reggie."

"Hold up a minute," Leslie said. "Are you saying the brother doesn't have his own place?"

Kim shook her head. "Obviously not. He's living in Reggie's house."

"Maybe I'll give you that one, Tam," Leslie offered. "A brother who doesn't have his own place usually doesn't have a job."

"Too late," Tam said. "He's a little too flashy for me. I'll take the other one. Nate. Right, Kim?"

"Uh uh, that's Nate. I think you'll like him, Tam. He seems really nice."

"Does he have his own place?" Leslie asked.

"I guess so," Kim answered with a shrug. "But I never really asked. It doesn't matter anyway, Leslie? We're just going out to have some fun. You don't need to know the guy's net worth."

Leslie mumbled some reply that Kim refused to acknowledge. She glanced in the men's direction again and saw that they still hadn't spotted them.

"My hair is okay, isn't it?" Leslie asked as she fiddled with the curly strands feathered around her face. All three had gone out earlier and gotten their hair done.

"We've told you fifty times your hair is fine," Tam said. "Give it a rest, Leslie."

"Well," Leslie said. "You know sisters can't hook-up a hair-do like the brothers. I knew I should have asked for a brother."

"Whatever," Kim said, dismissing her friend's babbling. "Now, let's meet the guys."

"Wait a minute, Kim," Leslie said, grabbing her arm. "I need to check my makeup one more time. Let's stop by the restroom."

"Les-lie." Kim was beginning to feel like a college student on one of those dreaded group dates. She wondered if she, Leslie and Tam would still act this way when they were fifty and getting ready for a date. She hoped not.

Heck, she wanted to be settled down with grandkids when she was fifty, not still dating. "There's nothing wrong with your makeup." Leslie was notorious for being late and Kim didn't want to get hung up in the restroom with her. "Besides, we don't want them to think we went to too much trouble."

"That's the whole point of make up," Leslie said. "To make you look like you didn't go to any trouble."

"Whatever," Kim said again. "Come on, let's go meet them. The sooner we get this evening started, the sooner it'll be over."

"Look, Kim, you've got to have the right attitude if this evening is going to work," Tam said. "I want to have some fun and we won't if you're going to have an attitude all evening."

"I don't have an attitude," Kim said.

"Well, you've got something," Leslie agreed. "I just hope it's not catching." She hooked arms with her girlfriends. "Show time, girls," she said. "Let's do this."

"You guys remember the plan, right?" Reggie asked Luther and Nate. He wondered what he'd been thinking when he'd agreed to Kim's suggestion of this triple date business. Obviously, he hadn't been thinking at all or he would have nixed the idea immediately. Every time he, Nate and Luther got together they reverted to their elementary school days and ways. Not exactly the way to impress a lady.

"You've gone over it a hundred times," Luther said sarcastically. "I think we have it."

"That's right," Nate said. "Luther and I take our dates in my car and you take Kim in yours. We've got it, man, so you can calm down. She's really got you going in circles, doesn't she?"

"I just want to be alone with her," Reggie said. "Let's not make more out of this than there really is."

"Whatever you say, man," Luther said. He turned to Nate. "And I get the first pick of the women. Don't forget."

Nate shrugged. "I don't know. With all these rules, I may forget my name."

"Wouldn't be the first time, I'm sure," Luther mumbled. "Now describe them one more time for us, Reggie."

Reggie really couldn't remember Kim's friends in much detail. He'd focused his time and attention on her. "Let's see, Leslie is the short one, cute, about five-four, really thin, big flirt. Tam's the taller one, she's heavier than Kim, cute, kind of quiet."

"Okay," Luther said, rubbing his hands together. "It looks like it's going to be me and Leslie. No giant-sized wallflowers or church mice for me." He poked Nate in the side. "You get Tam, old buddy. She sounds about your speed. I just hope the two of you don't bore each other to death."

"Remember," Reggie said. "You guys are to be on your best behavior. These women will be reporting back to Kim and I don't want anything you do to reflect badly on me. I'm trying to clean up my reputation, not flush it completely down the toilet."

"We've got it, man," Luther said. "We'll be perfect gentlemen." He poked Nate in the side again. "Did you get the roses?"

"What roses?" Reggie asked.

Nate shook his head. "You're trying to make a good impression and you come to pick up the woman empty-handed? It's a good thing I left our roses in the car. Otherwise, we'd show you up."

"You guys brought roses?" Reggie cursed himself for not getting a gift for Kim. He wouldn't have gone the roses route, though. Too predictable. Too common. No, he should have gotten something that she'd always associate with him. Unfortunately, he'd spent most of his time trying to figure out how to keep his date from turning into a group picnic. "How many?"

Luther tugged at the lapels of his jacket. "One each. A perfect rose for a perfect woman."

Nate chuckled. "That's the oldest line in the book. Please don't use it. They'll think we're corny."

Luther shook his head. "No they won't. They'll think we're gentlemen. Trust me," Luther said. "I know my way around women. The roses will add the perfect touch. And the line may be old but it'll work."

Reggie wondered again if he'd done the right thing by bringing Luther and Nate along. Maybe he should have asked some other friends. Luther and Nate were turning into Martin and Cole right before his eyes.

"Whatever you do," Reggie pleaded, "don't embarrass yourselves or me. The key word for tonight is *good impression*."

Nate grinned. "That's two words."

Luther laughed at the lame joke and Reggie turned his head to look for Kim and her friends. Just when he thought they hadn't come down yet, he saw them headed their way.

"Here they come," he said. "Follow me and act sane."

Reggie greeted Kim with a kiss on the cheek that he knew surprised her by the brightness he saw in her eyes when he pulled away. "You look great," he whispered, taking in the red column dress that hugged her body and whose thigh-length front slit showed off her long legs. The pearls she wore on her ears and her wrist matched the pearls that were woven into the bodice of her dress. He took her hand in his and smiled at Leslie and Tam. "Hi, ladies. You're looking lovely tonight," he said because they did. Tam wore a purple scarf dress with a V-neck column while Leslie wore a daring black mini dress.

Reggie introduced the women to his friends and waited for Luther to say something stupid, but his friend surprised him when he said, "We've heard a lot about you ladies, but we think Reggie was holding out on us. He didn't tell us you were beautiful."

It was a line, Reggie thought, but it wasn't outrageous and the smiles on the women's faces indicated they appreciated it. They did look nice, though not as nice as Kim. But then, he freely admitted his bias.

The two couples then paired off rather easily with Luther taking Leslie's arm in his and Nate and Tam sharing shy smiles. Reggie was feeling a little bit better about the prospects for the evening by the time they left the lobby.

Kim was relieved when Leslie and Kim easily paired off with the man of their choice. It would have been a bit awkward had the men had other choices in mind. Since the evening was warm they waited outside while Reggie and Nate went for the cars.

"Reggie tells me you're moving to Atlanta," she overheard Luther say to Leslie.

She turned to Tam. "So what do you think of Nate?"

Tam lifted her shoulders slightly. "He's seems nice enough. Kind of shy, but I think I like that."

Kim was about to respond when Nate drove up. Luther immediately took Leslie's hand and helped her into the back seat.

"Are you ready, Tammy?" Nate asked.

Tam turned to Kim, then back to Nate. "I guess so, but what about Reggie and Kim?"

"Ah," Nate said awkwardly, "Reggie will be around with his car. We couldn't all fit in mine."

Though Kim kept a smile on her face, she silently cursed Reggie Stevens.

Nate turned to her. "He's pulling up now."

"Are you okay with this, Kim?" Tam asked.

Kim looked at her friend and decided not to ruin everyone's evening. She touched Tam's arm. "Go on. I'll see you when we get to The Club."

Kim watched as Nate opened the door for Tam, then handed her a single rose before she got in. A simple gesture, not very original, but Tam's smile told her it had paid off.

"Ready?" Reggie asked, bringing her attention to him.

She turned around and had to stop herself from smiling at him. He looked too good for words. "I don't know about you, Reggie Stevens."

He took her arm and led her to the car. "What did I do now?"

"You know what you did," she said easing into the front seat of his Maxima. This car was definitely more Reggie than that sports car she'd seen Luther driving.

Reggie closed her door with a smile on his face. "You're a hard woman, Ms. Washington," he said. "You've got to be a little more trusting. Give a man a break, will you?"

She flashed him a low wattage smile. "I'll think about it."

Reggie chuckled then walked around and got in on the driver's side.

"So when did you decide we'd go in two cars?" she asked after he pulled his car out into street.

"Right after I counted six people. Don't you think we would have been a little cramped in here?" He raised a brow in her direction. "I guess I should have thought about the fringe benefits before I made that decision though. With six of us in the car, you wouldn't be able to hug your car door. What's wrong? Are you afraid of me or something?"

Kim thanked God he didn't know just how close to true his words were. She had good reason to be afraid of Reggie. The man was lethal. So lethal he almost made her forget what a rat he was. "What's to be afraid of?" she returned.

"Why don't you slide away from that door, then."

Kim moved a couple of inches away from the door. From the way she was behaving, a person would think she was out on her first date.

He cut another glance in her direction. "A little closer," he urged.

"This is close enough. How long before we get to this club?"

"It depends on which route I take."

She took comfort in the fact that she could see Nate's

car ahead of them. "Have you forgotten why we're going out?"

"To have fun?" he suggested.

"I can think of other ways to have fun. In case you *have* forgotten, we're going out so that you can show me that you're a true nice guy. I have to tell you though, Stevens, you're off to a bad start."

"But the night is young. I have plenty of time to redeem myself."

"Or to dig yourself further into a hole," she murmured.

"I heard that, Ms. Washington. Why don't you just relax and enjoy the evening? Forget about the article for now." He inclined his head toward the dash. "There're some CDs in there or you can turn on the radio." When she didn't move to do either, he added, "Unless you want to continue this wonderful conversation we're having."

Kim had to fight not to laugh. She leaned forward, opened the dash and shuffled through his CDs. Johnny Taylor, Marvin Gaye, The Temptations, The O'Jays. She looked over at Reggie. "How old are you, again?"

"What?" he asked, looking at her.

She held up one of the CDs. "Don't you listen to any music recorded in the nineties?"

He laughed, then leaned forward and clicked on the CD. Herbie Hancock joined them. "Not all my music is Stone Age. I just like quality music."

"So now you're a music critic? Are you planning any articles on the downfall of the music industry?"

"I don't think so. I'm through with writing articles. Look at the trouble that first one got me in."

The sincerity in his words caught her attention. "You really don't like all the publicity, do you?"

He shrugged. "Not really. I'm basically a quiet person and having my photo plastered across the newspaper every other day and reporters camped out in my front yard kinda upsets my life-style. Let's just say I'm glad things have quieted down."

"Hmmm."

"And what does that *'Hmmm'* mean?"

"Nothing," she said.

"Come on, Ms. Washington. No need to hold back anything now. I think it's a little too late for that anyway."

She knew he referred to her alleged quotes in the paper, so she guessed his point was valid. "I don't know," she began. "But I'd think there'd be an upside to all this attention."

"You'll have to tell me what it is, because I don't see it yet. Unless you're talking about meeting you. In that case, you *could* have a point."

Reggie definitely knew his way around women. If she didn't know him better, she'd think he was serious. "You're on the right track, just with the wrong woman."

"Meaning?"

"Meaning I'm sure a lot of women have responded to your article." She had gotten her share of mail from male and female readers of *her* article. She'd received a packet of letters addressed to her in care of the magazine from Jim today, so she knew Reggie had to have received his share as well. "Am I right?"

"Now what makes you think women would respond positively to my article when you didn't?"

She smiled a syrupy smile. "Not all women are as wise as I am."

"Good one, Ms. Washington. You're pretty good at this, aren't you?"

"This what?"

"Flirting."

"I'm not flirting with you."

"What do you call it then?"

"Conversation or some semblance of it. But definitely not flirting."

"If you say so."

"I do, and stop trying to change the topic. About the letters. You've gotten a lot of them from women, haven't you?"

"Jealous?"

"Please. I'm just trying to get some information for my article."

"Then where's your notebook? You don't want to forget something and misquote me, do you?"

She tapped her forefinger on her head. "My notebook's up here. Don't worry. I won't misquote you."

They were quiet a few minutes, and then she noticed that Nate made a right turn while Reggie kept going straight. "I think you missed your turn."

"I told you there was more than one way to get to The Club."

She eyed him cautiously. "Are you sure we're going to The Club?"

"Would I lie?"

She didn't really think he would. For some reason, she trusted him.

"Now tell me about the letters you've gotten."

Though she hadn't had a chance to go through all of them yet, there seemed to be a general consensus. "The women agree with me, though a few of them thought I was too hard on the brothers."

"Maybe I need to talk to those women. Remind me to ask you for their names and numbers."

"That wouldn't be ethical," she said.

"Somehow I knew you'd say that. Now what about the men?"

"What about them?"

"I know you've gotten your share of letters from men. What did they say?"

"You still haven't told me about the women who write to you. What do they say?"

Reggie sighed, resigned to give in and give her the information she wanted. "Most of them tell me that I haven't met the right woman yet."

"And then they suggest that they're that woman?"

He grinned at her. "How'd you know? Did you write one and use a fake name?"

"Sure I did, Reggie. My letter was the one in the perfumed pink envelope." Kim felt good about that jab. It was a good one even if she did say so herself.

"You'll have to be a bit more specific. I've got a couple of boxes of letters that fit that description. I guess all you women think alike."

Kim conceded round one to Reggie. He'd beaten her fair and square.

Chapter 12

When Reggie finally escorted Kim through the golden double doors of The Club, she said, "Next time just follow Nate. For a while there, I thought you'd gotten lost."

He rested his hand on the small of her back and led her through the crowded room. It was difficult to focus on finding her friends with the heat his hand stirred, but she tried. Though the building was large, it was packed. People milled around the bar area, some sat in tables around the now-empty stage while others were further away strutting their moves on the dance floor.

"I see them," Reggie said, pressing close against her back. She told herself such intimate contact was inevitable in the crowded room.

"Where?" she asked.

"Over there. On the dance floor."

She turned to her left away from the tables to the dance floor. "Where? I still don't see them."

Reggie waved his arm and soon she saw Luther and Tam emerge from the dance floor. Then Reggie applied pressure to her back and ushered her in their direction.

"We wondered if you two were going to make it," Luther

said, Tam's hand in his. "I'm glad I had them save us a table. Do you want to dance or sit?"

"Let's sit," Kim said. She wanted to find out why Tam was with Luther instead of Nate, but common courtesy didn't allow her to inquire. As she sat down in the chair Reggie held for her, she watched Luther do the same for Tam then drape his arm around the back of her chair.

"Where are Leslie and Nate?" Reggie asked, taking the words right off her lips.

"On the dance floor somewhere," Tam said leaning close to Luther. "We were going to eat dinner first, but since you guys were taking so long to get here, we decided to dance while we waited."

Reggie looked down at Kim. "Hungry?" he asked.

"I can wait a while," she said. "What time's does the comedian come on?"

"Around ten," Reggie said, looking at his watch. "We have plenty of time to dance and eat before the show starts."

The tempo of the music slowed and Luther turned to Tam, "Ready?" he asked.

Tam's eyes sparkled. "Definitely." Luther stood, pulling her up with him. "We'll see you when we see you," he said. "Let's eat around eighty-thirty, okay?"

"Sounds good to me," Reggie said and the couple was off. "I wonder what happened?" he asked Kim.

She didn't have to ask what he was talking about. "Me, too. I would have sworn that Luther and Leslie would hit it off."

"Me too," Reggie said, looking down into her eyes. "But you never know what attracts one person to another. Take us, for instance."

Kim sucked in her breath. "Let's not."

Reggie continued to stare at her as if he wanted her to read some message in his gaze. Apparently he didn't know that she couldn't think when she looked into his eyes.

"Let's dance," he said, getting up out of his chair. She

had no choice but to give him her hand and allow him to lead her to the dance floor.

Once she was in his arms, he asked, "Having fun yet?"

She pulled away slightly so she could look up at him. "We just got here."

"I know that, Ms. Washington. I'm talking about the entire evening."

"It hasn't been bad, but I wonder why I didn't get a rose."

"You certainly know how to put a guy in his place, don't you? I was hoping you didn't notice the two roses on the table."

"Oh, I noticed when Nate gave Tam hers back at the hotel. But it wasn't until I got here that I realized Luther had given Leslie one as well. So where's mine?"

"You didn't strike me as the type of woman to be moved by something as simple or as predictable as a single rose. I thought you'd go for something more original."

"Like a driving tour of Atlanta?" she asked.

He chuckled. "For starters."

"Well, let me give you a tip. The rose would have been better."

He pressed her head against his chest and pulled her closer. "Had I known you were one of the women who sent me a scented pink envelope, I might have gotten a rose for you. And here I was thinking you were a woman of originality."

Kim felt the laughter in his chest and was surprised at the comfort she found in it. She decided to take his advice and try to enjoy the evening. She didn't think it would take much effort at all.

The six of them were having a perfect evening until it was time for them to leave. Reggie, Luther and Nate excused themselves for a minute and left the women alone at the table.

"What happened?" Kim asked her girlfriends as soon

as the men were out of earshot. "Why did you two switch dates?"

"Ask Ms. Flirty here," Leslie said. "She and Luther talked all the way over here."

"We did not," Tam said with a big smile. "We discovered that we had some common interests. Nate wasn't saying much and Luther was just trying to keep the conversation going."

"It might have worked better if you two had talked about something Nate and I understood," Leslie complained. "Who gives a flip about stars and constellations anyway?"

"Luther's into astronomy?" Kim asked, surprised. She never would have guessed in a million years. Nate, yes. Luther, no.

"Don't sound so surprised," Tam said. "Luther's a deep brother. You'd find out if you took the time to get to know him."

Leslie rolled her eyes. "Tam, you've known the man less than eight hours. I don't see how that makes you an authority on him."

"You're just upset because he preferred me to you," Tam said with obvious pleasure. "You and Nate seemed to hit it off anyway, so I don't know why you're complaining."

Kim suspected Leslie was complaining because her pride was hurt. A man preferring Tam to her was a definite first and no doubt a blow to Leslie's considerable ego. Kim thought it just that things had worked out the way they had.

"What do you think about Nate?" she asked.

Leslie smiled a shy smile. Another first for her. "He's a sweetie. Different. A little slow, but you know what they say about slow hands."

"You need to get your mind out of the bedroom," Tam said, shaking her head. "You've known the man all of five hours and you're talking about going to bed with him."

Leslie was nonplussed. "At least I get to talk about it *before* I do it. With a fast talker like Luther, you'd better

watch yourself or you're going to be flat on your back
before you realize what hit you."

Kim listened to the back and forth between her friends,
amazed at the happenings of the evening. Luther and Tam
were acting as if they'd known each other for years. And
Leslie was talking about Nate like a lovesick teenager.

She didn't even want to think about herself. Here she
was, out with Reggie Stevens, and having the most fun
she'd had in a very long time.

"That wasn't the plan, Nate," Reggie said. "The four
of you are supposed to ride together so that I can be alone
with Kim. Now what's the deal?"

Nate looked down at his shoes. "Leslie's not ready to
go. She wants to dance some more and I told her I'd stay."

Reggie turned to Luther. "Then why don't you and Tam
stay?"

"Because Tam doesn't want to. The music is getting to
her. She's not up for clubbing all night."

Reggie wondered if aliens had inhabited his friends'
bodies. Nate wanted to stay at the club longer and Luther
wanted to leave. Something was definitely wrong here.
"How did you two end up switching dates, anyway?" he
asked.

"Tam and I just hit it off," Luther said. "It surprised
me as much as anybody, but I like her and she's a lot of
fun."

"So you dumped Leslie for Tam?"

"I didn't dump her," Luther said. "We just didn't click."

Reggie looked at Nate. "But she did click with you?"

Nate grinned the widest grin Reggie had ever seen on
his face. "Seems that way. Now what are we going to do
about the driving arrangements?"

"I don't see that we have a choice," Reggie said. "Tam
and Luther will have to ride with me and Kim. Remind
me never to ask you guys for a favor again."

"Look," Luther offered. "If you're that put out by it, Tam and I can take a cab."

Reggie shook his head. He knew he was behaving childishly, but damnit, he wanted to be alone with Kim. "That wouldn't make any sense, man. We'll ride back to the hotel together, but when we get there you and Tam had better make yourselves scarce. I want to be alone with Kim."

"Don't worry about it," Luther said. "I'd rather be alone with Tam than with you and Kim anyway. Now, can we get back to the ladies? I'm going to try to talk Tam into one more dance before we go. If I'm lucky, it'll be a slow one."

"All right, but I want you guys to remember tonight before you think about asking me for another favor. Because I'm telling you right now, the answer is going to be no."

Kim noticed the difference in Reggie as soon as the guys came back to the table. Their last dance was nice, but the tension she'd felt in him had taken some of the pleasure out of it for her. Things hadn't gotten any better during the drive home. She, Luther and Tam had tried to engage him in conversation, but all he'd given were short, clipped responses. Soon they'd given up.

Luther and Tam started talking to each other and she was left to stare out of the front windshield wondering what had happened to her perfect evening. This was supposed to be her date, but her friends seemed to be having a better time than she was.

When they pulled up to the hotel, Luther and Tam hopped out first. She reached for her door and said, "I can see myself in, Reggie. You don't have to get out."

"Forget it, Kim," he said. "I'll get the door."

He was out of the car and at her door in a flash. He opened it and helped her out. "How about going for a walk around the block?"

"It's late," she said.

"Don't think I can protect you?"

Something in his voice reached out to her and she shook her head. "It's not that."

He tossed his keys to the valet and reached for her hand. She slipped it in his and allowed him to pull her close to his side. When they reached the sidewalk, he squeezed her hand and said, "I'm sorry for acting like such an ass."

She couldn't find fault with his description of himself. "What happened to make you so upset?" she asked.

"Not what," he corrected. "But who. More like four whos."

"Why are you upset with them?"

He dropped her hand and stood in front of her, staring down at her face. "Because Nate and Leslie wanted to stay at the club, Tam and Luther had to ride back with us. That wasn't exactly the way I had planned to end the evening."

Entranced by his eyes in the moonlight, she asked, "How had you planned it?"

In answer, he leaned his head down to hers slowly so that she had time to move away if she didn't want his kiss. She didn't move because she did want it. She hadn't known how much until that moment.

He placed his hands on her waist when his lips met hers and pulled her close. The taste of him was better than she'd imagined and God help her, she *had* imagined. She'd imagined being in his arms this way when she'd first seen his picture, when she'd first spoken with him on the phone, when she'd first met him, when she'd watched him during his photo shoot, when they'd shared dinner at The Inn and tonight when he'd picked her up for their date. It was only natural that she put her arms around his neck and give herself fully to the kiss.

Reggie had wanted to kiss Kim all evening, but he hadn't dared hope she would allow it. He'd tried to tell himself to give her time to get to know him, but he hadn't been able to. He needed to kiss Ms. Kimberla Washington right now as much as he needed to breathe. In this kiss he shared with her, he found liberty and an ability to drop the fury he felt toward Nate and Luther. From the sweet way she responded, he assumed she needed him as much.

Kim ended the kiss. She had to, because he wouldn't have been capable of doing so. And when he looked down at her kiss-swollen lips, he wanted to kiss her again. He leaned toward her to do just that, but she stopped him with a hand to his chest. "You'd better walk me back to the hotel now."

He looked into her eyes to see if she was serious or just saying what she felt she should say. Unfortunately, her expression said she was serious. Without saying anything, he took her hand, pulled her to his side and walked her back to the hotel. They reached the lobby just in time to see Luther and Tam share a passionate good night kiss of their own. The act heightened Reggie's need to kiss Kim again, but he decided not to push his luck.

They walked to the elevator in each other's arms. He pushed the button for a car and massaged her neck while they waited. When the car door finally opened, she looked up at him and whispered good night. He brought their entwined hands to his lips and kissed her knuckles. "I'll call you in the morning," he said.

She nodded and got on the elevator. As the doors closed separating them for the night, he took satisfaction in the questions he saw in her eyes because he knew they were also reflected in his.

After the elevator doors closed, Kim pressed her hand to her mouth, closed her eyes and savored the lingering taste of Reggie. She knew she was in trouble, but, for once she didn't care.

Reggie Stevens was the sweetest and dearest man she'd ever met. They might share different philosophies on some subjects, but she knew in her heart that he was a good man, a man who could be counted on.

When the elevator stopped and she got off, she was surprised to see Tam get off the one next to hers.

"Luther didn't want Reggie to wait," Tam said, her eyes full of excitement. "I had a great time tonight."

"I could tell," Kim said, leading the way to the suite. "You like Luther, huh?"

"He's an okay guy after you get past all the flash."

Kim used her key to open the three bedroom suite she and her friends shared in the all-suite hotel in Atlanta's midtown. "Seems to me you got past the flash pretty quickly."

Tam walked into the sitting room and dropped down on the couch. "Pretty good as first dates go; excellent for a blind date. How about you and Reggie? You seemed to hit it off."

"I like him, Tam. I really like him. And I think it's mutual. We'll have to see what happens."

"Are you going out with him again?"

She hoped so. "He said he'd call in the morning, so we'll see."

Tam hugged her friend. "He'll call. Just wait and see. I saw how Reggie looked at you tonight. He's a goner, if ever there was one."

Kim hoped her friend was right, because she felt she was a goner too. "Don't get carried away, Tam. This was only our second date."

"So what? You know more about the guy than most women know about men they've dated for years. I wish I had that kind of info on Luther. It sure would save me a lot of time."

"I don't know about that," Kim said. "There's something to be said for discovery."

"There's also something to be said for knowing what you're getting yourself into. Anyway, what do you think about Nate and Leslie? Do you think she's really interested in him?"

Kim shrugged. "I never would have thought Nate was her type, but you never know with Leslie. She seemed to like him, but who knows."

"I think the grief she was giving me at the end of the evening was a sham. She prefers Nate to Luther."

"I—," Kim began, but a phone rang. They both listened to see which one it was. They soon realized both their phones were ringing.

"Laughing, Tam said, "Bet I can guess who's calling."

"I can too," Kim said. "Good night, girl. I'll see you in the morning."

"Night," Tam said, heading for her bedroom and her phone.

Kim went into her bedroom and lay down on the bed before picking up the phone.

"I couldn't wait until morning," Reggie's deep masculine voice said when she picked up the handset. "I miss you already."

His words made her feel warm and content. She shared his feelings, but wasn't yet ready to voice hers. She needed time to test them, to get used to them first.

"What are you doing?" she asked.

"Thinking about you."

He couldn't have said more perfect words. "Good night, Reggie," she said.

"Good night, Ms. Washington."

Kim hung up the phone and closed her eyes. Sleep and sweet dreams of a nice guy soon claimed her.

Reggie hung up the phone after saying good night to Ms. Washington and lay on his bed, hands behind his head, thinking about her and the evening they'd shared. Holding her close had been nice, very nice, and kissing her had been even better. He could still feel the warm response in her lips and the softness of her arms around his neck. He closed his eyes and savored the memory. After a few minutes, he opened his eyes, got up from the bed and headed for the shower. That's what savoring memories had done for him.

Chapter 13

Reggie lowered his head to kiss her just as the phone rang. "Let it ring," he said as he pressed his lips against hers.

Kim relaxed against him and tried to enjoy the kiss, but the ringing phone seemed to get louder. "I'm busy," she murmured but the insistent ringing would not stop.

"Who is it?" she demanded and opened her eyes. She was in her bed—alone—and the phone was still ringing. *Just a dream,* she thought as she touched her fingers to her lips. Shaking her head to rid herself of sleep, she reached for the phone.

"Hello," she said, trying to keep the sleepiness out of her voice.

"Kimmy," Jim's voice boomed. "I thought you would be expecting my call. What's this? The third or fourth time I've called you this early?"

Kim's disappointment that the caller wasn't Reggie didn't surprise her. "What do you want this time, Jim?"

"How'd your date go with Reggie last night? Did any reporters follow you two around?"

Kim thought Jim was getting a bit carried away. "No,

Jim, there were no reporters. They must have all believed that joint press release you and Reggie issued."

"I wouldn't be too sure about that if I were you, Kimmy girl. You know how sneaky reporters can be. Remember that article about you?"

Did he think she could forget it? That article had led to this dating between her and Reggie. "Well, let's hope they weren't so sneaky last night."

"Wrong, Kimmy girl," Jim said. "We want them to be sneaky. The Nice Guy Contests being sponsored by the radio stations are keeping *Urban Style* in everybody's mind, but it wouldn't hurt for you and Reggie to generate a little publicity for that column you'll be doing. Now when's your next date?"

Kim didn't like discussing her time with Reggie as though it were a business arrangement. It had started that way, but she had the feeling it was turning into something more. "We haven't planned our next date," she said.

"Why not? He did ask you, didn't he?"

"No, he hasn't." She felt contrary enough not to tell him that Reggie would be calling this morning.

"You didn't say anything to turn him off, did you, Kimmy?"

"What's that supposed to mean, Jim?"

"Well," Jim began. "You know how you can be sometimes."

"No, Jim, I don't know how I can be sometimes. Why don't you tell me?"

"Forget it, Kimmy. There's no need to go down that road."

"No, Jim," she insisted. "You brought it up. Now finish it."

Jim sighed. "You're a good kid and all, Kimmy, but sometimes you can be a little hard on the young men."

"What?" she sputtered. "Me a little hard on men? You've got to be kidding."

"Don't go getting angry with me now. You asked me

and I'm just telling you what I see. You're hard on men, Kimmy. Maybe too hard.''

Kim didn't think so. She'd just kissed enough toads to begin to wonder if there were any princes left out there. "Because I don't put up with any BS, you think I'm hard? If that means I'm hard, then I think I'll just stay that way."

"That's not what I'm saying, Kimmy. You need to be hard with some of them. That Derrick for instance. I don't even know why you still talk to him. But Reggie Stevens is different. Kimmy, there's something about him that's different. Don't prejudge him based on your other experiences. And that's all I have to say on the subject. Now back to Reggie. He's done well so far but it's not over yet. You two have got to keep it up.''

"What do you mean he's done well so far?" Kim asked, suspicious again of Jim's motives and his possible actions.

"You'll find out as soon as you see the Sunday paper," he said. "Now I've got to go. You make sure you and Reggie go out tonight. And try to play it up for the papers, Kimmy. We need all the publicity we can get.''

"Wait a minute, Jim," Kim began, but Jim had already hung up. "Sometimes that man—" she started, then covered her mouth with her hand. "The papers. What was in the papers?''

She jumped out of bed, quickly pulled off her pajamas and dragged a pair of jeans and a shirt from her closet. She had to see the newspaper. A sense of foreboding told her she wasn't going to like what she read.

What has Jim done? she asked as she made her way out of the suite and to the elevators. And what role had Reggie played in it?

She stepped into the elevator and then pressed the button for the lobby as soon as the doors closed. As the elevator made the seemingly slow trip down, she tried to prepare herself for what she was going to see. *What could be worse than that article?* she asked to reassure herself. If she could handle the article, she could handle anything.

The elevator came to a short stop at the lobby level and

she quickly exited, making a beeline for the gift shop. As luck would have it, the shop was closed. "Figures," she muttered then turned and headed for the front desk. If she was lucky they'd have a copy of the paper on the counter.

She saw a stack of papers as she approached and was grateful for her good luck. When she picked it up and flipped to the Lifestyle page, she quickly changed her mind.

"I'm going to kill him," she said. "I'm going to kill both of them."

Reggie's first thought when he answered his front door and found Ms. Washington standing there was that his day was off to a great start. Unfortunately, that thought was quickly replaced with a feeling of dread when he saw the anger blazing in her big, brown eyes. "What did I do now?" he asked, deciding his best route was a solid offense.

"You've got some nerve asking me that question," Kim said, brushing past him and entering the house.

He closed the door and followed her into his living room. "What's the problem? Why don't you just tell me what's going on?"

She slapped the newspaper that he suddenly realized she was holding against his belly. "Jim says to tell you that you did a good job."

Grasping the paper to keep it from falling to the floor, he asked, "What's Jim got to do with this?"

She dropped down on the couch and crossed her legs. Her top leg rocked back and forth rapidly. "Why don't you check out your handiwork in the paper? I don't *believe* you did this. You almost had me fooled last night." She shook her head. "You're a piece of work, Reggie Stevens."

Reggie unfolded the paper. After scanning the headline, he said, "I still don't know what you're so angry about."

She gave him a look that scorched. "Turn to the Lifestyle page."

He quickly did as she directed. "Ah, hell," he said. Right there in the paper for all the world, or at least all the city, to see was a picture of them sharing their one and only kiss last night. He looked down at her. "You can't really think I had anything to do with this, can you?"

"Why shouldn't I? You were the one who suggested we take a walk around the block." Her leg still rocking back and forth, she began shaking her head to the same tempo. "I can't believe I was so naive. It was all a set up."

He dropped down on the floor next to the couch. "It wasn't a set up. I have no idea how this picture came to be in the paper."

"Sure you don't," she said. "Just one of those things, right?"

"Right." He said the word but even to him it sounded inadequate. "I swear, Kim. I didn't have anything to do with this photograph."

"Then explain how it was taken," she challenged.

He caught her gaze with his own, needing her to see the truth in his eyes. "I don't know how. I just know that I didn't have anything to do with it." He could tell she was struggling with herself. Should she believe him or shouldn't she? "What would I have to gain by getting this photograph in the paper?"

Kim didn't know. She just knew that she'd been upset when she'd seen the photograph. To be more precise, she'd felt like an idiot. Here she'd been having dreams about that kiss and he'd been staging it for some cheap publicity shot.

"Answer me," he demanded. "What would I have to gain?"

"Look, Reggie," she said, realizing he was turning the situation against her. "I'm the one asking the questions."

"And I'm answering them. I did not, repeat, did not, have anything to do with this photograph showing up in the paper. If you were rational about this, you'd see that you get more out of this kind of publicity than I do. Maybe I should be offended."

"Oh, no you don't," she said. "You're not going to turn this one on me. You're the one who set up this whole dating fiasco with Jim. What else did you two cook up? Did you tell him where we were going to be and when so that he could have the reporter there? Did he specifically tell you he wanted a kissing shot?"

Reggie stood up and stared down at her. "Have you lost your mind? Do you really think that kiss was staged?"

She hadn't at the time and even now she hoped it hadn't been. That kiss had touched her in ways she hadn't been touched in a long time. It hurt to think it had meant nothing to him. "Sometimes a woman can't tell what's real with a man and what isn't. There are too many games, Reggie. Too many moves. How do I know that kiss wasn't just a move on your part?" She saw what she thought looked like hurt in his eyes, but she didn't stop. "Maybe," she added, "you just wanted to put me in my place?"

He folded his arms across his chest, which she could see through the opening in his robe. She wondered that, even in the midst of their argument, she could still admire how gorgeous he was.

"And maybe you're regretting what happened last night and now you're trying to find some way to discount it?" he suggested. "Is that it, Ms. Washington? Do you want me to be a bad guy so much that you're willing to believe something as ridiculous as my staging our kiss for some photographer?"

"I know what lengths you go to when you want something, Reggie. What did you hope to gain this time?"

He dropped his arms and again stooped down next to the couch. "Look, I don't know what kind of men you've interacted with in the past, but I'm not them. I don't play games, Kim. Last night wasn't a game for me and I'd hoped it wasn't one for you either."

Kim didn't like the turn the conversation had taken. She'd come there to tell Reggie off, not to hear his words of endearment. "But Jim said—," she began, but he cut her off.

"Forget what Jim said. I want to know what you feel." He raised his hand and placed it across her heart. "I want to know what you feel right here. What does your heart say?"

Her heart said she was in deep trouble. Her heart so wanted to believe he wouldn't play with her emotions. But her heart hadn't always been reliable, had it? "All I want to do is figure out who took the photograph. We spent the entire evening together. How did they just happen to get that shot? It's too much of a coincidence, Reggie. If I had gone straight into the hotel instead of taking you up on your offer of a walk none of this would have happened. Don't you think that's a little too much to be a coincidence?"

Reggie shook his head as if defeated. "I don't know whether it was a coincidence or not. Maybe reporters were following us. Maybe Jim sent a photographer to follow us. I don't know. But in the end, what does it matter? That somebody took a picture of us doesn't make what we shared any less real or any less important."

How could she explain to him that it did lessen it for her? She wanted what was happening between them to remain between them so it could flourish. "Obviously, we feel differently about this. I don't like having my personal life smeared across the newspaper."

"I don't like it either, Kim, but I guess that's the way it's going to be. In a way, our relationship *started* because of the paper. Don't you think it's sort of impractical to think the paper won't keep track of it?"

The rationality in his words made her feel small. But she couldn't bear to think that Reggie was using her when her feelings for him were very real—more real than she wanted them to be. "Okay," she said, "maybe I over-reacted."

"Maybe?"

She got up from her seat on the couch and retrieved her newspaper from Reggie. "Okay, I admit it. I overreacted."

Reggie smiled and pulled her into his arms. "How big

of you to admit it, Ms. Washington. You are indeed a woman among women."

Reluctantly, she pulled out of his arms. While she wanted to be close to him, she also needed some time to figure out how she felt about what was happening between them.

He looked at her as if he was going to question her action, but when he opened his mouth he asked, "So what do you want to do tonight?"

When Kim made it back to the hotel, Leslie and Tam were having a room service breakfast. "Where've you been?" Leslie asked as soon as she walked into the suite.

"I should be asking you that question," Kim responded, taking a piece of buttered toast from Leslie's plate. "Where have you been and what time did you get in?"

"Wouldn't you like to know?"

"That means she was out all night," Tam explained. "I guess old Nate isn't as quiet as we thought."

"Guess not," Kim teased. "So you and Nate got along well, huh, Leslie?"

Leslie sipped from her cup of coffee. "He's all right," she said. "A lot different from the other men I've dated though."

"Different how?" Tam asked.

"You know," Leslie said with a shrug. "I usually date flashy, flirty, out there guys like Luther. I never could imagine myself with someone like Nate."

"But—" Kim encouraged.

Leslie shrugged. "But nothing. He's a sweet guy and he makes me feel good."

"Wait a minute." Tam lifted her palms upward. "We don't want details."

"Girl, it's not like that," Leslie said. "Sure, I spent the night at his house, but nothing happened."

"Right, Leslie," Kim said, knowing her friend's track record. "You expect us to believe that you spent the night with him and nothing happened?"

"I don't care what you believe," Leslie said a bit defensively. "I know what happened and we didn't make love."

"Then what *were* you doing all night?" Tam asked. "Crocheting?"

"We talked," she said simply. "We just talked."

"You talked and he listened, you mean?" Tam said.

Leslie shook her head. "That's not what I mean at all. We talked. He talked and I listened and I talked and he listened. You guys don't have to believe me."

"I believe you, Leslie," Kim said and she did. "I'm glad your evening went so well."

"Me, too," Tam added. "I didn't mean to be so negative."

"That's all right," Leslie said. "I don't know if I would believe me either. But like I said, Nate's different from any man I've ever dated. I can't remember the last time I had a guy actually listen to what I had to say and enjoy hearing it. Most of the time, they're just waiting for their turn so they can brag about something they've done or something they've bought. Nate's a refreshing change."

"Sounds like he's a keeper," Tam said.

Leslie sipped from her coffee again. "I don't want to start making predictions. I like him and right now that's enough. Enough about me. I don't think I was the only one who had fun last night. Come on, tell me."

Kim was relieved when Tam spoke first, telling Leslie how things had progressed between her and Luther. "And he's picking me up this morning," Tam said. "We're going to spend the day together. And then tonight we'll watch the stars."

"Oooh, sounds romantic," Leslie said. "Be careful, girl," she warned in a playful manner. "Don't do anything I wouldn't do."

Kim knew it was her turn when both her friends looked at her. "There's not much to tell," she said.

"Well," Leslie said. "First you can tell us where you went so early this morning."

"I bet she went to meet Reggie," Tam teased. "They had a good time last night. A very good time."

"Did you meet him, Kim?" Leslie asked.

"Not exactly," she said, not wanting to give her friends the details. "I sorta took a drive over to his house."

"Couldn't bear to be away from him, huh?" Leslie teased.

"Not exactly." Kim pulled the paper out and placed it on the table. "Take a look at the Lifestyle page."

Tam stopped eating and reached for the paper. Her bubble of laughter told Kim she'd found the picture. "Nice shot," she said, passing the paper to Leslie. "But when did you become an exhibitionist?"

"Whoa girl," Leslie said. "That must have been some kiss. I can feel the heat through the paper."

Kim knew she could do nothing but allow her friends' teasing to run its course. "I'm glad you two think it's funny."

"You're not upset, are you?" Tam asked. "It's not like this is the first time you and Reggie have been in the paper."

"I was a bit upset when I first saw the picture," she admitted. "But I guess I'm okay with it now."

"Is that why you went to see Reggie? Because you were upset?"

Kim nodded. "I wanted to find out if he had anything to do with it."

Leslie snorted. "If anybody had anything to do with it, I'd start looking in Jim's direction. He's the one who's trying to milk the situation for every drop of publicity he can get."

"You're right, I know," Kim said. "But when I spoke with Jim he intimated that Reggie might have somehow been involved."

"So you went over and confronted Reggie?" Leslie asked.

She nodded, feeling stupid now for her actions which had seemed very reasonable at the time.

"What did he say?" Tam asked.

"He said he didn't have anything to do with it."

"I wouldn't think he'd do something like that," Tam said. "He doesn't seem the type."

Leslie chuckled. "You know something, ladies? This is the first time we've all had positive vibes with men at the same time. Let's not screw things up by getting too serious too fast, or by being overly critical. Let's just have some fun for a change without thinking about ten years down the road."

Kim knew Leslie had spoken words of wisdom. But she wondered if the words had been spoken too late to do her any good. Things between her and Reggie were moving briskly and in a serious direction. She didn't think she could change either at this point. She wasn't even sure she wanted to.

Chapter 14

Reggie hung up the phone from talking to his mother, dropped down in his office chair and wiped his hands down his face. They're family, he told himself. And they love you. His words didn't help.

After the picture of him kissing Kim appeared in yesterday's paper, he'd expected another call from Oklahoma City. That it had been from his mother told them how serious his family was taking his new-found celebrity. His mother was already rating Kim's daughter-in-law potential.

Reggie checked the ebony and ivory clock on his desk. Any minute now, Kim and Marty would arrive to take pictures of him at his office. In his opinion, there was not much to photograph, but what Kim wanted she usually got. She was one persistent woman.

His thoughts automatically went to the kind of lover she'd be. How would her persistence translate in the bedroom? He bet she'd get her way there as she did everywhere else.

Reggie heard noises in the outer office and assumed they had arrived. He got up, his eagerness to see her, no longer a surprise.

"Ms. Washington," he said when he pulled his office door open and leaned against the jamb. "Looking for me?"

Kimberla turned her hundred-watt smile to him and he wondered how she'd managed to go so long without some guy snatching her up.

"Who else is around?" she asked saucily.

He pushed away from the doorjamb and took the few steps that took him to her. Ignoring the warning in her eyes, he dipped his head and gave her a light peck on the lips. "I don't want Carol here—"he nodded to the young, petite woman who was his secretary—"to get the impression that you don't like me."

Kim gave Carol a tight smile. "Is he always this arrogant?"

Carol shook her head and smiled. "Never. It must be the new company he's keeping."

Reggie's masculine laughter made her turn to him. She refused to respond to his smug grin and turned to Marty instead. "This is your show."

With that, Marty took over. After an hour, Marty had finished and was gone, leaving Reggie and Kim in Reggie's office and Carol at her desk beyond his closed door.

"Now this is better," Reggie said, pulling her down on his lap. "I've wanted to do this since I saw you standing there talking to Carol." He placed soft kisses against her neck, savoring the sweet, clean scent of her skin.

Kim tried to move away from him but he pulled her close. "Shouldn't we be discussing the article?"

He stopped kissing her neck and looked down at her. "I don't believe you."

"What?"

"I'm kissing you and you're thinking about some article. Maybe I'm losing my touch."

"So you have a touch, Mr. Stevens? And here I thought you were moving on pure emotion."

"Oh, no," he said, leaning back in his chair. "Please don't tell me we're going through this again."

She punched him in his side. "I'm supposed to be getting to know the real Reggie Stevens, aren't I?"

"But sometimes actions can tell you a whole lot more than words," he said with a wide grin.

She bet he was right, but she wasn't yet ready to find out. "Come on, Reggie. Talk to me."

"Okay," he said. "What do you want to talk about?"

"You," she said. "I want to know more about Reggie Stevens."

He grinned. "Let's see. He's handsome, responsible, and good to women and old folks—especially old women folks."

She giggled and punched him in the side again. "I'm serious. Tell me something I don't know."

"I don't know what you don't know. You ought to be telling me. Have I finally convinced you that I'm a true blue nice guy?"

"Let's just say your stock is rising," she said, not wanting to give too much.

"That's not all that's rising," he murmured against her neck.

"Reggie!" she exclaimed. "I don't believe you said that."

"Said what?" he asked with an innocent expression on his face.

She shook her head. "I've heard high school boys use more finesse than your 'That's not all that's rising' line."

"High school boys? I think you've just insulted me."

"Just calling 'em like I see 'em," she said, enjoying his discomfort. She folded her arms across her stomach and waited for his explosion.

"Now I know you've insulted me. Maybe what you need is a demonstration of my moves."

She gave him a syrupy, sweet smile. "I've seen enough." She patted his chest. "Maybe you should come up with another line before trying again."

He placed his hand atop hers and stopped her patting motion. "I'm not talking about a demonstration of my verbal moves," he clarified, with a twinkle in his eyes that challenged her. "I'm talking more about my physical ones."

She tugged her hand away from his. "Now you're really getting corny."

"I bet I can make you forget all about corny," he said. "I bet I can make you forget everything. Except me. And you."

The challenge in his eyes burned. Visions of her and Reggie, naked, filled her mind.

He held her closer. "And I didn't think it was possible."

She blinked away the vision. "What?"

"I can't believe you don't have a sharp comeback ready for me. I think I've finally found a way to shut you up."

She cast him a short glance down her nose. "Some things are so outrageous they don't rate a response."

Reggie studied her face and in his eyes she saw the look she'd seen the other night right before he'd kissed her. "But there's only one way to be sure."

Kim knew he was going to kiss her, but she wasn't ready for a repeat of the fireworks from the other night. Not yet, at least. She gave a nervous giggle then got up from his lap. "I don't think so, Mr. Stevens. I'm here to write about your amorous pursuits, not participate in them."

"Too late," he said, reaching for her arm and tugging her back down. "You don't issue a challenge like that, then walk away. You've insulted my masculinity. I can't let that slide."

The warmth of his touch made her look up at him. The challenge in his eyes made her blink and she pulled her hand away. "You don't have a choice this time," she said, feeling weak. Maybe she had gone too far.

He pulled her hand to his mouth and kissed her palm. "I always have a choice."

She tugged her hand away from his again. "And so do I." She got up again. "And my choice is to go home. Now." She reached for her purse and headed for the door.

"You know this matter isn't settled, don't you," he said,

as he opened the door and escorted her out of his office building and to her car.

"In my mind, it is," she said, but she was lying. She was very attracted to Reggie and the thought of making love with him had certainly crossed her mind. But thinking about it and doing it were different things.

When she pulled her keys out of her purse, Reggie took them from her and opened her door. After she was seated in the driver's side, he said, "It's not over, Kim."

"Think what you will, Reggie." She switched on the ignition. "But all you're going to get from me is an unbiased story in *Urban Style.*"

He stepped back from her car. "I'll see you tonight."

She smiled sweetly at him. "You sure will. Right now, you're my job."

"What are you doing, Reggie?" Kim asked later that night when they were alone at his house. They'd had a quiet dinner in and she knew they should be talking instead of necking. Unfortunately, since their conversation earlier today she hadn't been able to keep her thoughts off the idea of making love with him.

"I'm helping you with your article," he said, pressing soft kisses against her neck.

It was impossible to ignore the warm feelings his kisses caused to spread across her body, but she knew she had to try. "Did you seduce all those women who nominated you for the contest?" she asked, seeking to distract both of them.

He pulled back and a wide grin split his face. "Jealous?"

"More like curious."

He tilted her chin up and kissed her softly on the lips. "Those women are in the past. You don't have to worry about them."

She placed a hand on each of his cheeks and kissed him back. "I'm not worried. I'm just trying to get some insight for my article. So, *did* you seduce all of them?"

"I don't want to do this, Kim." He took her hand in his and kissed her palm.

"Come on," she said, loving the feel of his tongue against her skin, but still unsure how far she was ready to go. "This is business. I need the information for the article."

"Somehow I don't believe you're going to tell the readers of *Urban Style* whether or not I seduced my nominators."

"Of course not," she said. "I need to know for background information. Your answer could give me a slant for the article. So did you?"

"You're persistent, aren't you?"

"I'm a reporter," she said with a smile. "Now stop stalling and tell me."

He kissed her again. "No way," he said. "Nice guys don't kiss and tell."

"So that means you did?"

"No. That means I'm not telling you."

"Come on, Reggie," she pleaded. "I need to know."

"No, you don't."

"Yes, I do."

He pulled away from her and gave up his seduction attempt. "Give me one good reason why you need to know. And don't give me that bull about your needing the information for the article."

"But I *do* need it for the article," she explained. "I need to understand why those women dumped you. Look at you," she said. "You're handsome, you're considerate, you're stable financially and emotionally. I just don't understand why they let you go."

Reggie gave her the sweetest smile. "You know, Ms. Washington, those are the kindest words you've said about me. Thank you."

Though she'd spoken her feelings, Kim felt exposed by her openness. "I'm not trying to flatter you. I'm trying to understand. Why do you think they dumped you?"

Reggie shrugged. "I don't know," he said. "That's the

question I was trying to answer when I wrote that first
article. I think I'm a nice guy, but I've dated women who've
dropped me to go back to some guy who treated them
bad in the past or to go on to some slick-talking guy who
probably had no real interest in them. You tell me. Why
do women make those kinds of choices? They say they
want a nice guy, but they'll choose the player every time.''

Kim didn't have an answer to his question, but his words
helped her understand him better. His article had really
been written in an attempt to gain a better understanding
of women. "Maybe you just haven't met the right woman
yet."

"Then again, maybe I have."

From the way he looked at her when he spoke the words,
she wondered if he was talking about her. "Christina?"

"You're full of questions, aren't you?"

"I'm a reporter."

"Are you sure it's the reporter asking the questions?
Maybe it's the woman."

Maybe he was right. Then again, maybe he wasn't. "You
loved her, didn't you?"

He brushed her hair back from her face with his hand.
"I thought I loved her at the time, but now I'm not so
sure."

Kim leaned into his hand, bringing her face closer to
his. "Why aren't you sure? You asked her to marry you so
you must have loved her."

"You would think so, wouldn't you?" he asked, his finger
now stroking down her cheek.

"Yes."

Reggie dropped his hand from her face. "Are you sure
you want to know?"

She nodded.

"Okay then. When I asked her to marry me, I thought
I was in love with her, but now I'm not so sure. I cared
about her a great deal."

"Oh," she said, feeling as if a big weight had been placed
in the pit of her stomach. She heard the deep affection

he still felt for Christina and she was jealous. The emotion wasn't rational given the circumstances, but she coveted the space, however small, that Christina still held in his heart. "Does it hurt to think about her?"

He shook his head. "Not anymore. She's happy. That's what's important."

Reggie might not be sure whether he'd loved Christina, but Kim knew he must have loved her a great deal if her happiness meant so much to him. She almost wished she hadn't asked about her.

When Kim and Reggie got together again at his house the following night, she teased, "I think you're taking me for granted. You don't even take me out anymore."

"We can go out if that's what you want. After our picture showed up in the paper, I just thought you'd prefer we have some privacy."

She did prefer the time alone, but she was sure Jim wouldn't. He wanted them out, preferably with a reporter or a photographer at their side. "And here I thought you were trying to seduce me."

"Nice guys don't do seduction," he said, guiding her to the dining room table. "It's against our code of ethics."

"Says who?"

"It's right there in The Nice Guy Handbook. Page one-hundred and two. I'll show it to you if you don't believe me."

She looked at the table he'd laid out before her. "Is cooking for your dates in that book, too?"

He shook his head. "That comes from my mother's book. She taught me and my brothers how to cook. She said a man shouldn't expect a woman to do all the cooking. She also said a man wouldn't always have a woman to cook for him. I guess she wanted us prepared for anything."

"Smart woman," she said. "Maybe she did write the Nice Guy Handbook and you just don't know it?"

Reggie chuckled. "If she did, she co-wrote it with my father. They do everything together."

"Even cook?"

He chuckled again. "Everything but that. Dad can cook, but he doesn't. And I think Mother is secretly glad. She likes cooking."

Kim wondered what life was life in the Stevens household. She bet there was lots of laughter and lots of love.

"What does your family think about the contest, your article, all of this?"

"They're curious about it all. My mother's especially interested in the woman I was kissing in the paper. You've got them curious."

"You told them that we were working together, didn't you?"

"After seeing that picture, I don't think they would have believed me. I just told them that you were a special friend."

A special friend. What exactly did that mean? "And what did they say to that?"

"Trust me, you don't want to know."

From the look on his face, Kim decided to do as he asked and trust him. "Did they meet any of the women who nominated you?"

He shook his head.

"Why not? I thought nice guys always went to mother for approval."

"Nice guys aren't Mama's boys, Ms. Washington," he said a bit harshly. "Don't mistake courtesy and kindness for weakness. They're not the same."

She hadn't meant to insult him, but she had. "I know they aren't and I didn't mean to imply you were a mama's boy."

"Then what were you implying?"

"I just figured if you cared deeply for some woman, you'd want her to meet your family."

"I guess that tells you how special they were to me."

"So you never took any of them home to meet the family?"

He shook his head.

"Not even Christina?"

"Not even her."

His answer pleased her. "So have you thought any more about why those women dumped you?"

"No, I haven't. I've been too busy thinking about you."

"Me?"

"Don't look so surprised, Kim. You have to know that I like you and am very much attracted to you."

She realized it, but it felt good hearing him say the words. "Yes, I knew."

"So, how do you feel?"

"I like you, too."

"But you're not attracted to me?"

"I didn't say that."

"Then you are attracted to me."

"I didn't say that either."

"I think you are," he said. "I can see it in your eyes sometimes when I look at you. I can feel it in your kiss on those rare occasions when you kiss me."

She didn't say anything. What was there to say? He was right.

"I want to make love with you, Ms. Kimberla Washington."

His words made her suck in her breath. "You don't mince words, do you, Reggie?"

"Another nice guy trait. We're straight and aboveboard."

"That could be a problem, you know. Sometimes a little seduction is better than straight and aboveboard. Maybe that's the reason the other women dumped you. Maybe a little subtlety would go a long way."

He stared at her for what seemed to be a long time. "You seem a bit pre-occupied with what I did and didn't do with other women. Is my lovemaking on your mind that much, Ms. Washington?"

"No," she lied. "I'm just trying to be helpful. Maybe you should consider revamping your moves."

Reggie got up and began removing the dishes from the table.

"I didn't mean to insult you," she said again. "I was only making an observation."

"I guess you'd like it a lot better if I threw you over my shoulder, carried you into the bedroom and had my way with you. Is that what women want?"

The idea of him becoming so overcome with passion and need for her that he tossed her over his shoulder held interesting possibilities. "Now you're being defensive."

"Hell, yes, I'm defensive. You'd be defensive too, if you were in my shoes."

She got up and followed him into the kitchen. "I'm sorry."

He rinsed the dishes and quickly placed them in the dishwasher. When he was finished, he slammed the door shut and pushed the button to start.

Then he turned to her, picked her up, and threw her over his shoulder.

"What are you doing?" she yelled.

"I want to make love with you so I'm taking you to bed."

"But I don't want to make love with you."

"Yes, you do," he said, moving quickly down the hall. "You just don't want to admit it."

He entered the bedroom, threw her on the bed and proceeded to undress. "This is what you wanted, isn't it? A big, strong man to take charge?"

"No, Reggie," she said, getting up from the bed. "This is not what I want."

His shirt off, he turned to her. "What did you mean then? You don't want honesty, you want subtlety. What the hell does that mean?"

"This is not what I want," she said again.

Reggie sat down in the armchair next to the bed and pulled off his shoes and socks. Then he stood and unhooked his belt. When he was about to unzip his pants, she said, "Stop, Reggie. This is not funny."

"I'm not being funny. I'm giving you what you want. If I don't, you may dump me too. Isn't that what you said?"

She went to him, hugged him around his neck and rested her head on his bare chest. The *thump, thump* of his heart sounded loudly in her ears. "Don't be this way, Reggie. This is not you. I said I was sorry."

He pulled back from her and looked down in her face. "What do you want from me, Kim? One minute you're calling me the plague of the male sex and the next you're telling me I'm straight out of The Nice Guy handbook. In actuality, I'm neither. I'm just a man who tries to treat people as he wants to be treated. Why is that so hard for you to understand?"

She moved back into his arms. "I don't know. Sometimes I just think you're too good to be true. I keep looking for a hole in the armor, but I can't seem to find one."

"I'm not perfect, Kim, and I don't claim to be. But I'm not a dog trying to get every woman I meet into bed either. That's not and never has been, my style. I'd hoped you would know that by now."

"I do know it, Reggie," she said. "I do."

He moved her away from him again, reached for his shirt and pulled it on. Then he stepped into his shoes. "Come on, I'm taking you home."

Kim looked into his eyes to see if he was angry with her. She saw anger and she saw disappointment. Both hurt. "I said I was sorry," she repeated.

"Don't worry about it, Kim," he said. "You're just doing your job. I don't fault you for that. I'll take you home."

Kim couldn't think of any other words to say. She felt she'd somehow ruined whatever was between them and that made her sad.

Chapter 15

Kim lay in bed unable to asleep. Thoughts of her evening with Reggie kept running through her mind. She feared she'd gone too far tonight, though she really hadn't meant to. All she'd wanted was to slow things down a bit. She and Reggie were reaching a turning point in their relationship and she wasn't sure she was ready for the change.

She glanced at the clock. Five-thirty. And she hadn't gotten any sleep all night. Neither had she gotten any calls. Not the good night call from Reggie which she'd become so used to and not the wake up call from Jim which had become just as expected.

Rolling over onto her side to face the clock, she hugged her pillow. Would Reggie call? she wondered. Or had he written her off as one of the double-minded women he'd written about in his article? She wasn't, but she knew her actions spoke differently.

She heard the faint sound of a door opening and closing and wondered which one of her suitemates was coming in. In need of someone to talk to, she got up from the bed, grabbed her robe and went to greet the late comer.

"Leslie," she said as she saw her friend rush toward her bedroom, shoulders shaking. "What's wrong?"

Leslie leaned her forehead on her bedroom door, not turning around. "It's Nate. Why'd he have to mess everything up?"

Kim rushed to her friend, put her hands on her shoulders and turned her around. The tears in Leslie's eyes surprised her. Crying over a man was definitely a new one for Leslie. "What happened?" Kim asked. "What did Nate do?"

Leslie brushed wildly at the tears streaming down her face. "Men can be such jerks," she said. "Why do they have to be jerks, Kim?"

"You'll have to tell me what you're talking about," Kim said, leading her friend back to the living room area. "Here, sit down. Do you want some coffee?"

Leslie shook her head and Kim sat down on the couch next to her. "So tell me what happened."

"There's nothing to tell," Leslie said. "Nate's a jerk. I should have known better than to go out with him. And making love with him was definitely a foolish move. How could I have been so stupid?"

Had Nate slept with Leslie, Kim wondered, then decided he didn't want to see her again? Probably. Sometimes men could be so callous. "It's his loss, girl," Kim said. "I'm sorry I even got you two together. But he seemed like such a nice guy."

"Yeah," Leslie said with a sniffle. "He's a nice guy, all right. Too nice. I can't believe him."

"Tell me exactly what happened, Leslie. It'll make you feel better to get it all off your chest."

Leslie stood up and paced in front of Kim, rubbing her hands together as if she didn't know what else to do with them. "It had been a wonderful evening. We went back to The Club. We talked, we danced, we ate, we laughed. And all the while I was thinking what a special guy he was."

Leslie's voice broke then and tears filled her eyes. "Why did he have to be a jerk, Kim? Why?"

Kim got up to embrace her friend, but Leslie shook her head. "I've got to finish this, now or I won't finish it."

Kim nodded, sat back down and waited for her friend to speak. She was already planning the harsh words she was going to give Reggie. He should have told her what kind of man Nate was. He was as much responsible for Leslie's pain as Nate was.

"Then," Leslie continued, "we went back to his place. Again, it started out so beautiful, so sweet. First we were sitting on the couch talking, sharing our lives, cuddling. And the next thing you know we were in his big old king sized bed."

The rat, Kim thought. She bet Nate pulled that shy routine on lots of women. Another get over persona from another get over brother.

Leslie closed her eyes and smiled through her tears. "It was beautiful, Kim. It's like I was there but then I wasn't. I can't explain it." She opened her eyes and looked at Kim. "Have you ever felt like that?"

Sadly, Kim shook her head. She'd been through her share of men in her thirty-two years, but she'd never come close to feeling what Leslie described. *Until Reggie,* a soft voice in her head said. Kim's envy of what her friend had experienced was only surpassed by her anger with Nate. How dare he play with Leslie's emotions the way he had?

"Then," Leslie continued, her eyes dry and her mouth angry. "He blows it. He blows it, Kim. He should have kept his mouth shut. He should have kept his damn mouth shut."

"What did he say?" Kim asked, feeling righteous anger toward the man who'd betrayed her friend.

Leslie's eyes filled with tears again and she covered her face with her hands. She mumbled something, but Kim couldn't understand her. "What did he say, Leslie? I didn't understand you."

Leslie wiped her hands down her face then dropped them to her side. "He said he loved me. Can you believe it? He said he loved me. How could he be such a jerk, Kim?"

Kim's mouth dropped open.

"You look exactly the way I felt. I mean, can you believe it?"

"Wait a minute, Leslie," Kim said, totally bewildered now. Men were always telling Leslie they loved her. She'd come to expect it by now. "You're telling me that you're all upset because Nate told you he loved you?"

Leslie dropped down on the couch next to her. "How can he love me? He doesn't even know me. And here I was thinking he was different, that he wanted to get to know me." She stabbed a finger to her chest. "The me in here." She shook her head. "I must have been crazy to think that."

Kim's envy immediately left as she turned and embraced Leslie.

"I know I can act all cold sometimes, Kim," she said. "But I'm no different than you or Tam. I want somebody to love me the same way you two do."

"I know, Leslie," Kim murmured, and she did know. But sometimes she forgot. It was easy to forget with Leslie. The girl had everything—looks, brains, body, and personality. But men tended to stop at the looks and body and not dig deep enough to appreciate the brains and personality.

"Did you know that Nate was the first guy in a long time who really talked to me?"

Kim shook her head.

'Well, he was. And he didn't just brag about himself. He told me about his firm, his latest projects and he asked my opinion. That was the biggest turn-on of all. He didn't see me as another pretty face and it felt wonderful. Then he had to go and ruin it." She stopped her sniffles and looked at Kim. "Maybe it's my fault," she said. "Maybe I shouldn't have slept with him so soon. It was only our fourth date."

"It was kinda fast," Kim said. "But no faster than usual for you."

"Which has always been faster than either you or Tam. What's wrong with me, Kim?"

"There's nothing wrong with you. You're a strong woman. You know what you want and you go after it. You're that way in every aspect of your life. I can't imagine your sex life being any different. You're safe, you're discriminating, but you're Leslie and you do things the Leslie way."

Leslie stopped her sniffles. "Then why am I sitting her blubbering over some jerk?"

Kim shrugged. "You tell me."

Leslie sighed. "Because I thought he was different. I broke my own first rule: Don't get serious until you're sure the guy is worth it. That way you don't get hurt."

Kim thought about her and Reggie. "Sometimes your heart doesn't line up with your brain, Leslie. Don't be so hard on yourself. You and Nate weren't a match. You'll meet another guy."

"That's what I'm afraid of," Leslie said with a dry laugh. "Anyway, I'm back to myself now and I'm just gonna write Nate off. I'll never meet the man of my dreams if I spend all my time mooning over the ones who couldn't cut it."

Two hours later, while Leslie was in bed and probably sleeping soundly Kim was still thinking about their conversation. She and Tam had often been envious of Leslie's seeming success with men, not stopping to think how the attention made Leslie feel. Though their friend seemed to always get her pick of men, in reality, she didn't fare any better in relationships than she and Tam did. Leslie wanted a man who loved her for herself—the person she was inside—just the way she and Tam did. Sometimes the outlook for the three of them looked bleak, then she remembered the happy sisters out there who'd found the man of their dreams.

Sometimes she wondered if she and her friends were at fault. Were they too hard on men as Jim had accused? Did they demand too much? She didn't think so. Actually, she

THE NICEST GUY IN AMERICA   177

thought the opposite was true. Sure, if a guy who held no appeal for them came along, it was easy for them to brush him off and forget him. But with a guy with potential, they seemed to lose their backbone and their mind. Why was that?

She turned her head when she heard the suite door open and waited for Tam—who else could it be at this hour—to enter. From the wobegotten look on her friend's face, Kim guessed her evening with Luther hadn't gone well, either. Though not usually a superstitious person, she wondered if there had been a full moon last night. Or if all the black cats had escaped from the zoo and had walked across their paths.

"Morning, Tam," Kim said brightly, hoping her friend would give a smile.

"Morning," Tam said, not looking directly at Kim. "What are you doing up so early? Or did you just get in?"

Kim shook her head. "I was in before ten. I got up when Leslie came in."

Tam scanned the room. "Where is she?"

Kim inclined her head in the direction of Leslie's bedroom. "Probably sleeping like a baby."

"Good," Tam said, dropping down on the couch and kicking off her black pumps. "I don't want to hear her, I told you so, this morning."

Without bothering to ask, Kim poured coffee for herself and a cup for Tam then took it to her friend.

Tam smiled up at her. "Thanks, though I could use something a bit stronger."

Kim smiled too, since Tam didn't drink. "The coffee's strong enough."

"I don't know, Kim," Tam said. "Sometimes life requires something a bit stronger."

Kim placed her cup on the table. "Something happen with you and Luther?"

Tam shook her head, the sadness in her eyes speaking volumes.

"Do you want to talk about it?" Kim suddenly wondered

about psychiatrists. How did they spend all day listening to people's problems and making comments on their lives?

"There's nothing to talk about," Tam said, staring down at her coffee cup. "Not really."

"I don't want to pry, Tam, but you look so down. Is it Luther?"

"I'd rather not talk about it, Kim," Tam said.

"Talk about what?"

Both Kim and Tam turned their heads in the direction of Leslie's voice. "When did you get up?" Kim asked.

"I never went to bed," she said, dropping down on the couch on the other side of Kim. "What's up, Tam? You having man problems too?"

"Too?" Tam asked.

"Yes, girl," Leslie began. "Nate turned out to be a jerk, after all." She then explained what had happened.

Tam turned back to Leslie. "You're the jerk, Leslie. I don't believe you. Frankly, I don't see what a nice guy like Nate wants with you anyway. You're nothing but a selfish, stuck-up—"

Kim grabbed Tam's arm and cut off her words. She knew Tam was speaking out of frustration at her own situation but she also knew that some things said couldn't be taken back. "Don't take whatever happened between you and Luther out on Leslie," she said softly. "Just tell us what happened."

Tam got up, taking her coffee cup with her. "Nothing happened," she said.

"Yeah, right," Leslie said. "I don't know why you fell for that brother's line anyway. Any man without enough money to get his own place doesn't need to be dating. Please tell me that the two of you haven't been having sex in Reggie's house."

"That's enough, Leslie," Kim said, stepping into the familiar role of referee. This time she couldn't just leave the room and hope her friends would work out their differences.

"That's all right, Kim," Tam said. "I don't pay much

attention to what Leslie says anyway. As usual, she doesn't know what she's talking about. How she ever got a promotion is a mystery to me.''

"Hey, I got a promotion because I'm good at my job," Leslie said. "I'm damn good at my job. Now, your Luther, it doesn't take much brainpower to figure him out."

Tam poured herself some more coffee and took her time coming back to join her friends. Instead of sitting on the couch with them, she took the armchair that faced the sofa. "So you think you know so much about Luther, huh?"

"I know the brother doesn't have his own place. Now, it doesn't take a genius to figure out he probably can't afford one which means either he doesn't have a job or he has a piece-a-job that pays crap."

Kim cut her eyes at Leslie, wondering how a woman who'd been practically blubbering over a man a few hours earlier could be so unsympathetic to her friend's pain. "He must have some money," she said. "You should see the car he drives."

"Like that means anything," Leslie said, clearly cynical. "It just means the brother has priority problems on top of everything else."

"You know The Club?" Tam asked Leslie.

"Sure," Leslie said. "Nate took me there again last night."

Tam smiled. "I'm sure Luther will be glad to hear it. He owns the place."

"What?" Kim and Leslie asked at the same time. While Kim didn't think Luther was a bum or anything, she surely hadn't suspected he owned The Club.

"He's lying to you, girl," Leslie said. "No way does that brother own The Club. Though he's probably spent enough money there to have purchased it."

Tam nodded her head toward the phone. "Why don't you call the county office and ask them who owns The Club? They'll tell you."

"You're serious, aren't you, Tam?" Kim asked, surprised but believing her friend's words.

"Dead serious. That's why he's here in Atlanta. He said it was a shame a town this size didn't have a place for the over thirty crowd to go for a nice night out. And it's doing well too."

"Well, I'll be damned," Leslie said. "Maybe I made a mistake by choosing Nate instead of him."

"And maybe you have selective memory," Kim reminded her. "You *did* choose Luther. Unfortunately, he chose Tam."

Leslie flinched. "In a manner of speaking." She turned to Tam. "So what happened? Did you and lover boy have a fight? I told you to watch yourself."

Kim watched the sadness cloud Tam's face again. "It's none of your business, Leslie," she said.

Leslie looked from Tam to Kim. "Okay, I can take a hint. I'll leave you two alone." She got up and went toward her room, then turned back. "I know I can be a bitch at times, Tam. But you know I love you, don't you?"

Tam smiled through her sadness. "I know you do, Leslie, but sometimes you drive me crazy. Now, if you're a good girl, you can listen to my story. But no wisecracks, okay? I just can't take them this morning."

Leslie quickly moved back to her chair. "My lips are sealed," she said, making a motion of using a key to lock her lips.

"It's nothing really. I just thought we were getting along so well," Tam began.

"What happened?" Kim asked.

"You know we've gone out every night since Saturday and every night we'd talk about what we're going to do the next day. When I made a suggestion tonight, Luther didn't pick up on it. He made no comment at all and when he brought me home, he didn't say he'd call. He *always* says he'll call."

"Maybe he had something on his mind," Kim offered. "Could be he's having problems with The Club."

Tam shook her head. "I don't think so. I think it's because I have a child. I told him about Melissa tonight and he lost interest." She shrugged her shoulders in a defeated motion. "Another brother who doesn't want a woman with children."

Leslie raised her hand as if she were in elementary school. "May I say something here?"

Tam nodded. "You may as well."

"He's just one guy, Tam, and there are plenty of other guys out there. I say if Luther doesn't recognize what a prize you are, then to hell with him. Anyway, you shouldn't be getting serious about a guy after only a few dates. We're not in college anymore. Real relationships take time."

Kim turned to Leslie, amazed that such logical words could come from the woman who'd only hours ago had been crying because some guy told he loved her. "She's right, Tam."

"I know she's right," Tam agreed. "But knowing it doesn't make the situation any easier to deal with. Do you know how many brothers have never called back once I told them about Melissa?" She didn't wait for an answer. "A lot and I'll bet almost all of them had kids themselves. Men seem to want as little responsibility as possible. It's depressing sometimes."

"You're right, girl," Leslie said. "But we have to keep moving forward. Just chalk it up to experience and forget it. Thinking about it is only going to bring you down."

"She's right, Tam," Kim said. "Luther's just one guy. Don't blow the situation out of proportion."

"It's good you found out how he feels before you slept with him," Leslie said, again to Kim's amazement. "Just think how much worse you'd feel if you'd slept with the guy."

Later that morning while her friends slept, Kim sat in the quiet of the suite's living room and tried to do some long overdue work on her article. It was difficult to concentrate though since her thoughts continually strayed to Reggie.

What was really going on between them? she asked herself. What did she want to happen between them?

Maybe she was jumping the gun with Reggie as Tam had done with Luther and as Leslie had done with Nate. Before she could decide where she wanted her relationship with Reggie to go, she needed to know what her feelings were. And before she knew what her feelings were, she had to know who Reggie was. She didn't know that yet. She hadn't known him long enough to know.

Now that's the first lie, her inner voice said. *You do know who he is and he doesn't deserve the jibs you've been throwing his way. Either tell the guy you want to keep this, whatever it is between you, on a professional level and do it. Or be honest with him and yourself and let him know that you want to take it further.*

Chapter 16

"Are you sure you don't want to go with us?" Leslie asked. She and Tam had awakened feeling much better about their situations and had decided to spend a manless day roaming the city. They'd found Kim seated on the couch with papers spread out all over the coffee table.

Kim shook her head and rubbed her eyes. "Not this time. I really do need to put some thought into this article."

"Hey, what's this?" Tam leaned against the back of the sofa and dropped her purse down on the seat. "If you're working on your article, then why aren't you out studying your subject?"

"I don't have to spend all my time with Reggie, Tam," Kim hedged.

"Uh oh," Leslie said, taking a seat next to Kim. "Did you two have an argument or something?"

"Not really," Kim said.

"That's a definite yes," Leslie said. "We told you our problems so you have to tell us yours. What happened?"

"Nothing really," Kim said again. How could she explain how immature she'd been without seeming even more immature?

"We love you to death, Kim," Tam said, "but we want to get out of this hotel before dark. So do us a favor and just tell us. You know we're going to harass you until you do."

Kim knew Tam was right. "Okay," she said. "Reggie and I didn't have a fight. Not exactly."

Leslie rolled her eyes then looked at Tam. "They had a fight."

"Right," Tam said. "It was a fight. Now tell us what you fought about."

"We did *not* fight. We just had a difference of opinion."

Her two friends looked at her with eyes that said they didn't believe her. "Okay, maybe we had a little disagreement."

"What was it about?" Leslie asked. "What did he do?"

"He didn't do anything," Kim explained. "It's more like what I did."

"Out with it, Kim," Tam urged. "It can't be that bad."

"Well, I sorta said that those other women might have dumped him because of his performance, or lack thereof, in the bedroom."

Both Tam and Leslie howled.

"No, you didn't, girl," Tam said when she stopped laughing.

"Was he that bad?" Leslie asked between guffaws. "There have been a couple of guys I wish I'd had the nerve to say that to. You go, girl."

Kim lifted her palms to them. "Hold on a minute. You guys are getting ahead of yourselves. Reggie and I haven't been to bed together."

"Huh?" Tam asked.

"Then how do you know about his performance?" Leslie asked.

"That's just it," Kim said. "I don't. We were talking and he said something and one thing led to another and I just said it."

"Were you joking or what?" Tam asked.

Kim shook her head. "I wasn't exactly joking, but I wasn't being serious either."

"What did he do?" Tam asked.

"Obviously, he got mad, Tam," Leslie said. "Otherwise, Kim wouldn't be here trying to explain the situation to us." She turned back to Kim. "Go on."

"I don't know what happened. One moment we were flirting and the next moment I'd said it."

"She got nervous," Tam said to Leslie. "And started flapping her lips without thinking."

"You said he did something," Leslie said to Kim, ignoring Tam's comment. "What did he do?"

She shrugged to downplay what she knew had been a major happening. "He sorta picked me up, threw me across his shoulder, carried me to the bedroom and tossed me on the bed."

"Oooh, caveman. I like it," Leslie said.

Tam shot her friend a warning glance. "Les-lie."

"Well, there wasn't anything to like about it. Reggie was angry. And hurt." Kim didn't think she'd ever forget the hurt and disappointment she'd seen in his eyes.

"Did he hurt you?" Tam asked.

Kim shook her head. "No, Tam. Reggie never had any intention of doing anything to me. He was making a point."

"Hey, I'm missing something here," Leslie asked. "What was his point if it wasn't to have sex with you?"

"Leslie, you can be so dense sometimes. Before I'd made my comment, he'd told me that he wanted to make love with me. And I told him that he lacked style. Then he did what he did to show me that he could play the uncaring, macho guy that I seemed to want."

"Dog," Tam said.

"Double dog," Leslie added.

"I know," Kim said. "I tried to explain, to tell him I was sorry, but he wasn't listening. He brought me back to the hotel and I haven't heard from him since."

"I can't say I blame him," Leslie said. "You know men

have fragile egos, especially about sex. You hit below the belt that time, Kim.''

"She's right, Kim," Tam agreed. "You went too far."

Kim didn't like hearing her friends say she was wrong but she knew their assessment was correct. "Tell me something I don't know."

"You have to call him, Kim," Tam said. "If you didn't mean what you said, you owe him an apology."

Again, Tam was right. "I don't know what to say to him."

"Don't blow it out of proportion. Just tell him you're sorry."

"That's right," Leslie added. Then honestly respond to his request. If you want to sleep with him, tell him. If you don't, tell him that too."

"What if I don't know how to respond to his request?" she said, voicing her primary concern. Did she want to sleep with Reggie? The answer to that question was an easy Yes. But was it wise for her to sleep with him? That was the question she couldn't answer.

"Well, we can't help you with that one," Leslie said, getting up from the sofa. "Are you ready to go, Tam?"

Tam grabbed her purse and go up, too. "She's right, Kim. This one you have to figure out all by yourself. We'll see you tonight."

Kim watched as her friends made their way out of the suite. Once she was alone, she thought about their advice and tried to figure out what she really wanted.

Kim took a deep breath before ringing Reggie's doorbell later that afternoon. She hoped to catch him before he left for his weekly visit to the Boys Club. As she stood waiting for him, she thought about the first time she'd stood in front of his house. There'd been other reporters there that day, but today there were none.

"Ms. Washington," Reggie said when he pulled open the door. The surprise she saw in his eyes was quickly replaced with wariness. And maybe boredom. "Here to ask more questions for your article?"

"I'd like to talk to you, Reggie," she said, feeling awkward. "Is it okay if I come in?"

Reggie stepped back and waved her in the house into the gallant fashion of old. "Why, of course, Ms. Washington," he said. "Forgive my rudeness."

She tried not to be hurt by his formality. In the past, there had been a wistfulness in the way he said "Ms. Washington." Today there was a hardness.

"About last night," she said after she was seated on the couch in his living room.

He took a seat in the chair across from her. "What about it?" His voice was hard. Stiff.

She really couldn't blame him for making this difficult for her so she tried not to take his coldness to heart. "I know what I said was out of line."

"Out of line?" he said as if the words were inadequate to describe what she'd done.

"Okay, more than out of line."

He nodded. "Go on."

"That's it. I was wrong and I'm sorry."

"And?"

"And what" she said, her feeling of godwill strained. "I've said I was sorry."

Reggie stood up. "Okay, you've said it. I'll escort you to the door."

"That's it?" Kim said, eyes wide. "I come here and apologize to you and all you have to say is 'I'll escort you to the door.'"

He lifted his arms. "What more do you want?"

She didn't know what she wanted him to say or what she'd expected him to say. But she hadn't expected to be dismissed out of hand. She stood up. "My mistake," she said. "Thanks for listening. I'll let you get back to whatever you were doing."

"Fine," Reggie said and walked her to the door. As she was about to exit, he asked, "So when is our next date?"

"Date?" The man couldn't be serious. He was tossing her out of his house one minute and asking for a date the next.

"For your article and our column. I had a deal with you and your publisher, remember?"

Now she felt really stupid. "Of course, the magazine. When are you available?"

"How about tomorrow night? We could go out to The Club." He shrugged as if it didn't really matter to him. "Or someplace else if you prefer."

She shook her head, a bit disappointed he hadn't asked her to go to the Boys Club with him. She'd enjoyed herself the last time she'd gone. "No, The Club is fine. What time?"

"I'll meet you there at eight."

"Meet me there?" she said aloud, though she was really talking to herself.

"Okay, I'll pick you up," he said, a noticeable lilt in his voice that made her wonder if he was making fun of her.

"No, I'll drive."

He shook his head. "I insist. I'll pick you up at your hotel at seven-thirty."

She wanted to protest, but she had a feeling that doing so would only make her seem silly. "Seven-thirty is fine. I'll see you then."

She walked past him and out to her car, feeling his eyes on her all the while. If he'd wanted to stare at her, he could have walked her to her car, she thought, a bit ticked with him.

"Kim," he called.

She turned around at the sound of his voice and fought down the desire to scream: *What?* "Yes."

"I accept your apology."

The words she'd thought to say left her when she saw his grin. He *had* been making fun of her. She gave him a small smile and turned back to her car. She'd see who was making fun of whom.

* * *

Reggie knew he was in trouble as soon as he saw Ms. Washington in the hotel lobby. Dressed in a black beaded dress with thin, thin straps, and her long legs in black heels, she looked as if she were prepared for battle. The smile she fixed on him told him he was the opponent. And his body's response to her told him he was going to be the loser. But he was determined to go down happy.

"Ms. Washington," he said, going up to greet her. "You certainly look gorgeous tonight. All the men at The Club are going to be envious of me."

She smiled and his stomach did flips. She'd smiled at him before but never like this. "Why, thank you, Reggie," she said. "You don't look too bad yourself."

Reggie had taken special care in choosing his all black ensemble tonight, so he accepted her words as truth. "I do my best," he said.

"Hmm. So modest."

"Are you ready to go?" he asked. When she nodded, he took her arm in his and escorted her out of the hotel and to his waiting car. Once they were both settled, he turned on the radio.

"Did you tell Jim we were going out tonight?" she asked.

He cut his eyes at her. "I'd think that was your job. He's your boss."

"But, if I remember correctly, *you* made the deal with him." She had him there.

"I haven't talked to Jim since I made him the offer. For the record, it wasn't Jim or the offer I was interested in."

She turned and looked out the window.

"Aren't you going to ask what I was interested in?"

She looked back at him. "Why? You said you wanted me to find out for myself what a nice guy you really were so I could tell the truth in the magazine. That was your reason, wasn't it?"

He shrugged. Leave it to Ms. Washington to remember word-for-word what he'd said. "That was part of it."

"Just part of it?"

"I know you know what I'm talking about, Kim. You know as well as I do that I made that offer because I wanted to spend some time with you."

"So that I could write the article?"

"That was as good an excuse as any."

She raised her brow and eyed him suspiciously. "So you lied and all this was just a scam for you to get over on me?"

Reggie shook his head. He wondered if he could ever win with this woman. She turned everything he said around on him. "It wasn't a lie, Kim. I just told you part of the reason."

"I don't get it. You didn't even know me. Why did you want to spend time with me?"

Reggie wondered the same thing. But there was something about Kimberla Washington that had attracted him from the first. "I can't explain it, Kim," he began, deciding to be honest with her. "But I felt this connection with you. I'd thought we were getting along well when the interview started, then you turned on me. And the next day, I see this article in the paper with scores of negative things you'd said. I couldn't let you continue to believe those things about me. What you think is important to me. Very important."

"Why is what I think so important to you?" she asked.

Reggie shrugged, his eyes focused on the road ahead. "I don't know, but I want to find out." He glanced at her. "Don't you?" When she didn't answer immediately, he thought she was going to deny what was happening between them. He opened his mouth to challenge her, but she spoke.

"I remember going through the nominations for the contest and seeing your picture," she said with amazement in her voice. "There was something about you. I can't explain it. I'd read the letters, then I'd look at your picture and I'd wonder if those women were crazy. They said all those wonderful things about you, yet they dumped you.

I couldn't understand it. I tried to tell myself there was something wrong with you, but I couldn't find it in any of those letters. And I couldn't find it in your face."

He glanced at her again. "Do you really think it's because of my bedroom moves?"

She placed her hand atop his on the steering wheel. "I'm sorry. I shouldn't have said that. I didn't mean it. It was something smart to say and when I saw that it made you uncomfortable, I just went with it."

"So you enjoy making me uncomfortable," he teased.

"Let's just say, seeing a little chink in the armor makes you a little more human."

He chuckled, glad the tension between them had lessened. "You're a hard woman, Ms. Washington."

"And you're a nice guy, Mr. Stevens."

"You'd better watch it or I'm going to start thinking you like me." He winked.

"Of course, I like you," she said. "I've never denied that."

He arched his brow. "Not with words, but your actions have been anything but consistent. You run hot and cold on me a lot, Ms. Washington."

"No, I don't."

"Oh, yes you do."

"No, I don't."

"What do you call what happened at our first interview? You went from hot to cold pretty fast that day. What happened?"

"You said you wanted a nice woman. That phrase *nice woman* rings my bell."

"Why's that?"

"Because men sometimes get "nice" confused with gorgeous, sexy. They're not talking about a woman. They're talking about an ornament."

"And you don't like being an ornament?"

"Who would? Though I'm not considered the ornament type. The men who'd say they want a nice woman tend to consider me the buddy type. I'm the one they tell their sob stories to.''

"They must be crazy," Reggie said.

"Who?"

"Those men, your friends. They must be crazy if they don't consider you the gorgeous, sexy, ornament type, because Ms. Washington you definitely ring all my bells."

Kim knew she should be outraged with his blatant flirting, but instead she was flattered. "So that's how you think of me?"

"That's one of the ways. You're sexy as hell—but you're also easy to talk to. I enjoy just being with you. Surely you know that by now."

She didn't know, but she'd hoped so. "I enjoy being with you, too."

He turned his head and smiled at her. "Then no more nights like the other night, okay?"

"Okay," she said.

"Good. Now that all that's out of the way, we can have a good time tonight."

Chapter 17

"Take five, guys," Reggie said as soon as he glimpsed Kim entering the gym. "I'll be right back." In shorts and a tank top, Kim demanded his attention. It was hard to believe it had only been nine weeks since she'd first called him about the contest, three since their first date and just one since they'd acknowledged their feelings for each other. He felt as if he'd always known her.

As he ran to greet her, he heard some boys call, "Hey, coach, she's looking good." He just waved them off without looking back.

"Hi, gorgeous," he said before placing a kiss on her cheek. "I didn't expect to see you tonight."

She gave him a smile that made his heart pound. "I wanted to surprise you. How's it going?"

He wiped sweat from his brow with the white towel around his neck. "I think I'm too old for this," he said. "They're running me ragged."

"Poor baby." Kim patted his jaw. "I should have brought you some iron tablets to build up your strength."

He kissed her again quickly. "You are definitely a hard woman."

"How's it really going?"

"Luther and I are doing our best, but we miss Nate."

"Why isn't he here?"

"He fell hard for your girl Leslie. She really did a number on him."

"That's a matter of opinion," Kim said, not wanting to violate her friend's confidence.

"I knew he was no match for Leslie."

She cocked her head to the side. "The way Tam was no match for Luther?"

"I'm not too sure about that. Luther seems to be making changes in his life. He moved into his own place today."

"I'm sure Tam will be glad to hear that," she said wryly.

"Don't get mad with me." Reggie held up both hands as if to ward off blows. "It was your idea to pair them up in the first place."

"Don't remind me."

He kissed her lips. "Enough about them. I'm really glad you came tonight."

Her lips curved in the soft smile he'd come to cherish. "Does that mean you won't mind if I hang around until practice is over?"

"I wouldn't have it any other way. We'll only be about another half-hour."

"Reggie," Luther called from across the court, "we need to get started."

Reggie kissed Kim again. "They're going to kill me."

"Well," Kim said, "if you need some relief, just yell for me. I've been known to play a mean game of basketball."

Reggie grinned. "You're joking, right?"

She did a mock dribble. "No way. I've got moves that would make you holler."

"I bet you do," he said, staring into her eyes. From the passion she saw there, she knew he wasn't talking about her moves on the basketball court. "I think that's a challenge, Mr. Stevens," she said, her gaze trapped by his. "Want me to show you?"

Reggie sucked in his breath. "More than anything, Ms. Washington. More than anything."

She finally tugged her eyes away from his. "You're on. Do you want me to join you now or do we go one on one after practice is over?"

Reggie leaned in and kissed her again. Unlike his previous kisses, this one was long and demanding. When he pulled away, she was breathless. "You'd better get back to your team," she said, her hands still around his waist.

"I guess I'd better," he said, but he didn't move away from her.

"Reggie," Luther called again. "We'd like to finish this practice *tonight* if you don't mind."

"Yeah, coach," one of the boys called. "You and your lady can get it on later."

Reggie tapped her on her nose. "Sometimes I hate all of them. You know what I mean?"

She chuckled and dropped her hands from around his waist. "Get out there. I want to see what I'm going to be up against later."

He backed away from her. "I play a very physical game," he warned. "You'd better do some stretches before we get started. I wouldn't want you to pull anything."

"Don't worry about me," she teased. "Just make sure you don't give everything you've got before you get to me. I prefer opponents who give as good as they get."

Reggie took a step toward her then stopped. "Do you have any idea how much I wish I could make everybody else in this gym disappear so that we could have our match-up?"

"I was thinking we could have them hang around. Luther could referee and the boys could cheer."

Reggie stared at her for a long second then chuckled. "You're definitely a hard woman, Ms. Washington. I just hope you're up to all your big talk. I'd hate to get all excited only to be let down."

Kim shook her head. "Don't worry about it. My moves

more than match my words. You won't be let down." She
paused. "At least, not until the game is over and you lose."

"Lose?" Reggie quirked his brow. "Somehow I don't
think that's possible."

She shoved him toward the court. "Go, Reggie. The
sooner you finish the sooner we can get started."

"You don't have to tell me twice. Get ready for the time
of your life, Ms. Washington."

"I didn't do too badly for a guy who'd been run ragged
by a group of teenagers, now did I?" Reggie asked.

"Not too badly," Kim said, across from him. They'd
returned to her hotel after their game and were taking
advantage of the empty and inviting hot tub. "Though I
did almost beat you. A two point win over a poor, feeble
woman is nothing to brag about."

"Poor, feeble woman, my foot," he said. "You were a
powerhouse out on the court and you know it. My muscles
know it too. You ran me as hard as those boys did."

"You're just a little out of shape," she teased. "But stick
with me and I'll have you at one hundred percent in no
time."

He encircled her legs with both of his. "You're reading
my mind, lady."

"What are you doing, Reggie?" Kim asked, pushing at
his legs.

He leaned his head back and rubbed his legs up and
down her thighs. "Just kicking back, trying to rest my bones
until all my energy comes back."

She tried to get free of the confines of his legs, but he
tightened them around her. "No fair," she said.

"Never said I was fair," Reggie murmured. "Just said I
was nice."

Kim raked her nails lightly down his legs and he felt a
bolt of electricity go up his legs and to his crotch. He
opened one eye and looked at her. "You'd better watch

that. What you're doing is better than the Energizer Bunny."

"So romantic, Mr. Stevens. Energizer Bunny. Surely you can do better."

He closed his eye and pursed his lips tight as she continued her gentle assault. Erotic visions of the two of them naked on a sunset beach filled his mind. "Keep that up and you're going to be in trouble."

"I doubt it," she said. "You've done all you're going to do tonight. Expelled all your energy so to speak."

"Hmmmm. That feels good." He massaged her thigh again with his leg. "And you feel good. Did you know you have the softest skin?"

"Could be your rough feet."

His eyes shot open and he saw her wide smile.

"Just joking," she said.

He closed his eyes again. "Don't give up your day job. You wouldn't make it on the night club circuit."

"Oooh," she teased. "You do say the sweetest things. You just set my little heart all aflutter."

"That's not all I'm going to set aflutter, if you don't stop."

"Is that a threat?"

He opened one eye. "More like a promise."

She sank down a little in the tub and closed her eyes. He followed. "I had a good time tonight," she said. "When are we going to do it again?"

"So, you want another try at the title?"

"Don't flatter yourself. I just want a chance to play you when you're at one hundred percent. I had to go easy on you tonight."

"Losers usually have some excuse."

"Is that a yes or a no on the rematch?"

He ran his leg up hers again. "You have to qualify for a rematch. I'd be belittling the title if I gave you another shot just because you wanted one. You have to prove yourself worthy to go another round with me."

She tickled the bottom of his feet.

"Stop that," he said, dropping his legs from around her.

She scooted off her seat and grabbed his foot. "So the big, bad man is ticklish." She giggled and tickled him again. "How cute!"

"Cute, huh," he said, trying to get his foot away from her without hurting her. "Stop it, Kim."

"Not until you say Uncle."

"Grrrr." He gave short bursts of laughter. "This is not funny, Ms. Washington."

She giggled. "Then why are you laughing?"

"You're going to pay for this," he said. "It's time for you to pay."

She tugged harder on his foot as he tried to twist it away from her. "It'll be worth it, Reggie. I had no idea you were such a wuss."

"A wuss? Now you've done it." Reggie quickly leaned over, picked Kim up and seated her on his lap facing him with her legs on either side of his hips.

Still giggling, she pushed at his chest. "Let me up," she said.

"No way, you big talker. I told you that you had to pay."

"Let me up, you wuss," Kim said, still giggling.

"Take it back," he demanded. "Take it back."

"Not on your life. Just wait until I tell Luther and Nate. Reggie is a wuss," she sang, "Reggie is a wuss."

Kim's movement on his lap fueled his already budding erection. "You'd better stop wiggling around, or I'm not going to be responsible for what happens." He opened his eyes and found himself facing her bikini top clad breast.

Kim moved again, then stopped suddenly and looked down at him.

Reggie leaned forward and pressed his head against her breast in a motion as natural as drinking water. When she responded by placing her hand behind his head and pulling him to her, he groaned. "Kim," he said. "Sweet, sweet Kim. Do you have any idea how long I've wanted to hold you like this?"

Her answer was a matching groan from deep in her throat and a laxness in her hands around his head. He reluctantly moved his head from her breast and looked into her eyes. Seeing the passion and wariness there, he pulled her head down to his and captured her mouth in the kind of kiss he'd always wanted to give her. A kiss that said he wanted more than to hold her in this hot tub. A kiss that promised protection and consideration if she trusted him. If she trusted her instincts with him.

Her response was as much as he could want. She uttered sounds he couldn't understand, but her body spoke to his in a language of its own. He moved his hands up and down her soft skin and reveled in the knowledge that she was with him, that she wanted to be with him. A feeling of rightness and completeness surrounded him when he realized he wanted the right to hold her like this forever. To be the only one with the right to do so.

Kim gave herself to Reggie's kiss and took pleasure in his touch. She acknowledged that she'd longed for him, for the feel of his hands against her bare skin. She pressed herself closer, needing to be closer, needing to get as close as she could get. But she couldn't get close enough.

Reggie felt the urgency and the need in Kim and was further aroused because they matched his own. He tightened his arms around her back and pulled her closer. He needed more, as he knew she did, and sought it from her.

The distant sound of laughter somehow managed to break-through his thoughts and make him realize where they were. He reluctantly broke the kiss, but kept up the stroking motion down Kim's back. In return, she relaxed against him, resting her head on his forehead. Then, with his help, she moved off his lap and back to her seat across from him.

At that moment, the sources of the laughter entered the room—a couple. "Ooops," they said.

Reggie looked at them, then at Kim. The passion in her eyes erased any doubts or concerns he had. "We were just leaving," he said. Then he reached for her hand and they

got out of the hot tub and walked hand-in-hand past the
staring couple.

He kissed her once more before releasing her hand so
she could enter the women's locker room and change.
The look they exchanged before they parted told him that
she knew the night wasn't over.

They didn't talk much during the drive from Kim's hotel
to Reggie's house because there wasn't much to say. If Kim
admitted the truth to herself, she knew their relationship
had been coming to this point since the first day she'd
picked up his picture from the stack of nominations for
the contest. Even then, there'd been something about him
that that had called out to her. She hadn't known then
what it was, and she still didn't. She just knew that what
she felt for him was right, that being with him was right.
More right than anything she'd ever done in her life.

He guided her into the house before him, placed his
arms around her waist and kissed his forehead. "Hungry?"
he asked.

She shook her head. Food was the last thing on her
mind. She needed sustenance, all right, but food wouldn't
meet that need.

His finger stroked her cheek. "What do you want, Ms.
Washington?"

You. The word sounded loud in her mind, but didn't
flow from her lips. Instead, she raised up on her toes and
pressed her lips against his. When he moaned and pulled
her tightly to him, she knew he'd gotten her message.

"Do you know how much I want you?" he asked when
he finally pulled his mouth away from hers.

Her eyes studied his and she believed she did know. He
wanted her as much as she wanted him. "Tell me," she
whispered, needing to hear the words from his lips.

"More than I've wanted anyone in my life," he said
hoarsely. "More than anything in my life. I have to have
you, Kim."

She pressed her head against his chest and wrapped her arms tight around his waist. "I need you, too," she murmured.

Reggie joined in the embrace, pulling her even tighter to him. His hardness against her aroused and comforted her. Unfortunately, his belt buckle was another matter.

She pulled back a little and looked up into his passion-filled eyes. "You're going to have to pull off your belt. It's poking against my skin."

His eyes darkened. "I think I can handle that," he said, hugging her to his side and leading her to his bedroom.

As she walked with him to her destiny, she thought about the first time she'd been in his bedroom. That time she hadn't had the honor of walking. She giggled at the memory.

He looked down at her. "What's so funny?"

She told him.

He grinned down at her and brushed his hand softly across her hair. "Maybe next time I'll carry you. This time I want to conserve all my energy for more important endeavors."

His "next time" stuck in her mind. She found comfort in the knowledge that he didn't consider their coming together a one time thing. Not that she'd thought he would. It was just good to hear the words.

When he opened his bedroom door, she felt as if she were in a dream. There was no hesitancy or awkwardness on her part. This was where she was meant to be. She had no doubts.

She looked at Reggie and found him watching her. Waiting for her to make the first move. Without losing his gaze, she moved to undo the buttons on her blouse.

"Let me," Reggie said, stepping close to her. "I want to undress you."

Her mouth went dry and her legs went weak. All she could do was nod.

He unbuttoned first one button and then the other, placing soft kisses against her skin as he revealed it to his hungry, seeking eyes. When her blouse was completely undone, he pressed his head against her bra-covered breasts and inhaled her scent. "I love the way you smell," he said.

Kim had to hold onto him to keep from sinking to the floor. The gentleness in his touch and the sincerity in his voice almost undid her.

He lifted his head long seconds later and undid the hooks on her bra, pushing the garment away from her breasts and onto the floor. His sharp gasp was met with one of her own when he placed his wet mouth around one of her already erect nipples.

"Reggie," she moaned as he softly sucked.

A deep moan was his only response as he moved from one breast to the other, as if concerned he'd neglect one. The more he sucked the weaker Kim felt, until she finally sagged against him.

He pulled himself away from her breasts, lifted her in his arms and carried her to his bed. Once there, he leaned over her, kissed his lips and ran his finger teasingly from her neck to the waistband of her shorts.

"Reggie," she moaned again as she twisted so that her body could be closer to him.

"I'm here," he said. "I'll always be here."

With one hand holding her to him, he used the other to unbutton and unzip her shorts. Then he pushed them and her panties down her legs. She had to kick off her sneakers before he could get the shorts and undergarment completely off.

Despite her protests, Reggie pulled away from her so he could see the body he'd so often dreamed about. He studied her from head to foot, filing every inch of her in his brain for future reference. "You're beautiful," he finally said. "So very beautiful."

And she felt beautiful when he looked at her the way he was looking at her now. Her skin wasn't too dark; it was perfect. Her hips weren't too wide; they were just right. Her thighs weren't too heavy; they were sexy. She saw herself as he saw her and a feeIng of total satisfaction enveloped her.

As he lifted himself above her and caressed her face with his gaze, she wondered if this was what real love felt like. She lost focus on her analysis when he quickly and surely entered her. Her arms tightened around him and her hips moved in motion with his.

He'd been right. There was no room in her mind at this time for anything or anyone but him. And she wouldn't have had it any other way.

Chapter 18

Kim woke first. She felt the strong arms around her and smiled, safe and secure in Reggie's embrace. It had been so good with him, so right, that it could have been a dream because reality couldn't be that good, could it?

She rested her hands atop Reggie's to assure herself that what they'd shared and what she'd felt wasn't a dream. He was real. She was real. They were together. And they had been together in the truest sense of the word. She couldn't imagine being anywhere else, with anyone else. Not after being with Reggie.

She closed her eyes and wondered if the experience had been as life-changing for him as it had been for her. Had being with her been any different than with the other women in his life? She hoped the answer was *Yes*. She couldn't bear to think that what had been so special, so dear, for her had been only ordinary for him.

As she thought about the other women who'd passed through Reggie's life, she couldn't help but wonder again why they'd let him go. "They must have been fools."

"What are you talking about?" Reggie asked, pressing

a kiss atop her head and tightening his hold around her waist.

She smiled and snuggled closer to him. "I was just thinking about the women in the contest."

Reggie rolled her over onto her back and quickly straddled her.

"What are you doing?" she asked, her eyes open wide.

"If you have to ask, I must have done something wrong the first time."

The man must be crazy if he thought something so outrageous. "And there must have been another man with me if you think you did anything wrong."

He grinned the grin of a conqueror. "I guess that means you enjoyed yourself."

"Fishing for compliments, Mr. Stevens?"

"Well," he said, "you're the one who woke up thinking about the other women who've been in my life. Emphasis on *been,* as in past tense."

She pressed her palm against his cheek, needing to do something to show him how much she cherished him and appreciated the sweetness of his touch. "I'm not jealous, Reggie."

"Then what were you mumbling about?"

"I was just thinking that those women had to be fools to let you go."

He grinned again and this time he rubbed his pelvis against hers. "I was that good, huh?"

She punched him in the shoulder, at the same time pressing her lower body against his. "Stop fishing for compliments. I'm the woman here. You should be telling me how wonderful I was, how wonderful I am."

His movements stopped immediately and he pressed her palm to his lips. "You are the most beautiful, the most wonderful, the most generous, the most loving, the most sensuous, the most satisfying, woman I've ever known," he said, punctuating his words with soft kisses against the palm of her hand.

He sounded so earnest that she had to believe he meant it. "And you're very good with words."

His serious expression lightened and he pressed himself against her again. "How about my moves?"

"Still fishing for compliments!"

"Unless my hearing has gone bad, you haven't given me one yet."

"Yes, I have," she said.

He pressed a kiss against her lips. "Well, tell me again. I missed it the first time."

"No way," she said with a playful pout. "You should pay closer attention."

Reggie stretched out his body against hers. "I bet I can make you tell me again."

"And I bet you're heavy," she said, though his weight didn't bother her. She actually enjoyed having him rest on her.

"Want me to get off?" he offered, then moved to lift himself away from her.

She placed her arms around him to keep him right where he was. "You aren't going anywhere, buster."

"Bossy, aren't you?"

"Only when I have to be."

"Hmmm," he said, dropping kisses along her neckline. "I think I'm beginning to get a new appreciation for bossy women. Boss me around some more."

Kim giggled. "I will not. Anyway, you seem to do well enough on your own."

"That's not much of a compliment on my outstanding performance," he said. "But I guess that's all I'm going to get."

She pulled his mouth to hers. "I'm not so sure about that," she said. "Not sure at all." Then she kissed him and again gave her entire self to him.

Reggie stared at the sleeping Kim, thinking how fortunate he was to have her. There had been something special, something so very right about being with her. About having the freedom to hold her, caress her and love her.

He stroked his finger lightly across her lips and smiled when she moved to knock his hand away as if he were some annoying gnat. Even in her sleep, she was bossy and demanding. In her lovemaking, she was the same.

His amazement at the total surrender with which she gave herself to him had given him the power, for the first time in his life, to do the same in return. He'd given Kim all he'd had and she'd taken it and given back even more. Had he not experienced the phenomenon, he wasn't sure he would have believed it.

He touched her jaw again, as if he were a kid unable to wait for his baby brother or sister to awaken, and quietly spoke her name. When she didn't budge, he said, "Wake up, sleepyhead."

This time his words roused her and her eyelids slowly fluttered open. He took advantage of her obvious disorientation and placed a nice, wet kiss on her still pouty lips. "It's about time."

She rubbed at her eyes in a way that made her seem a child. "What time is it?"

"Time for breakfast." He threw back the covers and exposed her nakedness to his hungry eyes. "Or at least it was. But maybe breakfast can wait."

"Oh, no," she said, now fully awake. "Don't you ever get tired?"

He leered at her. "Never of you. Now, come here."

Kim shook her head, grabbed the edge of the sheet, pulled it around herself and then got out of the bed. "I'm tired enough for both of us."

"No you're not," he said, stalking toward her. "And if you drop that sheet, I'll show you just how much energy you have."

Kim held her hand out to stop him, but it did no good. He reached her and pulled her back into his arms. "Now are you going to drop the sheet or what?"

"Or what."

He could see her crumbling resistance in her eyes. He reached for the sheet pressed tightly against her breast, but the ringing of the doorbell stopped him.

A slight smile crossed Kim's face. "Saved by the bell," she said.

"Not by a long shot," he said. "I don't have to answer. They'll go away."

The doorbell seemed to ring louder and longer.

"I don't think so," she said, trying to scoot away from him. "Anyway, all that noise destroys the moment, don't you think?"

He grunted, not taking his eyes from her. "Not for me."

"Answer the door, Reggie," she said, heading for the bathroom. "I have to get dressed. I'm supposed to be working, remember?"

Reggie cursed under his breath as he struggled between the desire to follow Kim to the shower and the need to answer the door. He made his decision and headed for the bathroom door. When he found it locked, he cursed her slick thinking, pulled on his robe and headed for the door.

"Hold on a minute," he yelled, taking out his frustration on the unknown visitor. "Who the hell visits this early in the morning in the first place?"

His mouth dropped open when he saw his parents standing before him, luggage in hand.

"You see, I told you he was home, George," his mother said to his father.

"How are you doing, son?" His mother turned and gave him a great big Stevens hug. "I knew you'd be here. We tried calling, but you didn't answer and you know how I hate those answering machines."

"What are you doing here?" Reggie asked after his mother pulled away and he was able to get his mouth working again.

"We came to visit our boy," she said. "Now are you going to let us in or what?"

He stepped back. "Oh, I'm sorry, Mom, Dad. Come on

in." After his mother passed, he said to his father, "Let me help you with those bags."

"No need, son," the elder Stevens said. "I've got them now. Just tell me where to put them."

Reggie's thoughts went to Kim in the shower and he immediately recognized how awkward the situation could quickly become. "I insist, Dad. Let me take these." He practically had to fight to get the bags from his dad's hands but he did so. Then, with a forced smile, he said, "Why don't you two sit down while I put these in your room. I'll be right back."

Reggie made sure they were seated in the living room. Then he rushed back to the room Luther had recently vacated, dropped their bags and headed to Kim and the shower. Unfortunately, the door was still locked. He tried calling her name, but not too loudly because he feared his parents would hear him. He didn't want to think about the conclusions they would draw if they heard him yelling some woman's name. Unable to think of anything else to do, he turned and went back to join his parents.

When he returned, his mother was seated on the couch and his father was standing in front of the window. "So, how was your trip?" he asked, praying that Kim would be dressed when she came out of the bedroom. He hoped she would think someone was there since she'd heard the bell, but then again, she might think he'd gotten rid of whoever it was. And he would have if the whoever had been anyone other than his parents.

"Come here, boy," his dad said, with open arms. "Give your old dad a hug."

Reggie did as requested and hugged his father as he had countless times in the past. They were a close family and embraces were normal.

"Now that's better." His dad pulled away after a final slap on his son's back. "To answer your question, we had a good trip."

"You must have taken an early flight out," he said.

"We drove," his mother said. "Didn't you see our car parked out front?"

Reggie hadn't noticed the car. He'd been too surprised at seeing his parents standing at his door.

"Of course, the boy didn't see the car, Katherine," his father said, saving him from having to make up an excuse. "He looks like he just got out of bed. It's a wonder he saw us standing at the door. Isn't that right, son?"

"That's right, Dad," he said, then faked a yawn. "You two must be tired, if you drove all the way."

"Well," his mother said, "I could lie down for a little while. How about you, George?"

"I'm not that tired, but I guess I could use a little rest."

Reggie wanted to shout his relief. If he could get his parents into their room before Kim got out of the shower, he'd have a chance to prepare her for meeting them.

"Okay, then," Reggie said, "why don't we all go back to bed?"

Reggie led his parents down the hallway. As they neared his bedroom, he held his breath and prayed Kim wouldn't come out. Not that he didn't want her to meet them. He just knew she'd be embarrassed as would his parents. Just as he was about to release a sigh of relief, his bedroom door opened, and Kim,—fully dressed, thank God, stepped out. He looked from her to his parents and back again. It was a toss-up as to who was more surprised.

It should not have surprised him when his mother spoke first. "We don't have to ask who this is." With a big, pleased smile on her face, she extended her hand to Kim. "Hello, Kimberla. You're even prettier than that picture of you that ran in the paper."

Kim knew as soon as she had opened Reggie's bedroom door and seen the two older people that they were his parents. At that moment she'd both wished she could fade into the woodwork and thanked God that she'd had the sense to slip on her shorts *and* top before coming out of the room. She'd never been so embarrassed in all her life. Of course, she was an adult and Reggie was an even older adult, but parents were still parents. And she knew she wasn't the only woman who would prefer to meet her man's parents under different and more conventional circumstances.

Mr. and Mrs. Stevens, on the other hand, seemed to take things in stride. They'd greeted her as if they'd known her forever. After a short while, she'd felt as though she'd known them just as long. It wasn't until Mrs. Stevens suggested that she join her in the kitchen to prepare breakfast while the men talked that Kim became nervous.

"So, how long have you and Reggie been seeing each other?" Mrs. Stevens asked as soon as they were in alone the kitchen.

Kim knew the question wasn't a loaded one, but it sure felt like one. She wondered what Mrs. Stevens would think about her sleeping with her son when she found out how short a time they'd been together. "Long enough, I'd say," she said.

Mrs. Stevens smiled at her, a feminine version of Reggie's warm smile. "Good answer. I like you, Kimberla. And I like your name too. You're good for my Reggie. I can see that already."

Surprised didn't exactly describe Kim's internal response to that statement.

"Don't look so surprised," Mrs. Stevens said. "I knew something was going on with Reggie as soon as I saw that picture in the paper. He's a good son, but he's a little slow sometimes."

Kim sat down on a stool at the counter while Mrs. Stevens rummaged through the refrigerator and the cabinets for something to cook. "I'm going to have to go shopping for that boy before I leave. He doesn't have anything in here worth cooking."

Kim didn't see a need to respond, so she didn't. She determined then that she liked Mrs. Stevens. The older woman reminded her of her mother.

"Okay," the older woman said, "I may be able to pull something together after all." When she turned around she had eggs, milk, cheese and butter in her hands. From the cabinets she pulled out grits and a can of pink salmon. "This'll have to do. You like fried salmon, don't you?"

"Yes, ma'am," Kim said, though she remembered having the dish only once.

"Good," the older woman said, proceeding to pull the can opener from the cabinet. "So," she said to Kim. "Tell me how you and Reggie met."

Kim considered what and how much to tell Mrs. Stevens, then decided on the truth. When she told her about the contest, Mrs. Stevens face grew somber. "Reggie goes about relationships the wrong way," she confided. Then she smiled at Kim. "Except with you."

Kim couldn't resist asking the question that was on her mind. "How do you mean?"

Mrs. Stevens pulled out a black iron skillet, put it on the stove and turned on the burner. "Well, it's the women he's chosen in the past. They've always been in need. If Reggie goes to a coliseum filled with thousands of women, he's going to come out with one who just lost her job or the one whose husband just left her or one who's about to kill herself. It's become his way."

Kim considered Mrs. Stevens's words and realized they accurately captured the women who'd nominated Reggie for the contest. All but one. "Christina was different."

Mrs. Stevens looked up from her salmon. "So you know about Christina. Did she nominate him for the contest too?"

Kim nodded.

"Christina was different at first, but things changed when she got pregnant."

"Pregnant?" Kim couldn't keep the dismay she felt out of her voice. Knowing Reggie had loved Christina was one thing, but knowing they'd made a child together was a whole other matter.

"Calm down," Mrs. Stevens said with a chuckle. "It

wasn't Reggie's baby though he did volunteer to marry her and give her baby a name.''

This news almost floored Kim. Now she understood what Christina had meant about Reggie's sacrificial offer. ''He loved her that much?''

Mrs. Stevens shook her head. ''Not love, Kim. Caring. He cared about her and he felt she needed him, so he offered to help.''

Kim wasn't so sure. She didn't know many men who'd marry a woman they didn't love just to give her unborn child a name. Not even Reggie was that magnanimous. He must have felt he was getting something out of the deal.

''Can't believe it, can you?'' Mrs. Stevens said.

''Honestly, no. Reggie's a good man. One of the nicest and kindest men I've met. But I don't think even he'd go that far.''

''Then you don't know him as well as I thought you did.'' Mrs. Stevens studied Kim for what seemed to be minutes before extending her hand to her. ''Come, sit with me a minute,'' the older woman said, inclining her head toward the dinette set in the breakfast nook. ''I'm going to tell you a story that I think you need to know.''

Kim grew anxious as she seated herself across from Mrs. Stevens. The serious look on the woman's face told her that she considered what she was about to say very important. Kim wasn't sure she wanted to hear it. Her relationship with Reggie was moving along so well. She didn't want anything to change that. ''You don't have to—'' she began, but Mrs. Stevens cut her off.

''Yes, I do,'' she said. ''I love my eldest son very much. And even though he's a man now, he'll always be my little boy. You'll understand that when you have children of your own.''

Kim nodded because she thought it was expected of her. It was difficult for her to think of the Reggie she knew as someone's little boy though.

''Reggie has a strong need to rescue women who need help,'' Mrs. Stevens began. ''It started his first year in college when one of his old girlfriends committed suicide. Even though there was nothing he could have done to stop her, he's always felt responsible. The way he still seeks out women in need today is proof that I'm right. He's either trying to make up for not being there for his friend or trying to make sure that no other woman he knows ends up the way she did."

Kim's heart contracted and she felt very full of love for Reggie Stevens. He was definitely a special man. "So that's why the women left him," she said, for the first time understanding the dynamics of his past relationships.

"You catch on quick," Mrs. Stevens observed. "Yes, that's the reason. When Reggie finds them, they're like little birds whose wings have been clipped. He nurses them back to health and when they get well they leave his security nest and go back to tackle their own lives."

"Do you think Reggie knows what he's doing?" Kim asked.

"I think he's beginning to. That Double-Minded Women article of his gave me my first clue. I knew things were changing with him. And I think you're part of that change, Kimberla."

Kim hoped Mrs. Stevens's words were correct, but she didn't think it appropriate to comment on her relationship with Reggie before he did.

"Oh, you don't have to say anything. A mother knows. Reggie's in love with you. It's all over his face."

"No, he's not," Kim rushed to say.

Mrs. Stevens gave her a knowing smile. "I've loved the same man all my life," she said. "So I know love when I see it. It's in his eyes and in yours too. He's in love with you and you're in love with him. You're both just too bullheaded to realize it, but you will. And soon." Mrs. Stevens pushed her chair back from the table. "Enough of this. Let's get back to the food. You can help me roll out the biscuits."

Kim got up and did as Mrs. Stevens instructed, but she couldn't stop thinking about the things the older woman had said. About Reggie and his past relationships and about her and Reggie and their present relationship. Neither she nor Reggie had mentioned love and that was okay for right now. Leslie was right. Serious relationships took time to build and she wanted that time with Reggie.

As she thought about their relationship, a feeling of discomfort settled around her. Reggie's mother had said her relationship with Reggie was different. That his past relationships were based on his need to help. Could it be that there relationship was based on that same need? Could Reggie be responding to her because she needed him for her job? She shook her head to dislodge the crazy thoughts. Of course, that wasn't the case. Reggie had wanted to spend time with her because he'd wanted to clear up his reputation and because he wanted to get to know her. Her relationship with him was different, wasn't it?

Chapter 19

Reggie finally had a chance to be alone with Kim when his parents decided to go for a walk around the block. "I love my parents dearly," he said, taking a seat next to her on his living room couch. "But their timing couldn't be worse."

"Um, I don't know," she said. "Maybe their timing is exactly right. We were getting carried away."

He pulled her into his arms. "Speak for yourself, Ms. Washington. I was very much in control of my faculties and was doing exactly what I wanted to do." He increased the pressure of his hold on her and pressed a kiss against her forehead. "I love having you in my arms like this."

She leaned her head back and pressed her palms flat on his chest. "I bet you say that to all the women in your life."

"You're right about that," he said with a grin. "I give every last one of them this same line. Seems to be working too."

She thumped his chest. "I bet you and your brothers drove your parents crazy."

"We did, but fortunately they loved it." He released his

hold on her, took her hand and led her to the couch. "What were you two talking about in the kitchen?"

"I'm not telling you. It was girl talk anyway."

"Well," he said, stroking her arms, "if you don't want to talk, we can always go back to bed."

"And have your parents find us there? No way."

"Hey, it's a pretty long block. We could be in and out before they get back."

She shook her head and chuckled. "Sometimes I don't know about you, Reggie Stevens. Are you sure you're thirty-eight and not eighteen?"

"I know you aren't criticizing my moves again after the way you were screaming last night."

She socked him in his arm.

"Ouch," he said. "I was just telling the truth. You were screaming."

"I was not and you know it."

"You just don't remember it. I do."

She folded her arms across her chest. "I was not screaming."

He pulled her to his side and chuckled. "Don't be embarrassed. It was a sexy scream. Matter of fact I enjoyed hearing it and wouldn't mind hearing it again."

She leaned away from him. "What you enjoy is teasing me."

"True, but not as much as I enjoy making you scream with passion. We have about twenty minutes before my folks get back. Are you sure you don't want to give it another go?"

"Look," she said getting up from the couch. "Since you seem to be losing your mind, I think I should get ready to go home."

"Don't go," he pleaded. "I want you to stay for the rest of the day and I'm sure my parents do too."

"But you need some time alone with them and I need to go home and put on some fresh clothes."

He knew she was right, but he didn't want her to go.

"Will you stay until they get back so I can drive you to the hotel?"

"I can call Tam," she offered. "I don't think she had plans for the day."

Reggie stood up and pulled her into his arms again. "Don't call Tam. I want the time alone with you. Do I have to toss you over my shoulder to make you understand?"

She leaned into his embrace. "No. Just hold me until your folks get back."

"That I can do. I wish I could hold you longer. My parents certainly picked the wrong time to visit."

"Don't let them hear you say that, Reggie. You'll hurt their feelings. Your parents are so proud of you and it's obvious how much they love you."

"I think they like you a lot too."

"Well, I like them too. They're a special couple. Married forty-one years and still happy. Maybe *Uptown Style* should do an article on them."

He leaned away from her so he could look down into her eyes. "One of these days I'm going to hold you in my arms and you aren't going to mention that magazine."

"It's my job, Reggie. In case you've forgotten, I'm in Atlanta on assignment. And I'll bet Jim is pretty upset that you and I aren't drumming up publicity for him."

"Can we just forget Jim and the magazine for a while?"

"It's my job."

"I know," he said, frustrated with her fixation on her work. "You know what?"

"What?"

"If you ever bring up your job when we're in bed, I'm going to dump you."

"No problem," she said. "When I'm in bed with you, I can't think of anything else."

Reggie stared down into her eyes thinking she couldn't have given a better response. He could think of only one way to show her how much her words meant to him. He picked her up and tossed her over his shoulder.

"What are you doing?" she demanded as he headed down the hallway toward his bedroom.

"You'll find out."

"But your parents?"

"We've got at least fifteen minutes, plenty of time. Plus, I'll lock the door so they can't surprise us."

"But—"

"But nothing." He kicked open his bedroom door, tossed her onto the bed and prepared to give her the most thrilling fifteen minutes of her life.

"What are you guys doing?" Kim asked when she walked into the suite a few hours later and saw suitcases arranged by the door.

"Going home," Tam said. "But don't worry. I'll be back. Maria wants to see Atlanta."

"That's right," Leslie added. "Don't forget we have this suite for nine more weeks. Right now, I need to get back and clear up some things in my old office. I should be back in a week or so."

"But I'm going to miss you guys," Kim said, feeling a bit betrayed. "Why didn't you tell me you were planning to leave?"

"We haven't exactly seen you a lot the last couple of weeks, Kim," Tam said. "You've been pretty busy with Reggie."

"You mean with my article," she clarified, though she realized she and Reggie had been spending a lot of time together.

"No," Leslie said. "We mean with Reggie. You don't expect us to believe that you've been out all night working on your article, do you?"

"But—"

Don't get us wrong, girlfriend," Leslie interrupted. "We're not complaining. As a matter of fact, just the opposite. We're happy for you. At least one of us ended up with a keeper."

Kim turned to Tam, figuring she could make her change her mind. "Why are *you* leaving, Tam? Isn't Melissa still with Marcus?"

Tam nodded. "I know, but I need to get back home just the same. I can only stay in a hotel so long, even one as nice as this one."

Kim nodded as the real reason for her friends' abrupt departure occurred to her. "This is about Nate and Luther, isn't it?"

"For me it isn't," Leslie said, a bit too quickly in Kim's opinion. "I haven't given old Nate a second thought."

Kim wasn't sure she believed her friend, but what could she say? "What about you, Tam? Are you sure you aren't running away from this situation between you and Luther?"

Tam shook her head. "There is no situation between me and Luther so there isn't anything to run away from. He hasn't even bothered to call since the night I told him about Melissa."

Kim knew her friend referred to the night things had gone sour in her relationship with Luther. "Have you called him?"

Tam shook her head. "And I won't. If the man can't deal with the fact that I have a child, we have nothing to talk about. I've never run behind a man and I'm not going to start now."

Kim couldn't blame her friend. In Tam's situation, she was sure she'd feel the same. "I wish you two weren't leaving," she said. "I'm going to miss you."

Leslie shook her head. "We'll be back before you know it. Besides, Reggie will keep you occupied."

Kim guessed she and Reggie would be spending a lot of time together, but that didn't mean she wouldn't miss her friends. "But I won't have you two to talk to when I run into a problem."

"I have a feeling there aren't going to be any problems with you and Reggie until it's time for you to go back home. Have you two talked about what's going to happen then?''

Kim shook her head. Neither she nor Reggie had even brought the topic up. Their energies and thoughts were focused on the now.

"But you aren't going to be here forever, Kim, or has Jim told you something that you haven't told us?''

"I haven't talked to Jim in a couple of days and I'm surprised. I was sure he'd be upset that Reggie and I haven't been keeping the papers jumping.''

"Knowing Jim," Leslie said, "he probably has some scheme in the back of his mind. Who knows, he may even have you moving to Atlanta?''

The idea of living in Atlanta appealed to Kim, though she knew that what really appealed to her was living close to Reggie. She was hooked on the guy. Why deny it to herself? "Somehow I don't think so. The Nicest Guy Contest issue runs in September and there's no way Jim's going to pay his share of my expenses for any longer than necessary." Kim looked from Leslie to Tam. "When are you leaving?''

"Tomorrow morning.''

"You can't leave that soon. We should at least spend one day together before you go back.''

Tam waved her ticket. "We have to.''

"You can change them," Kim said. "Come on.''

"Why don't we spend today together?" Leslie suggested. "What do you want to do anyway?''

"I can't today," Kim said.

"Let me guess," Tam said. "Plans with Reggie." When Kim nodded, she said, "See? I knew you weren't going to miss us.''

"I'd change the plans if I could," Kim insisted, "but his parents are in town and they want to take us to dinner.''

"His parents?" both friends said at the same time.

"You didn't tell us his parents were here," Leslie said. "This thing between you two must be serious.''

"Not exactly." Kim went on to explain to the unexpected arrival of Reggie's parents.

Leslie chuckled. "At least they won't forget meeting you. How did it go after that?"

Kim thought it had gone well and told them so. "They're going to be here for a week and Reggie had mentioned hosting a cook-out for them at his house and inviting a few friends over. I know he was thinking of Luther and Nate. And I was going to invite you two. Are you sure you can't stay a week longer?"

Her friends looked at each other, then at her. "No way," they said.

"I'm sorry your friends are leaving," Reggie said after he and Kim had dinner with his parents later that night. They sat in the lobby of her hotel.

Kim looked up at him. "No, you're not. Your expression says you're quite happy about it."

He rubbed his hand up and down her bare arm. "I'm not happy your friends are leaving because I know you'll miss them, but I won't say that I don't see the benefits."

"Such as?"

"Such as having a place to be alone with you while my parents are in town. I don't think I can go through an entire week without making love to you again."

His sweet words soothed her ruffled feathers a little, but not much. "Is sex all you can think about?"

"Not all, but it takes up a great deal of space in this old brain of mine. Don't you think about it?"

"Not much," she lied. Her thoughts didn't stray far from the memory of them together. Even the quickie earlier in the day had been satisfying.

He hugged her to him. "What am I going to do with you, Ms. Washington?"

She relaxed in his embrace. "Pretty soon, you won't have to ask yourself that question."

"What does that cryptic statement mean?"

"I have to go home at some point myself. I don't live here, remember?"

Reggie's hold on her tightened. "I remember, all right. I just don't like to think about it. Has Jim said anything?"

She shook her head. "But he will. I'm be sending in the Contest article in a day or so and we aren't exactly drumming up publicity with our relationshp. There's really no reason for me to be here."

He tilted her chin up and kissed her lips. "I could name a reason or two."

She knew she was being obvious, but she had to ask. "Okay, name them."

He kissed her lips. "First, there's me." He kissed her lips again. "Then there's you. I'd say those are two very good reasons for you to be here."

That he wanted her to stay warmed her heart, but the reality that she couldn't didn't allow her to take much joy from his words. "We have to be realistic. I'm not going to be here much longer."

He pressed a kiss to her forehead. "Let's not talk about that now. I don't want to start thinking about your not being here. I just want to enjoy you. By the time you have to leave, I'm sure we'll have come up with a scheme that will convince Jim to extend your stay."

She shook her head. "I don't know about you. It scares me that you and Jim think so much alike."

He chuckled. "Then don't think about Jim and me. Think about you and me."

"It's too bad things didn't work out between Leslie and Tam and Nate and Luther."

"There you go again," he said.

"What did I do now?"

"Talking about other people. I'm talking about me and you. And you're talking about our friends. I'm going to have to do something about that."

"Something like what?" she asked.

He kissed her again. "So far I've only found one thing that works. I guess I'll have to keep making love to you.

Heck, I may even have to do it three, four, five, times a day in order to keep your attention."

"You make it sound like a duty."

He nodded. "It's a hard job but somebody has to do it."

She punched him in the side. "I can see this conversation is going downhill. I think it's time to say good night."

She moved to get up from the lobby couch, but he pulled her back to him. "Not so quick. Let's just sit here a while."

"We've been sitting here for over an hour, Reggie. Your parents are going to think you got lost."

"They might be old, Kim, but they're not dumb. Believe me, they won't think I'm lost. Now, if I came home early they'd probably think I was losing my mind."

"Why?"

"They like you and they like us. Can't you tell?"

She could. Mrs. Stevens had come right out and told her so and Mr. Stevens went out of his way to be friendly. "You have nice parents."

"I think they're looking at you as daughter-in-law material."

The word *daughter-in-law* made her heart flutter. She'd fought long and hard not to think too far in the future about her relationship with Reggie. The two of the them were together now and things were good. She wasn't going to complicate the relationship unnecessarily.

"I told you I don't often bring women home," he continued.

"You didn't exactly bring me home, Reggie. It's more like your parents came looking for me."

He shrugged his broad shoulders. "Same difference. If I hadn't wanted you to meet them, I would have gotten you out of the house pretty fast."

"Umm, sounds like you have experience with that."

He pulled back and looked down at her face. Then he opened his mouth to speak, but closed it.

"What?" she asked.

"I'm not going to get into it."

"Get into what?"

"The way you bring up other people—women, friends—when all I want to talk about is us."

"But—"

He placed his finger across her lips. "I don't want to get into it. Let's talk about this cook-out we're giving my parents."

"Well, my friends can't make it so the guest list will be two shorter than we'd planned. Who are you going to invite instead?"

"Nobody, I think. If you don't mind being the only woman other than my mom, I'll just invite Nate and Luther."

"Maybe they'll bring dates?" she offered.

"Maybe. Does it matter?"

She shrugged. "Not really. It's just too bad they couldn't work things out with Leslie and Tam."

"You're doing it again," he said.

She squeezed him to her. "Sorry, you now have my undivided attention. I promise not to think about anyone or anything but you until you leave."

"That's better," he said. "But not good enough. I can't wait until we have some more time alone."

Kim cuddled against him. She couldn't wait either.

Chapter 20

When the ringing phone awoke Kim at five o'clock in the morning later that week, she wasn't surprised to hear Jim's voice. "You aren't still sleeping, are you, Kimmy girl?" Jim's thick voice asked.

"Not now, Jim," she said. "Did you get my article?" She'd Fed Exed it to him two days ago.

"That's what I'm calling you about, Kimmy. I got the article yesterday. It was damn good."

"I think I hear a but coming, Jim. Come on, tell me."

"Well, Kimmy, it's a good article, like I said, but it doesn't have any punch to it. Have you and Reggie stirred up any news down there in Atlanta?"

"Not really, Jim," she hedged. "But we've got a couple of ideas for our column." Kim knew she was lying but felt she needed to give Jim something to keep him off her back.

"Well, ideas are good, Kimmy girl, but what we need is a publicity grabber. Have you come up with anything like that?"

She hadn't and she didn't plan to, but she was wise

THE NICEST GUY IN AMERICA   227

enough not to give that bit of information to her boss. "What exactly are you looking for, Jim?"

"Something like that article you did or the article Reggie did. Something controversial or outrageous. Something like that picture of you two kissing that showed up in the papers. Do you have anything like that?"

"Not quite, Jim," she said. "I was thinking of something a little bit more sophisticated."

"Sophisticated doesn't sell magazines, Kimmy," Jim growled. "I thought you'd learned that by now. Are you and Reggie still dating?"

"Yes," she answered, unwilling to tell Jim how far their relationship had come. Who knew what he'd do with that information?

"How's it going?" he asked. When she didn't answer immediately, he said, "Come on, Kimmy girl, there could be something there that we could use."

"I don't think so, Jim. We're just dating, getting to know each other."

"But you do like him, don't you, Kimmy? He seems a nice enough guy."

"Sure I like him, Jim, but what does that have to do with anything?" A strong feeling of apprehension built up in her belly. Jim was up to something.

"Well, since the two of you haven't been drumming up any publicity, I've been trying to come up with something and I think I've found just the right angle."

She didn't want to ask, but she had to. "What kind of angle, Jim?"

"Don't go getting all nervous on me, Kimmy. It's not a biggie. Just something to drum up a little interest."

"What kind of angle, Jim?" she repeated.

"Well, I was thinking that if we're going to really kick off the contest issue and your column, we're going to need something really big to draw interest."

"Stop beating around the bush, Jim. Tell me what your idea is."

"Well, Kimmy, it would just be for show, you know, but I was thinking that you and Reggie could get engaged."

"Engaged?" she shouted. "Have you lost your mind?" Kim knew she could do a lot of things, but pretending to be engaged to Reggie wasn't one of them. Her relationship with him was serious and engagement was serious. She wasn't willing to jeopardize what they had by playing such a game.

"Hear me out, Kimmy. You wouldn't *really* be engaged, just engaged for the publicity. You wouldn't have to get married."

"Why, thanks a lot, Jim," she said sarcastically. "For a minute there, I thought you had my wedding gown already picked out."

"You're getting mad, Kimmy. I can hear it in your voice. Now just calm down and listen to me."

"Calm down?" she said. "You want me to pretend to be engaged just so we can drum up some publicity for the magazine. Don't you have any sense of integrity?"

"Wait a minute, Kimmy," Jim warned. "You're coming pretty close to crossing the line there. Don't forget that you've been down there in Atlanta on an expense account, *my* expense account, for weeks and you haven't come up with diddly. Well, I don't intend to lose money on this deal and if you want to keep your job you'd better go in for a little attitude adjustment."

"Are you threatening me, Jim?" Kim asked.

"I'm just telling you like it is. This is a business, Kimmy, and businesses are about making money. If you don't know that by now you just may be in the wrong business."

"Maybe you're right, Jim," she said. "Maybe you're right."

"It's up to you, Kimmy. I'll give you one week to think over my offer. As I see it, you've got two options. Go along with this fake engagement idea or start looking for another job. I'll give you one week."

"I don't—"

It was too late. Jim had hung up. She had half a mind

to call him back and tell him off. But what good would that do? She'd only be lowering herself to his level.

Surprisingly, the thought of losing her job didn't upset her. There was no way she was going to fake an engagement with Reggie for the magazine's sake. Their relationship was much too precious to subject to such a scam. She couldn't wait to tell Reggie what Jim had said. She was sure he'd get a good laugh out of it after he got over being angry.

"Nice cookout, Mr. Stevens," Kim said to Reggie. She'd spent most of the afternoon seated on his shaded patio with his parents while he'd slaved over the hot grill. This was the first private moment she'd found to talk with him.

"Nice outfit, Ms. Washington." He gave her yellow denim-like short set a positive masculine appraisal. "Nice body, too."

"Oooh, you do know how to tease a girl."

"I'm not teasing, darling. Just wait until we get my parents on the road."

"What'll we do with Nate and Luther over there?" She nodded in the direction of his two friends who were being taught the finer points of holding a golf club by Mr. Stevens.

He flipped one of the burgers on the grill. "Don't worry about them. I'll throw them to the curb before they realize what's happening."

She chuckled. "And here I was thinking you were such a wonderful host."

"I am," he said. "I just like to choose my guests."

"Hey," Luther interrupted. "What are you two talking about?"

Kim turned to Reggie's friend. "Nothing much. I was just telling Mr. Stevens here that he throws a pretty good party."

"You call this a party?" Luther asked with wide eyes. "I've had more fun at funerals."

"You can always leave, man," Reggie said with a wink to Kim.

"And do what?" Luther complained with a shrug. "Unfortunately, yours was my most exciting offer for today."

"Now, I don't believe that, Luther," Kim said. "I thought you were a ladies' man *extraordianaire.*"

"So did I," he mumbled. "Hey, why aren't Leslie and Tam here?"

She turned to Reggie. "You didn't tell him."

"Tell me what?"

Reggie shrugged. "It wasn't my business."

"What wasn't?" asked Luther.

Kim sighed. "They went back home earlier in the week."

"So she's gone," Luther said absently.

Kim thought Luther expressed a lot of concern for a woman he didn't care about. Could it be that Tam had read him wrong? "Yes, she's gone." She took perverse pleasure in letting him think it was forever.

"And she didn't even have the decency to call and tell me she was leaving. Go figure."

Kim rolled her eyes. "The way I heard it is that you're the one who didn't make any phone calls. You left her high and dry, Luther. What did you expect her to do?"

"You don't understand, Kim," Luther tried to explain. "Things were complicated with Tam and me from the beginning."

Kim waved away his excuse. "So she said. But whatever it was seemed to have gotten uncomplicated pretty suddenly. What was it? You decided a woman with a child wasn't your style and you weren't man enough to tell her."

Luther shook his head. "You don't understand," he said again. "You just don't understand." He looked at her and Reggie then walked off, his head down.

"I almost feel sorry for him," she said.

"You were hard on him, Kim," Reggie said. "Whether you believe it or not, he cared for Tam."

Kim snorted. "I thought so too, but his actions proved

otherwise. A man who cares about a woman doesn't treat her the way Luther treated Tam. Heck, a man who *doesn't* care about a woman can treat her better than Luther treated Tam."

Reggie studied her face as if looking for something. Then he shook his head. "You're so sure of yourself, aren't you?"

"What? Are you saying you think Luther was right?"

"No, I'm not saying that. I just think that we may not know all that went on between him and Tam."

"I know enough," she said. "I know Luther was interested in her until she told him she had a child. Then he dumped her before the words could even sink in."

Reggie shook his head again. "Sometimes you scare me, Kim. You don't cut a guy any slack. I wonder what I'll do that'll set you off on me. Again."

She knew from the look in his eyes that he was serious. "Why would you say something like that?"

"Because you can be so rigid at times. You only see things your way. Don't get me wrong. You're a strong woman and that's a very attractive trait. A very sexy trait. But it scares me."

"As long as you're honest with me, you don't have anything to worry about. I may be rigid, but I'm fair. You, of all people, should know that."

"I'm human. I worry sometimes."

"Well, you shouldn't." She walked to him and pressed a light kiss against his lips. "Now smile before your mother thinks I've done something awful to you."

She would have stepped away, but he kept her close. "Do you realize that's the first time you've been openly affectionate with me with my parents around?"

She did, but at the moment it was more important to ease the worry from his brow than to worry about his parents' reaction to their sharing a kiss. "Maybe I'm getting used to them."

He kissed her. "Maybe you're getting used to me."

"Could be," she said. "Now let me go before your mother begins to think I'm a loose woman."

He loosened his hold and she stepped away, but not before he slapped her behind.

"What was that for?" she asked.

"Nothing," he said with a wide grin. "I just wanted to do it. Do you have a problem with it, Ms. Washington?"

She was about to rattle off a list of problems she had with it, but she saw the teasing in his eyes. "No problem at all, Mr. Stevens, but remember that turnabout is fair play."

"I'll look forward to the payback. Now stop flirting with me and go talk to somebody else. I'd hate to embarrass myself in front of my parents."

She backed away from him with a smile on her face. "It's nice to know I have that kind of effect on you."

He pointed the spatula at her. "Go. Now."

She chuckled and walked over to talk with Nate.

Reggie hustled Nate and Luther out of the house as soon as his parents drove out of the driveway. "Whew," he said to Kim when he returned to the patio on the back of the house. "I thought they'd never leave."

"You're bad."

"Very bad." He opened his arms to her. "Come here. I've wanted to hold you all afternoon." His heart expanded when she came willingly and eagerly into his arms. "This is more like it. Is it as good for you as it is for me?"

"I don't know," she said. "How good is it for you?"

He slapped her bottom. "Smarty pants."

"Hey, you'd better watch it with the hands, buddy. I don't like to be manhandled."

He leaned back and grinned down at her. "That's not quite how I remember it."

"Maybe you have a bad memory."

"Maybe you're the one with the bad memory. And I

think I know just the thing to help you refresh it." He stepped back from her and lifted her in his arms.

She kept her hands around his neck as he carried her into the house and to the bedroom. After he'd dropped her unceremoniously on the bed, she said, "I think I liked it much better when you carried me over your shoulder."

"Variety is the spice of life, Ms. Washington, or haven't you heard?"

He stood before her and began pulling off her clothes. "No," she said, getting up from the bed and coming to him.

"No?"

She smiled. "Not *that* 'No', silly. I want to undress you."

He sucked in his breath. "Well, go right ahead. Do your duty."

When her soft hands reached under his golf shirt and rubbed his chest as she pulled the garment up and over his head, Reggie sucked in his breath and had to call on every ounce of his self-control to keep from pulling her into his arms and taking over. If she wanted to undress him, he was determined to let her. Even if it killed him. And right now, it felt like it just might.

She placed a soft kiss against his bare chest then she rose on her toes to get the shirt over his head. When she did so, her breasts grazed his chest and he groaned. Unable to help himself, he covered each of her breasts with one of his hands and squeezed lightly. When he felt the hard tips of her nipples, he groaned again.

After she pulled his shirt off, she looked at him. "No fair," she said, removing his hands from her breasts. "I'm running this show."

"You're killing me, Kim," he murmured.

Her smile told him that his words affected her. "Good," she said and turned her attention to his belt buckle. She unhooked it and slowly tugged it from its loops and threw it onto the chair next to the bed. Reggie bit his lip to keep from telling her to hurry up. He felt as if he were about to explode.

She hooked her fingers in his empty belt loops and backed up, pulling him with her. She sat down on the bed, pulled him between her legs, then unzipped his shorts. Ever so slowly, she slid them down his legs. "Kick off your shoes," she whispered.

He did as she bade and kicked his shorts off at the same time.

"You're getting ahead of me," she accused. "I'm in charge."

"You're torturing me," he said. "And I think you're enjoying it."

Her smile told him he was right. "All's fair in love and war," she said, slipping her hand into the waistband of his jockey shorts.

"And what's this, Kim?" he asked. "Love or war?"

She slid the garment down over his erection. When he was fully exposed to her, she looked up at him and asked, "Which do you think?"

He thought he saw bright, shining love in her eyes and his control snapped. He quickly disposed of his undershorts, divested her of her top, bra, shorts and panties and positioned himself atop her.

"I was supposed to be in charge," she complained.

"You are, Ms. Washington," he murmured as he placed soft kisses all over her face, her neck, her chest, her breasts, her stomach. "You have been ever since the first day I met you. You've controlled my thoughts and my will. What more do you want?"

Kim wanted to tell him that she wanted his love, but her mind moved to other thoughts when he touched her dampness. "You," she whispered. "I want you. All of you."

"And I want you, too. More than you'll ever know."

In short order, Reggie slipped himself inside her. He heard a loud, guttural scream and was about to remind her that he'd told her she was a screamer when he realized the sound came from his own lips.

Reggie's shout of pleasure caused a similar one to escape Kim's lips. What did this man do to her? she wondered.

What was so special about him, about them together, that made her feel this way? As she looked into his passion-glazed eyes now, she knew she'd loved him from the first time she'd seen his face. Of course, it made no sense. But how many things in life that really mattered made sense?

Reggie wondered at the feelings that encompassed him when he joined his body with Kim's. This was no simple coupling. This was a merging of two souls, two people who'd met out-of-time given a second chance. There was no doubt in his mind that he and Kim were destined to be together. Everything else and everyone else in his life had prepared him for this moment, for her.

More than anything, he wanted to be worthy of her. To be the kind of man she deserved. A man who would spend the rest of his life loving her and making her happy. A man who'd seek to pleasure her as much out of bed as in it. A man who'd cherish her independence, her willfulness. A man who'd rejoice in her just being her.

This was a new feeling for him. Every other woman he'd cared for had been a woman whose life he wanted to change, to make better. He'd seen himself as being what they needed in their lives and he'd taken fulfillment in being needed. He'd substituted being needed for being loved. Not so with Ms. Kimberla Washington. She was what he needed. His life was made better by her. She opened doors to new dreams and new possibilities for him. She presented him with an opportunity for a future of being loved rather than a future of being needed. Satisfied that their future together was secured, he led her to the brink of satisfaction then quickly followed.

Chapter 21

Kim turned in the bed expecting to roll into Reggie's arms and was surprised to find herself alone. She opened her eyes and scanned the room for him. Not finding him, she slid out of bed and slipped her naked body into the sleep shirt she used when staying over at his house.

After making a stop in the bathroom, she headed for the kitchen where she found him at the stove preparing breakfast. She leaned against the doorway and watched him, thinking how much she'd come to care for him in such a short time and amazed that her feelings were returned. Or so it seemed.

She walked over to him, wrapped her arms around his waist and said, "Morning, Mr. Stevens. What's for breakfast?"

He turned in her embrace, and smiled down at her. "It's about time you got up. You must have been very tired."

She quirked an eyebrow at him. "I wonder who's fault that is?"

"I guess I'll have to take the blame," he said with a grin. "Sorry."

That was the most contrite-less "Sorry" she'd ever heard. "I just bet you are."

He spanked her backside, then turned back to the stove. "Why don't you make yourself useful and get out a couple of plates."

"Slave driver," she said, opening the overhead cabinet. "First you keep me up half the night. Then you put me to work as soon as I wake up."

He scooped up an omelet and placed it on one of the plates. "You're the most contrary woman I've ever met. All I'm trying to do is satisfy your every physical need."

She opened the refrigerator and pulled out a carton of orange juice. "And yours in the process," she said, pouring them each a glass of juice.

He picked up the plates and took them to the dinette table in the breakfast nook and she followed with the juice. "I've always felt that one should bask in the joy that comes from giving service," he said.

"You're full of it," she returned, taking her seat. She cut her omelet with her fork and popped a piece in her mouth. "But you're also a good cook, so I think I'll keep you around."

He took a swallow of his juice. "Well," he said dryly. "I'm glad I'm appreciated."

"Don't pout." She patted his hand. "It's not becoming on such a fine masculine specimen as yourself."

He folded her hand in his and brought it to his lips for a kiss. "So what do you want to do today?"

She sighed. "I might need to start packing."

"What? Why?"

"Well, I talked to Jim yesterday morning and he doesn't think we're doing a good job of keeping a high profile."

"And?"

"And he wants me to drum up some publicity or I'm fired."

Reggie chuckled. "I bet he threatens to fire you five or six times a year."

She nodded. "But I think he's serious this time. He's

spent all this money for me to be here in Atlanta and he doesn't think he's getting the return he should be getting."

"But you're doing a great job," Reggie said, between bites of his food. "I could tell him that."

She grinned, pleased that he was ready to come to her rescue. "I'm sure you could, but unless you were willing to send the tabloids pictures of us in bed together, I don't think he'd be too impressed."

Reggie chuckled. "You may be right. Jim does seem to lean toward the sensational. But he'll change his tune once he reads your article."

She sipped from her juice. "He's already read it."

"Why didn't you let me read it?"

She raised a brow at him. "What's wrong? You don't trust me?"

"Of course, I trust you." He grinned that grin that she'd come to love so. "I just wanted to read the article. It's not everyday a man has his woman sing his praises for all the world to hear, or in our case, read."

She lifted a brow at cockiness. "You'll read it, Mr. Modesty."

"Yeah, but when?"

She shrugged. "You may have to wait until it hits the stands. If it hits the stands."

"What do you mean if? Surely, Jim's not going to pull the article at this point. That would be crazy."

She agreed, but it wasn't her decision. "I don't know what Jim's going to do. He said he liked the article, but he also said it lacked punch. In other words, it didn't meet his criteria for sensationalism."

"From the short conversation I had with Jim, I get the feeling he thinks of you as a daughter. You'll work through this."

Kim nodded. Jim's calling her Kimmy and his nosing into her business were perfect examples of the paternal role he sometimes played with her. "Jim and I have disagreed in the past, but we've always been able to come to a compromise that was acceptable to both of us. I don't think that's going to happen this time."

"Why not?" Reggie asked, finishing off the last of his omelet.

She cut off a slice of hers and placed it on his plate. "Because this time what he wants is too outrageous to even consider."

"What does he want?" He popped the omelet she'd given him into his mouth. "It can't be that bad."

She put down her fork and captured his gaze. "Get this. He wants us to get engaged."

Reggie choked on his omelet and had to chase it down with juice. "Engaged?"

"My reaction exactly."

He pointed his finger between himself and her. "You and me. Engaged?"

Kim felt a prickle of annoyance at his incredulousness. Was being engaged to her so far-fetched an idea? "Not a real engagement. He wants us to pretend to be engaged so that he can have a media hook."

"You can't be serious, Kim. He wants us to fake an engagement so he can get some publicity?"

"You've got it."

Reggie shook his head. "Fake an engagement? How did the man come up with something so crazy?"

Kim's annoyance began to fade as Reggie's reaction to Jim's suggestion matched hers. "Jim's always looking for an angle. This is exactly his kind of idea."

"You really think you're going to lose your job?"

She nodded. "It looks that way."

Reggie shook his head. "I don't think it'll come to that. As a matter of fact, I won't let it come to that."

Again, his willingness to help pleased her. "And how are you going to prevent it, Old Wise One?"

"Easy," he said. "We'll fake the engagement."

She stared at him, not believing he'd just spoken those words. Did an engagement mean so little to him that he'd fake one on a whim? "You might, but I won't."

"Fine," he said. "Then quit your job and move in here with me."

"Why would I want to do that?" Kim thought the conversation was going from bad to worse.

He sat back in his chair. "Because if you don't have a job, you won't have money. You can live here rent free while you find another job."

The matter-of-fact way he solved her problem irked her. "So you've got it all figured out, haven't you?"

"I'm just giving you some options, Kim," he said, leaning forward and covering her hand with his. "I don't see what you're getting all upset about. If you don't want to quit your job, let's go ahead and fake the engagement. It's no big deal."

She moved her hand. "It's a big deal to me. An engagement is not something you fake. An engagement implies a commitment between two people. I won't fake something so important."

"Fine," he said, seeming to get angry. "Quit your job then. The offer is still open for you to stay here until you find another one."

She wondered why he was angry. She hadn't done anything to him, while he had offended her royally. "Look, Reggie," she said. "I'm not one of your charity cases. I'm used to taking care of myself and I don't need you to bail me out."

"What are you talking about?" He placed both his hands face down on the table. "All I'm doing is trying to help and you're making me out to be the bad guy."

Kim thought about the letters from the women who'd dumped him and the conversation she'd had with his mother. Then she finally realized what was going on, what was irritating her so much about this entire conversation. Reggie wasn't responding to her specifically. He was doing what he'd do for any woman in need. He was acting on instinct, not out of love.

"No, Reggie." She got up out of her chair. "You're not a bad guy. You're a real nice guy."

"Yeah, right," he said, getting up too. "Then why are you yelling at me?"

Kim tried to rein in her emotions. Reggie was just doing what he normally did, she told herself. But she didn't want him to do the usual with her. She wanted things between them to be different. "I'm not yelling," she said in a calm voice.

"But you were," he accused. "And I don't even know what I did wrong."

She believed him. She could tell from the bewilderment in his eyes that he didn't have a clue. She loved him, but he didn't have a clue. "I know you don't, Reggie," she said sadly.

He reached for her and she went willingly into his arms. "Tell me what I did wrong, Kim. I'd never do anything to hurt you. You have to know that."

She pulled back and looked up into the eyes of the man she loved. "I know." She rubbed her hand down his cheek. "You're a wonderful man, Reggie. And I can see how those women fell for you, but I can also see why they left you."

She felt him go rigid in her arms. "What?"

"You can't solve everybody's problems, Reggie. Sometimes people have to fight their own battles."

He dropped his arms from around her and moved away. "So you're walking away from me because I offered to help you? That makes no sense."

She gave him a sad smile. "I know it doesn't make sense to you. You're a nice guy and you're doing what a nice guy does. You're being nice."

"And what's wrong with being a nice guy?"

She shook her head and fought back tears. "Nothing, if being needed is enough. It's not enough for me."

He laughed a harsh laugh that made her heart hurt. "I guess I was wrong again. I would have bet everything that you were different—that we were different." He shook his head from side to side in frustration. "I don't get what you women want."

She reached up and gave him a short kiss on his lips.

"I know you don't," she said. "That's the problem." Then she turned and walked away from the man she knew she'd love the rest of her life.

"Women," Luther lamented two weeks later. "They're nothing but trouble."

"You're right about that, man," Nate agreed. "Tell me, what is it they want from us?"

Reggie sat among his friends as they chugged beer and cried the blues. Three eligible bachelors bemoaning the state of their most recent relationships. "I know you're not asking me. It's obvious I don't have a clue. I thought Kim was different, but I guess in the end, women are all alike."

"No way," Luther said. "They're not all alike. Tam was different. You know, I could have fallen for that woman."

Nate chugged his beer. "You did fall for her, Luther. You were just too stupid to realize it."

Luther shot his friend a wild stare. "Maybe you're right, man. But I just wasn't ready to get involved with a woman who had a kid. Hell, I'm still a kid myself."

"Now that's a lie," Nate said, barely able to put his words together. "You're thirty-eight and you're gonna be hard-pressed to find a woman—not a girl—who doesn't already have kids. You're the odd ball, man, not Tam."

Reggie agreed with Nate but he didn't even feel like responding. Kim had thrown him for a loop when she'd rejected his suggestion that they go along with Jim's plan to fake an engagement or his alternative that she quit her job and move in with him until she found another one. She'd turned him down flat on both offers. No discussion. Nothing. Just, No. And where had that left him? Alone. Again. "If I just knew what they wanted, maybe I could adapt, but, so help me, God, I don't have a clue. I was good to Kim. Hell, I was even going to fake an engagement so she could keep a job."

"I can top that, man," Nate said. "I told Leslie I loved

her and you'd have thought I set off a rocket under her or something. She left just that fast. I thought women were the ones who wanted commitment.''

"Women don't know what they want,'' Reggie explained. "They think they want something until they get it and then they move on. Maybe women are the ones who like a challenge. And then once you fall for them, they lose interest.''

"Yeah,'' Luther said. "That's what they do all right. They make you fall for them and then they leave. They like to see a brother balled up in knots.'' He gulped down more beer. "Why couldn't Tam give me a little time, man? Why did she have to tell me about her kid so soon?''

Reggie didn't know and said so. "Who knows, man? We could sit here forever trying to figure them out and we'd never come to a conclusion.''

"Well,'' Nate said, struggling to stand up. "I'm tired of trying to figure it out. I'm going home.''

Reggie looked down at the beer bottles scattered around them and realized they'd been drinking for a while. "You'd better crash here, man. You don't need to get in a car.''

"Hey, I can drive,'' Nate mumbled.

"Drive yourself right into a ditch,'' Luther said. "Sit your tired behind down.'' He pushed his hand against Nate's stomach and he fell back in his chair.

"Maybe you have a point,'' Nate said. "I think I will spend the night here.''

"Good thinking,'' Luther said. "You might be boring, but you definitely aren't stupid.''

Reggie looked at himself and at his friends. If they told their anyone that they'd spent a Saturday night sitting in his den drinking themselves silly because of three women they'd known less than three months, no one would believe them. Yet here they were.

Reggie took another swig of beer. And he'd thought Kim was different. He'd thought she was the one. That goes to show how much he knew. Not a damned thing.

* * *

"So Jim didn't fire you, after all," Leslie said. "You should have known he wouldn't."

"Well," Kim said, curled up on her couch. "He had me going there for a while. When I told him there was nothing he could do to make me fake the engagement, he'd ordered me back here as though I'd said I was going to bomb Atlanta. I just knew he was giving me my walking papers."

Tam chuckled. "All that cheapskate wanted was a reason to get you out of Atlanta and off his expense report. He's never going to let you go. He knows a good worker when he gets one."

Kim stared down in her cup. Tam was right. What she'd thought was going to lead to her getting fired had actually turned out to be a career boon. Not only had Jim not fired her, he'd actually given her a raise and a fancy new title. He'd even agreed to drop the His/Her column idea he'd had for her and Reggie and just go with her article, which had suddenly become good enough.

"What do you say, Kim?" Leslie was asking.

"I'm sorry," Kim said. "What did you say?"

"She said we need to celebrate your good fortune," Tam explained. "Where do you want to go? Anywhere. We're footing the bill."

Kim looked at her friends and knew she was lucky to have them. But she didn't feel lucky right now. Right now, she felt empty. And she knew why. She missed Reggie. Missed him more than she'd ever missed anyone. More than she'd known she could miss anyone. While she'd been able to keep the sadness that hovered over her from consuming her, she didn't know if she could endure an evening out on the town. Unfortunately, she didn't know how to tell her friends without getting into another long discussion.

"You don't want to go, do you?" Leslie observed. She

turned to Tam. "I told you she didn't want to go. She's still thinking about him."

"Don't talk about me as though I'm not here, Leslie," Kim said.

"You're not here," Tam interjected. "Your body's here but your mind, your heart, is back in Atlanta. Why don't you just call the guy?"

Because she couldn't. What would she say? Hello, Reggie, I didn't get fired after all. Would you like to start up again? No, she couldn't do that. "There's no point," she said to her friends. "Long distance relationships rarely work."

"It's your own fault, Kim," Leslie said softly. "The guy asked you to get engaged and you turned him down."

"He didn't ask her to get engaged, Leslie," Tam corrected. "He offered to pretend to be engaged to her so she wouldn't lose her job."

Leslie threw up her hands. "What's the difference? The guy offered to be there for her and she turned him away. I don't get it." She turned to Kim. "What did you expect him to do after you told him you were going to lose your job? Would you have preferred he said, Sorry, can't help you."

Kim had wanted Reggie to be outraged at Jim's idea. She'd wanted him to resist the idea of making a mockery of their relationship. But, no, he'd gone and offered to help. To help. Just the way he'd helped all the other women in his life.

Dummy that she was, she'd wanted to believe Mrs. Stevens when she'd told her that she was different. Yes, she'd even resisted the thoughts that Reggie entered into the relationship with her in his helping mode. Kim wished now that Mrs. Stevens hadn't bothered to tell her why she thought Reggie's previous relationships had all failed.

Kim didn't want to be another one of Reggie's causes. She wanted to be *the* woman in his life. She wanted to be his love. But he wanted to turn her and what they shared into a cause, no different than his previous relationships.

Kim would have laughed out loud had not her friends
been in the room. What was wrong with her? Why couldn't
she choose a man who just wanted to love her?

"So," Leslie asked her again. "What did you want him
to say?"

Kim lifted her shoulders. "Maybe I wanted him to tell
me he loved me, Leslie. I wouldn't run away from love but
I had to run away from pity."

Tam shook her head. "I think you're wrong, Kim. It
wasn't about pity with Reggie. I saw the way he looked at
you. And the way you looked at him. You loved him and
he loved you."

Kim wanted so much for Tam to be right, but she knew
her friend was wrong. Reggie had never pretended to love
her. To want her, yes. To cherish her, yes even that. But
love? No. Those words had never crossed his lips. If they
had she'd still be in Atlanta. She loved Reggie Stevens and
she had a feeling she always would.

Chapter 22

Kim had been gone for a month now but Reggie sat at the desk in his den this Saturday morning missing her as much as he'd missed her the first day she'd left him, if not more. He'd lost women before, but never before had he ached the way he ached since losing Kim. It was as if she had been a part of him and that part had been severed. He suspected he would feel the pain forever.

Not a day went by that he didn't consider calling her and asking again exactly what the hell had happened. But he refused to break on his own rule: Never go back. When it's over, it's over. A man had to have some pride.

The ringing doorbell brought him out of his thoughts and he was glad for the interruption. When he opened the door and saw the UPS driver standing there, he was surprised since he hadn't been expecting a package. When he saw the flat parcel was from *Urban Style,* he quickly signed for it and pulled a few bills out of his pocket for the driver. Then he closed the door, eager to see what Kim had sent him.

Disappointment consumed him when he ripped open the envelope and found the yellow Post-it with a note from

Jim. "Thought you might be interested in this," the note said.

Reggie pulled off the Post-it note and saw the galleys for the article Kim had written. "The Nicest Guy In America" read the heading in big, bold letters and under it was his name, Reggie Stevens.

He leaned back against the wall of his foyer and read. "Sometimes women complain about the lack of nice men," the article began. "And many times I've been in that number. But," the article continued, "that was before I met Reggie Stevens."

Reggie's throat clogged up as he read the loving words Kim had written about him. There was no doubt in his mind as he read the article that her words were words of love, written from her heart to his.

"As with everything and everybody, The Nice Guy has his downside, though it seems strange to call the manifestation of The Nice Guy's primary trait a downside. Do you know what that downside is? Well, I'll tell you. The Nice Guy's downfall is that for him the old saying, "Actions speak louder than words," doesn't apply. Why? Because The Nice Guy is nice to everybody. Just because he'd go the distance for you doesn't mean you're the special one in his life. No, it simply means he's responding to your need as any Nice Guy would."

As Reggie continued to read, he began to understand why Kim had left him. And he felt like a fool when he realized what she had really needed from him. She didn't need help to keep her job or help keeping a roof over her head. No, what Kim needed had been much, much simpler. So simple in fact he'd totally missed it.

He wiped at the tears that now filled his eyes and rushed to the den, to his desk and to his computer. He opened his word processor and typed the words he hoped would forever change his life: "Simple-minded Men and the Women They Love."

* * *

Kim was sitting at her desk on Monday morning when she received an express delivery. When she saw the Atlanta return address, her heart rate increased. *Reggie,* she thought immediately. *It couldn't be,* she warned herself, afraid to build up her hopes only to have them dashed.

"Calm down," she said. "This is just a package." Taking a deep breath, she ripped open the envelope and pulled out two typed pages. "Simple-minded Men and the Women They Love, an article by Reggie Stevens," she read. As she continued to read, hope sprang in her chest and tears filled her eyes.

"I'm the most simple-minded man of all," the article read. "And I'm simple because I never told my woman how much I love her. Well, I'm correcting that grave mistake today. I LOVE YOU, MS. KIMBERLA WASHINGTON AND I ALWAYS WILL."

As Kim's scanned the two pages she realized both were filled with just the single I LOVE YOU line. Her tears flowed freely. He loved her, she thought with joy. He really loved her.

"It wasn't supposed to make you cry," the deep, familiar male voice said.

Kim, almost afraid to look up for fear she was dreaming, lifted her head slowly.

"I love you, Kim," Reggie said. "And I'm sorry it took me so long to realize you needed to hear me say the words."

Kim's heart was so full and she had so much to say, but she couldn't voice her thoughts. All she could do was cry.

Reggie came around her desk and stooped down next to her. "I hope those are happy tears."

She brushed at her tears and tried to stop her hiccups. She couldn't think of the words to tell him how happy she was. Even though she hadn't known it at the time, she'd waited all her life for him, her very own nice guy.

"I should have told you how I felt before now," he said.

"But I thought you knew." He tilted her chin up and wiped at her tears with his fingers. "The love I feel for you goes beyond anything I've felt for any woman. I need you, Kim, and I need to be needed by you. But I also love you very much. With you, I've learned the difference between love and need. There's no comparison. Your love is everything to me. It gives me hope and it makes me happy. Do you believe me?"

Kim fell into his outstretched arms. "I love you so much, Reggie," she said through her tears. "More than you'll ever know."

Reggie held Kim close to his heart, where he would always keep her. He had a surprise for her—a small, square box, but he'd wait until tonight to give it to her.

"It's about time," came Jim's gruff voice from behind them.

Reggie couldn't have agreed with him more.

Six months later, Kim, dressed in a sheer white negligée that had been a gift from her husband, stood on the balcony of the Hilton Hawaiian Hotel and watched the soothing waves of the Pacific. Tonight was the first night of her honeymoon and she couldn't be happier.

Warm arms encircled her waist and warm breath blew against her neck. "What are you thinking, wife?" Reggie's deep voice asked.

She folded her arms across his and relaxed in his arms. She didn't have to look around to know he was naked because she felt every angle of his body. "I'm the happiest person in the world, husband."

In reward, her husband turned her around to face him. "Impossible," he said, rubbing his fingers across her now open lips. "I'm the happiest person in the world. Do you have any idea how much I love you?"

Reggie's words humbled her and she had to fight tears. "As much as I love you?"

"Good answer," he said. He lowered his head to hers

and her mouth automatically opened to receive his kiss. When she sagged against him, he pulled back and smiled, "Ready to go back to bed?"

She nodded and he turned and led her back to bed. "I wish everybody could be as happy as we are," she said, thinking about Tam and Luther and Nate and Leslie. They'd all been in the wedding party and when she and Reggie had left the reception, they'd been standing next to each other.

"Oh, no." He sat down on the edge of the bed and pulled her between his legs. "You're not thinking about other people again, are you?"

He pushed open her gown and ran his hand across her breasts and her stomach. She could barely think of anything. "What do you think will happen to them?" she asked.

"I don't know, Kim," he said, pressing a kiss against her soft belly. "And at the moment, I don't really care."

She placed her hand on his head and lovingy caressed him as he make love to her with his mouth. "I just want them to be as happy as we are."

He looked up at her and the passion in his eyes fired her passion. "And I want to make you happy." He reclined back on the bed and pulled her atop him.

She lifted slightly and gave him entrance to her body, all thoughts of anything but him erased. Against all the odds, she'd found the Nicest Guy in America and she'd spend the rest of her life making sure he was also the happiest.

ABOUT THE AUTHOR

Angela Benson is a former engineer who now writes full-time while she pursues a doctorate in instructional technology. She's the author of seven novels and a novella. Her titles include *The Way Home, Between the Lines, For All Time, Bands of Gold,* and *Friend and Lover,* her contribution to the Holiday Cheer anthology.

To receive Angela's popular newsletter, Angela's Corner, write to her at P.O. Box 360571, Decatur, GA 30036, or send e-mail to abenson@mindspring.com.

Look for these upcoming Arabesque titles:

November 1997
ETERNALLY YOURS by Brenda Jackson
MOST OF ALL by Loure Bussey
DEFENSELESS by Adrienne Byrd
PLAYING WITH FIRE by Dianne Mayhew

December 1997
VOWS by Rochelle Alers
TENDER TOUCH by Lynn Emery
MIDNIGHT SKIES by Crystal Barouche
TEMPTATION by Donna Hill

January 1998
WITH THIS KISS by Candice Poarch
NIGHT SECRETS by Doris Johnson
SIMPLY IRRESISTIBLE by Geri Guillaume
A NIGHT TO REMEMBER by Niqui Stanhope